NIGHT OF THE RAPTORS

Book 2 of the Mind-Speaker Series

A Novel
by
W James Dickinson

This book is a work of fiction. Names, characters, places and incidents are a product of the author's imagination. Any resemblance to actual persons, living or dead, events or locales is entirely coincidental.

James Dickinson of Salt Spring Island
British Columbia, Canada
Illustrations & Cover Design by
James Dickinson

ISBN: 978-1-77084-949-5

Printed and bound by BookBaby

To my wife, Judy.

Dedication

This novel is a work of pure fiction, but the people who helped me to complete this book are very real.

Brian Cooley inspired me to start writing a novel, by working on his novel while we sailed together.

My wife Judy listened as I read out loud each chapter and revision, giving me the feedback I needed to guide the story. She always had the time to help, as I puzzled my way through the storyline and final text.

In my professional career I worked with Roberta Hursey for almost 20 years, and she coached me while I wrote proposals and letters. Without her as my English teacher, I would never have had the confidence to go public with any written material.

Marj Scheunert, Ken Fearnley, Pat Ross, Brian Cooley, Tricia Yersel, Felicity Perryman and Marie-France Berube carefully reviewed the manuscript giving critical feedback and corrections. Dorothy Weimer and Dr. Sue M. Scott, PhD took on the onerous task of editing the final text, with later help from Dennis Hayden.

All authors say it, but I really could not have done it without all of their help.

For those of you who have just picked up this book, I thank you for risking the few hours it will take to delve into the tale.

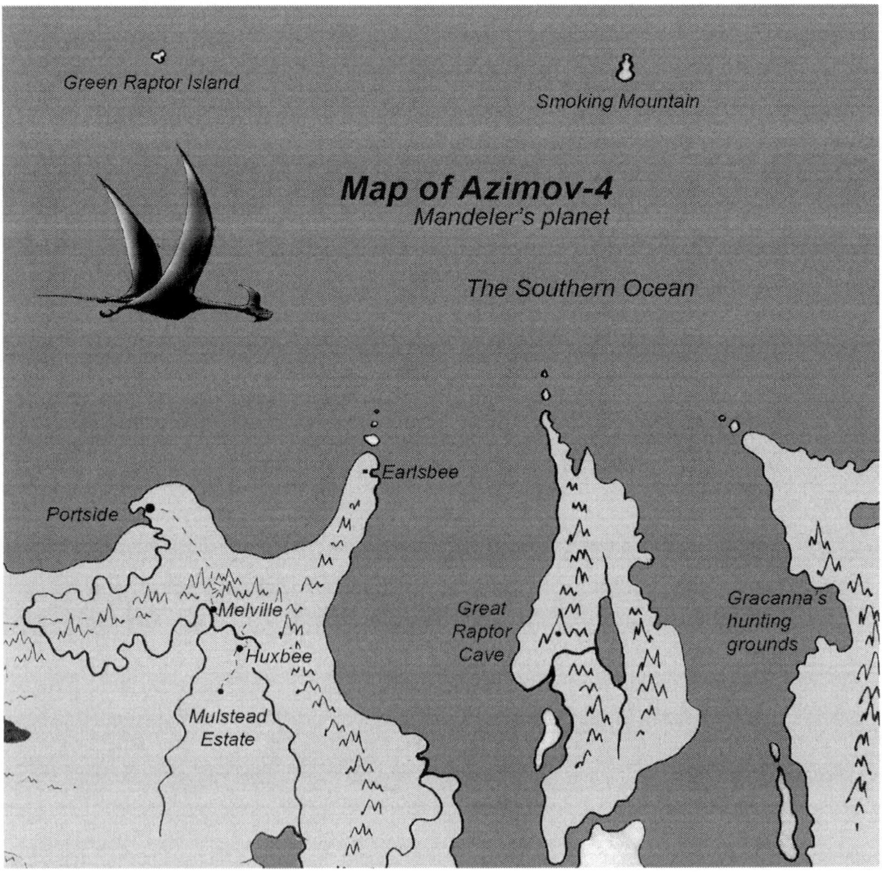
Green Raptor Island
Smoking Mountain
Map of Azimov-4
Mandeler's planet
The Southern Ocean
Earlsbee
Portside
Melville
Huxbee
Mulstead
Estate
Great
Raptor
Cave
Gracanna's
hunting
grounds

The night of Mandu's Manhood Ceremony

Out of Darkness

The prime hunter drew himself up, unfolding his massive leathery wings. For such large creatures their departure from the darkened cliff was almost soundless. Their black shapes cut across the star field as they made their way towards a small opening in the forest.

Mandu staggered as the room around him dissolved into the dark landscape where four huge creatures took to the sky. As quickly as the apparition appeared, it was gone, leaving him shaking.

His uncle Almar, turned to him asking, "Mandu, you look like you have seen a ghost!"

Mandu looked into his uncle's concerned eyes. "It's nothing really, probably just exhaustion from my manhood ceremony today. I'm really tired, that's all."

"Are you sure?"

"Yah, I'm fine, really!" Mandu answered, with more confidence than he felt.

"If you say so, " Almar paused while studying his nephew, "Alright then, let's finish getting you dressed because there is a party outside and they all want to meet the young man of the day. After all you will be called Mandeler from now on, and counted among the men in our community."

Moments later they stepped out into the yard, illuminated by dozens of glow globes. Mandu stopped to look towards the south-eastern horizon. Could there be something terrible coming from that direction? A cold shiver ran down his spine before he turned to follow his uncle.

Several days before and 413 years since the great solar storm

The Awakening

Mandu could see the muted colors of the canyon walls rapidly approaching. The wind roared in his ears and tears streamed from his eyes as he tried to focus on the blurred details of the gorge. He was diving steeply from a great height and as the trees suddenly loomed closer he willed himself out of the dive. His cheeks sagged with the force of pulling into level flight. Then in an instant he was clipping over the last of the dark trees and all that lay before him was the desolation of the canyon below. As he skimmed over a flat-topped hillock he caught a glimpse of a winged shape converging with his own shadow. He glanced over his shoulder just as the raptor screamed its attack. In the instant before the outstretched talons reached him, the dream cycle suddenly ended.

He sat bolt upright in the darkened room. He could still feel the effects of the wind on his face and the terror of seeing the attacking beast. How many nights had he awoken with this same dream, only to find himself tangled in his bedding and still laboring from the exertion of the chase? It felt so real and after each dream cycle it was getting more and more difficult to shed the feelings of exhilaration and dread.

Mandu rubbed the heels of his hands into his eye sockets trying to strip away the images now seared into his mind's eye. He turned to the shuttered window and slipped open the familiar retaining pins. As the panel rotated open he was washed with the cleansing chill of the pre-dawn air. Peering through the grill, he could make out a slight glow on the jagged eastern horizon that foretold of the day to come. He slid off his bed platform and felt the chill of the coarse stone floor under his bare feet. He pulled the damp night shirt over his head and shivered. On the back of his chair were the few homespun garments that made up his everyday wardrobe. As he pulled the thick tunic over his head the familiar scent of the animals filled his nostrils. He stood on one cold foot at a time and pulled on his breeches and then his favorite socks. Feeling warmer he reached for the wooden latch on his bedroom door.

He knew his way into the main hall by feel and as he drew near the great hearth there was a dim glow from last night's fire. He groped for his cloak, and wrapped it around his shoulders. Near the back entrance he found his work sandals and slipped them on. He sensed rather than saw his bonded denzel approach on padded feet. The warm snout in his hand was familiar and comforting. Soom gently leaned his smooth body against Mandu and matched his breathing with the boy's. In the dark no one could have seen the comfort that each one gave the other. As a child his parents had bonded him with a male denzel. It was unusual for a boy to be bonded with a male but the match was instantaneous. He called him Soom, and as he had grown they were inseparable companions.

Mandu straightened his back and gripped the coarse fibers of his cloak up under his chin as he released the back door and silently pushed it open. As he stepped out of the portal he noted the drop in temperature. The last cool nights of their short winter on the Mulestead Estate would be over soon. Outiside of the main lodge he was now unprotected. His uncle would not approve of him being out of the lodge before sunrise on his own, even with Soom at his side. Why was it that he felt no fear of the darkness but could still feel the real fear of his dream cycle? He took in several deep breaths of the pre-dawn air and turned towards the animal shed.

The frosty grass crunched under his feet as he turned his gaze to the night sky. Argil was in the full moon phase and the primary moon's rings shone amber with brilliance upon his planet, Azimov-4. The lesser moon, Izaic, in its new moon phase was just above the glow of dawn. A chill ran down Mandu's spine as he sensed movement in the star field and then out near the edge he saw it, a silent shadow crossing over the dragon constellation. Still caught in the world of his dream cycle, he knew in his heart that the shadow was one of the Great Raptors. So many legends told terrifying stories about his clan's early encounters with the raptors. There had not been an attack since he was a baby, but the distant shadow might foretell their return.

How many lifetimes had it been since his ancestors had come to this planet? The stories told of how Mandu's race had come here from Earth to set up two colonies and all had looked promising until the great tragedy wiped out their technology and left many of the people mutilated and dead. The legends told of a great storm on the sun that had crippled all the people's thinking boxes and their special machines, including the flying ones. Many died as a result of the storm and the survivors had to learn to live off the land. It had been four centuries since the calamity that wiped all knowledge from the thinking machines.

It was not long after that the raptors had appeared and brought the second wave of terror. Their crude fortified shelters gave little protection from the raptors. With the food desperately low, hope was fading. The exact details of that encounter are vague, but whether it was some intervention or not, they left just as quickly as they arrived. It was the denzels that made the first move to help. No one remembers how it happened but the denzels became part of their lives. They did not appear to speak but they understood how the planet and its ecosystem worked and somehow the people learned from them. How to use the local flora to support and protect life became common knowledge and in a few decades the people started to flourish again. They learned to live off the land and find better ways to fortify their dwellings against the night raiders. Along with this came the bonding of the denzels with the young people. During all this time there was never any contact with Earth again.

Mandu let his hand slip onto Soom's back. He felt the comforting reassurance of the warm body and slid his hand upon the neck ridge. The spines that looked so daunting were in fact soft to the touch. As Soom padded along beside him in the dark, it was hard to imagine what life would have been like without these sleek companions. He felt protected by the denzel as they neared the animal shelter.

Like the main lodge, the shelter was barred from the outside world. Mandu placed his hand in the wooden lock mechanism and slid the heavy door open, its weight moving easily on hidden hinges.

As he stepped inside he could feel the air change. It was laced with the scent of the animals and the temperature was noticeably warmer. On his right he found the illumination flask. A small shake brought buds of light springing to life from within the crystal globe. Its inhabitants came to life, each one glowing with blue light. Dozens of small flying creatures were buzzing about giving off a cool glow that lit the animals nearby. This was Mandu's safe haven and during the day he would bring the winter rations for the animals to eat. Some folks called it work or chores but Mandu never felt that way. To him all of these animals were in his care and it was only natural to make sure they were well fed and comfortable. It was not so much that they were beasts of burden, it was more like a partnership with both parties winning.

Stories of the days after the great tragedy told of the people's struggle. The colonists knew nothing about the indigenous plants. They could not tell what was safe or poisonous let alone what was nutritious or tasty, but with the help of the denzels, all that was needed for a well-rounded diet could be collected. The people started to thrive. After all, it was these animals that helped to make life here so much easier. Yes, in the wilds of Azimov-4 life and death played out in its natural way. Only the Great Raptors remained a mystery with little or no understanding of their sporadic attacks.

Mandu's uncle was one of the Clan's best animal handlers, making travel and collecting the bounty of the land much easier. One day soon Mandu would also be an animal handler. Stroking the beast he marveled at these tall creatures with the same smooth scales as the denzels. Their coloring was vivid with blues, purples and highlights of burgundy. The muzel placed its muzzle into Mandu's hand and he felt the warm rush of breath from the brow nostrils as the smooth forked tongue traced his fingertips. Sixteen years was considered the age of manhood in the Clan and that heralded the bonding and working with the animals.

He went around to each of the muzels and said his silent good mornings. Even though they outweighed him fifteen to one he had never felt any fear being near them.

As Soom leaned gently onto his thigh he asked himself, why was it that he kept having the same dreams over and over? Soom looked up at him at the same moment and for the second time that night Mandu felt a chill up his spine. Then a voice in his head seemed to say: *You are about to enter manhood and many of your questions will be answered!*

Breakfast

Mandu awoke with a start. He had fallen asleep in the shelter wrapped in his cloak with Soom curled up beside him. He sat up from his bed of herman nut leaves seeing the light piercing through the window slit above. It was the dawning of a new day. Mandu straightened up, brushing leaves from his clothes and made his way to unlatch the shelter door. He could see the shape of the main lodge with its stands of flat-topped conifers silhouetted by the rising sun. His Aunt Mirra would be stoking the morning fire and breakfast would be simmering in its clay pot. It was time to make an appearance.

"Where have you been at this time of day? Don't you know it is dangerous to be outside while it's dark?" barked Uncle Almar.

Mandu shuffled out of his damp sandals and raised his downy chin to his uncle, "I don't see what all the fuss is about. There hasn't been a Raptor invasion for years!" Even as he spoke the image of the dark shadow in the morning stars flashed through his mind. Was he being irresponsible and tempting fate?

"Twenty-seven times the Raptors have swooped down upon us and each time a foolish young boy like you has vanished!" Uncle Almar glared with brows drawn and Mandu felt every bit a child in front of his uncle. His shoulders slumped.

He said, "I know, I just had to get out of the house."

"Are you having those bad dreams again?" his uncle said with more kindness in his voice.

"Yes."

"Come sit with me. It is not easy being your father's son. Can you tell me any details of your dreams?"

Mandu shuffled uneasily despite his uncles concerns, "It's just more of the flying dreams. They are just dreams; I guess I wish I could fly is all."

Almar studied the young man's face looking for hidden answers, but could find none. "Alright Mandu, maybe they are just wishful dreams."

Mirra looked up at her husband and their nephew. They were so alike with their thick blond hair, the younger one showing the first traces of a man's beard, the older one bushy with a fringe of grey. The blue eyes were also the same but Mandu had his mother's straight nose and quick smile. He still had the slender body of youth but he had stretched up and his shoulders were now broad. She stirred the porridge and sprinkled in a few more of Mandu's favorite dried fruit. It would be ready in twenty or thirty breaths so she moved to the table and distributed the bowls.

She could hear movement in the back of the lodge as Jaida and Jamis, her twin daughters, came running around the partition pursued by their denzels, Nip and Tuck. The girls came bounding up and gave their mother hugs around her waist. They were seven season-cycles old and they had the bouncing curly green hair of their mother. They giggled as she fondled their heads. The denzels swept around to encircle them and leaned in to add to the hug. By the time Mirra had disentangled herself the gruel was getting thick and the bubbles were rhythmically snapping to the surface. "All right you lot, let's come to the table and have breakfast."

Mandu slipped onto the bench across from his cousins and leaned over his bowl. Jaida and Jamis were already blowing on their hot spoons of gruel. As he savored the first taste of breakfast his eyes drifted over the household denzels. They were seated on their lean haunches gently licking their own bowls of porridge from a low table. You could see in their eyes the same satisfaction as they took their first taste of the sweet mixture. He looked around the room at his family and wondered if it would always be like this.

Almar was halfway through his bowl before he spoke again, "How are the preparations coming for our trip? The last communication from Herbin Cochral said that all would be ready soon."

Mirra looked up at Almar but shifted her gaze to Mandu, “Any special reason?”

“Oh, we haven’t been off this property for ages, just call it a whim. Who wants to come along?” said Almar.

The twins were squealing, “Oh, can we come, can we come?”

“Of course you can come, we will all go. Herbin said they would host us after the Argil’s full moon and that was last night.”

Mandu shifted in his seat, “I would love to see the Cochrals but will we be back in time for my birthday?”

His aunt and uncle turned as one and gazed at him. Almar said, “Oh, this has everything to do with your birthday, Mandu.”

Mandu blushed and his family all smiled.

Cochrals

Mirra cast her eye over the packages and bundles for the trip. It was only half a day away but they would be spending the next three days there and the family would need extra clothing for the planned activities. Of course she had known about the upcoming event. It had been planned for months. Mandu was turning sixteen season-cycles and his manhood ceremony would be part of a larger community event. Still she double-checked her lists and made sure all the essentials were in place. She had made several trips out to the traveler and all was set for departure except for the participants.

The sun had cut through the thin morning frost and it felt more comfortable. In a dozen sun-cycles it would start to warm and the rain would sweep in from the high lands. Mandu pulled himself back to the task at hand and wheeled the hand cart back into the animal shelter with the loose sack of herman nuts. He had already shoveled out the shells from the previous feedings. He was putting enough of the hard rations in the self-feeder for two more days than necessary. During their departure the younger muzels would stay inside as tradition required.

Uncle Almar approached with the elder pair of muzels and their offspring. It was a common enough sight but there was still something remarkable about the huge animals getting into stride and moving with the same rhythm as their handler. As they moved towards the traveler each of the muzels would take turns nuzzling the other's slender ears. As they approached the traveler they separated and came in on opposite sides, lowered their heads and slipped into the drawing yoke with the ease of a well-practiced move. The offspring was about three-quarters grown and pranced about in a circle.

The traveler was a universal conveyance device with ample room for the five humans and their luggage. It had two rows of seats with a big tray at the back to strap the luggage. Its intertwining overhead structure was both functional and decorative with swirls completing the edge trim. Today it was sparsely packed with personal items and they did not have the cover in place since there would be no rain for some time yet. The vehicle was made of the local resilient green cane and held firmly together with iron weed. It was so light-weight and pliable that it was hard to imagine any better design.

Since all was loaded the family quickly took their places in the vehicle. The muzels stepped forward turning the traveler in front of the lodge and made their way down the lane. The three family denzels and the offspring flanked the departing traveler as the group picked up speed. Sitting in the back with his little cousins, Mandu felt the warmth of being part of this family. As they traveled, the landscape slipped by.

Soom pulled level with them moving with an easy, loping gait. Mandu glanced up at the pale blue sky and the rapidly passing terrain. Forest alternated with open areas dotted with low bare bushes. He must have come this way after his parents were taken. Why was it that the adults always referred to people as 'taken', instead of killed by Raptors? He knew they must have died in the attack.

He drifted into a daydream about riding abroad on an adventure of his own, imagining tall mountains and a distant sea. The ever-changing scenery blended in with his thoughts, and for a moment he was carried away in his waking dream. He felt a dark shadow flying overhead and shuddered, looking up quickly, but the sky was clear. As he came out of his reverie he noticed they had traveled far. There was still an echo of the outstretched wings in his memory. His dreams were starting to linger into the day. What that meant he did not know.

Herbin Cochral was standing on the steps of his lodge when he heard the traveler approaching. It drew up in front of his place in a cloud of winter dust. As usual the denzels had kept pace all through the journey and like the muzels, they stood without breathing heavily. His long-time friend Almar stepped down and gripped his hand and forearm in greeting. He could hear his wife, Petulla, coming out of the lodge behind him and soon everyone was talking and embracing each other. Herbin was struck by how much Mandu had grown since the visit last summer. The boy was looking more and more like his father with long legs and broad shoulders. He moved as easily as an athlete but when the youth looked up Herbin knew there was something much deeper about this boy. It was going to be a very interesting manhood passage.

The Hut

For the next three days, Mandu explored the areas around the Cochral estate. Sometimes he and Soom would take long walks in the morning, just spending time quietly together. The muzel offspring would often walk behind them, nuzzling his back and neck, until they were out of sight of the lodge and then it would romp back to be with the other muzels. Mandu's relationship with Soom was like a feeling of oneness, being an extension of each other.

At other times, they would take Jaida and Jamis with them to climb in the herman nut trees. Their two denzels, Nip and Tuck, were just as playful as the twins. The tangle of thick branches made a delightful maze to thread their way through. At first glance a denzel did not appear to be a climber, but with their long toes they could climb the lower limbs.

He took delight in playing with his cousins. Laughing and making up hiding games with the girls made him feel emotionally distant from the farm and that ever present sense of foreboding. Looking back into the distant past sometimes he thought he could remember that terrible night when his parents were taken.

The day Mandu turned sixteen he awoke without any dreams at all. He relished the feeling as he lay on his bedding at the end of the open common room. A faint light was coming through the narrow windows, painting the far wall in a reddish glow. It was then that he could smell the morning porridge, simmering over the low fire. Petulla must have slipped into the room earlier and started the first meal of the day. Suddenly he realized that it was his sixteenth birthday, with its secret manhood-passage. Today he would finally pass through the mysteries and be counted a man.

He sprang from his bed and hastily pulled on his clothes. Before he could finish, Soom was at his side looking every bit as excited as he felt. It would all be revealed today. He was just about to cross the room, when Uncle Almar and Herbin came from a side room beckoning him forward. He stared at the men, because neither was dressed in his usual rough work clothes. They were wearing thin cloaks that seemed to shimmer in the faint light. Herbin was clutching a bundle under one arm. Without a word, they motioned for him to follow them outside. Soom followed quietly.

Herbin led the way, as they emerged from the lodge, with Almar and Soom following behind. On a trail unnoticed before, they headed into the woods. They walked on through the mixed forest of conifers and herman nut groves. Mandu had not brought his cloak, and the morning chill, or anticipation, set him to shivering. As they cleared the last nut tree grove, he could see a small hill beside the river, and on top of it was a tall tree unlike anything he had ever seen. It had a massive trunk, and part way it split in two where it twisted around itself in a spiral, until it stood well above the other trees. Unlike the other trees this one had serrated purple-green leaves with red fruit hanging on its sparse branches.

As they climbed the little hill, what he had taken for a mound near the tree, looked more like a roundish hut with an opening that faced the river. It was covered entirely with the strange tree's leaves that gave off an odd odor. The pungent, yet sweet smell grew stronger as they approached it.

It was then that Uncle Almar touched him on the shoulder with a warm hand. As he turned, Uncle Almar reached up and undid the clasp on his cloak and let it fall to the ground. He stood there naked, except for a spectacular gleaming purple crystal suspended from a cord about his neck. It seemed to illuminate a mauve tattoo with swirling patterns upon his chest. How could he have lived his life with never having seen this before? Herbin gestured for Mandu to shed his clothing. Still shaking, Mandu pulled his tunic over his head and then unbuttoned his breeches. He stepped out of his undergarments and pulled off his socks, standing there in the sharp cold grass staring at these two men that he thought he knew.

As they turned towards the hut, Mandu saw two other men unclad like his uncle with their individual crystals standing on either side of the doorway. Again without speaking Mandu was directed into the hut, and as he drew closer, a curtain over the low entrance was pulled back, allowing the wisps of steam to drift up into the morning air.

Mandu crouched to follow Herbin into the dim interior. He immediately was struck with the damp heat. Following Herbin's lead, he went to kneel near the back of the cramped hut. He got a glimpse of a fissure in the center, where the steam rose, and the sound of gurgling water could be heard. His uncle and the others followed, and as the curtain dropped, Mandu was enveloped in total darkness.

The Crystal

A shiver of fear, tinged with excitement, ran up Mandu's spine and his whole body was on high alert in the darkness. The ground was spongy, and the air heavy with the smell of sulfur and sweetness. Despite the steaming hot interior, Mandu had goose flesh all over. His senses strained to make out what was around him. He had been on his knees and as he shifted to sit cross-legged, he touched his uncle's knee to his left. To his surprise the older man's hand came and rested on his damp shoulder. He said nothing but it was as if sparks of energy traveled through him. Within Mandu's head he heard his uncle's voice: *Just shut your eyes, they will do you no good in here. Listen to your own breath for it will guide you to a calm place inside.*

How long they sat there in the oppressive heat, Mandu could not tell but he felt a sense of peace washing over him. With one voice, the elders started to chant, low and rhythmic, in an unfamiliar language. Their voices rose and fell in a harmonic wave, and without knowing how, he too started to hum and then voice the song. It was like an ancient memory unlocked, as his voice flowed in unison with theirs. He could feel his heart pounding in his chest as the chant the same note. The only sounds to be heard, were the breathing occupants and the gurgling hot spring.

How had he been aware of that chant? It was as if he had always known it. While still rolling this around in his head, the curtain was thrust open, and Almar plunged into the brilliant light. On wobbly hands and knees, Mandu followed. Almar was the first to plunge into the river and without hesitation Mandu did the same. He was expecting ice water but it was tepid. Herbin's head came up beside him, and the older man's eyes locked onto his and again it was as if he spoke wordlessly into Mandu's head: *Do not drink of this river, for the minerals will make you sick. Wait, the reward at the end is worth the discomfort!*

Herbin watched Mandu stagger from the river, with wisps of steam trailing from his youthful body. He wanted to tell him there were still two more rounds to come, but silence was part of the ritual. He and the others had wrapped themselves in their cloaks, and now he motioned for Mandu to lay upon a new cloak spread upon the ground. They covered him all except for his chest, and kneeled in a circle around him.

Mandu saw one of the strangers take up a small pot and brush. His vision seemed to blur as a wave of fatigue washed over him. It started almost as a tickle, as the stranger dabbed the green paste on his exposed torso. Mandu lost track of time again, but when the stranger had finished, it was to reveal the most wonderful swirling pattern on his chest.

They took him back into the sweat hut two more times for darkness, heat and more chanting. He did not remember the end of the third round, for he awoke on the river bank wrapped in the soft glistening cloak with the others kneeling beside him.

Soom was crouching near him, with his gentle eyes fixed on his. With his last strength he tried to speak but his throat was too parched to make a sound, so he just lay there breathing heavily.

Since the sweat hut, two more denzels had joined them. The oldest one of the two held something deep burgundy in its mouth. A strange voice in his head said: *Take this fruit and eat it.*

It approached him, and gently placed the wrinkled red fruit on his chest.

The fist-sized burgundy fruit was leathery in texture and as he brought it to his nose, he recognized the smell from the sweat hut. Dizzy with thirst, Mandu bit into it and found his mouth filled with a spicy sweetness that numbed his tongue. His eyes filled with tears as he looked up at the group. Within Mandu's head, the same strange voice said: *You must eat all of the copeander fruit to get the full results!*

As he looked around the small group, he was overwhelmed by a sense of compassion. He took another bite and then another. With each bite, the spiciness was replaced with numbness. Feeling less thirsty, he swallowed the last bite whole.

A strange sensation spread through his entire body. Then as if a switch had been thrown, he could sense the feelings of the others on the hill. Soom stepped closer and seemed to say in his head: *There is one more thing you seek today.*

As Mandu went to stand, he found that his weakness was gone, and his mind felt sharp once again. The fruit had some incredible restorative power.

Except for the sweat hut chants, no one had spoken a word, and yet it was eerie how clear messages had come directly into his brain. How had that happened?

Follow us: came the command.

Mandu followed them along a narrow trail through the bushes by the river. It wound around the hill, and before long he could hear gurgling water ahead. He was the last to push through the foliage into an opening where sulfurous steam rose from a tall, irregular mound. It appeared to have been pushed up from within, to make a yellow, terraced form. Scalding water bubbled over the ledges to form small green-streaked streams that converged into a larger rivulet leading back to the river. To the side stood an outcrop of nodes, very much like a nest of rough grey eggs, beside a bubbling green mud pit.

Within his head came a faint tune, an ancient wordless song, like something long forgotten.

The half-circle of men and denzels kept their eyes locked on him. From under his robe, Herbin took out a mallet, placing it into Mandu's hands. His message came silently: *Take this tool. There is a crystal that beckons you. All you have to do is let it call and you will find it.*

Unsure what to do next, Mandu just stood there trying to tell where the music was coming from. The sounds seemed muffled, like they were trapped somewhere in the mound. To help focus, he closed his eyes and to his surprise the image of a dazzling green stone danced across the inside of his eyelids. It was dancing within the circle of stone eggs. His eyes flew open as he stepped towards the pool of bubbling goo. He could feel the heat and smell the sulfur, but the throb of the music grew stronger as he stopped in front of the outcrop of nodes. Heedless of the heat and discomfort, he knelt at the base of the outcrop where the music was most intense. Mandu grasped the mallet and swung it with all his might. The grey stone egg moved, so he hit it again and again, until it came loose. It was almost as long as his forearm and heavier than it looked, but soon he had it rolled out to the edge of the clearing.

Herbin kneeled down next to him, handing Mandu his amber crystal. He gestured for Mandu to use it like a chisel. The young man's hands were shaking as he placed the sharp point of the amber crystal on the stone. Carefully he tapped it with the mallet. A small crack opened at the base of the rock node, so he rapped it harder. This time, the stone egg split open to reveal a lining of white crystals that cradled a slender emerald stone within. He plucked it out and held it aloft where it flared to life emitting shafts of brilliant green light. The crystal had come alive! It was as if a flame burned from within.

As Mandu held the gleaming crystal, his whole world changed. All the colors seemed to vibrate with a new intensity but it was the people and the denzels that were more surprising. The men glowed with the color of their individual crystals and the denzels pulsed with tones of blue, purple and silver. Their long snouts seemed to smile at him.

His world blurred: *In the darkness a huge body with folded wings stirred restlessly, her red eyes glowed as she seemed to stare directly at him. What light there was reflected on the scales of her forehead and swept back cranial fin. Her mouth gaped open to reveal double rows of yellow teeth. Mandu's nostrils were filled with the stench of death, and in that moment he knew she hated him with a burning intensity.*

As quickly as it came, the vision was gone leaving him shaken and nauseated. Swallowing, Mandeler tried to settle his trembling limbs. This was his first waking dream of the great one. What was going on?

Almar stepped close, "Mandu, are you alright?"

Not wanting to seem nervous Mandu replied, "Yah, I am fine. Really I am just a bit tired."

"Somehow I don't think that's the whole story, but we can discuss this later."

Mandu looked about him, his eyes meeting those of Soom.

I greet you my friend, but like your uncle, I too worry that your dreams may be coming more frequently.

"How do you know about my dreams?" Mandu asked before he realized that nobody had asked that question aloud. He looked confused and then the voice came in his head again. *It is me, your childhood companion, Soom.*

Now Mandu looked shocked as he stared at his four legged friend. "This can't be happening, I'm dreaming again."

Again Soom seemed to speak directly into his head: *This time it is not a dream, let me explain. First we are telepaths and secondly my name is Alheeza. Soom was only the childhood name that you gave me. How we speak is the way our race has always communicated. We use pure thought, not the cumbersome words of your race. After the great tragedy that befell your people almost four hundred of your years ago, we discovered that there were those amongst you who could be tuned or trained to mind-speak this way. The crystals become a conduit for thought speech. There is much we need to share, but there will be time for that later.*

Almar mind-spoke: *Tonight you will be presented to the rest of our community along with your adult name, Mandeler Freedahson.*

You will no longer be known as Mandu. Unfolding a length of dark fine cord, he held out his hand for Mandeler's crystal. As Almar took the emerald stone from him, the world dimmed to its original dullness. With the skill of practiced hands, his uncle knotted a cradle for the gem with two long tails. The older man then laced the amulet around Mandeler's neck bringing back an element of the enhanced senses that he had felt while clasping the stone.

It was then that he noticed his feet and knees were bleeding. Almar took another copeander fruit from under his cloak, and using his knife, he cut it into several strips. He then motioned Mandu to sit on the grass while he gently rubbed the medicinal fruit on his abrasions. It took the sting out of the shallow cuts and stopped the bleeding.

The other two men came close, introducing themselves in mind-speak: *We are Vernyet and Freegate. Attending your manhood passage was a privilege for us. What a pleasure it is to meet you as a man. Now look at your chest.*

Mandeler glanced down to his gleaming green amulet as it lay against the swirling pattern. It seemed to make his chest tattoo come to life. Amongst the swirling letters was a winged creature like the one in his dreams. How could they know?

Freegate mind-spoke: *It says Mandeler Freedahson, seeker and heart friend. It is written in an ancient language of Earth and will be recognized by other telepaths of the brotherhood. In time the tattoo will fade to almost nonexistence, but when the stone glows, so will it. The more of your skin that touches the stone, the more powerful it becomes. Remember, except at formal gatherings such as this, we keep our identity and the stone hidden.*

The other two denzels now introduced themselves, they were Charleez and Vanzooth. It had been their pleasure to be the guardians for Herbin and Almar as they grew to manhood. Now they were bonded to another young pair in a distant community. They had made the trip especially for this manhood ceremony to stand in witness to this most special occasion. Charleez glanced at the sun already cutting a path low into the trees and indicated that it was time to return to the settlement.

Alheeza came to walk beside his former charge.

Mandeler asked: *How is it that I can hear you so clearly now and I could not hear you before?*

When your people were in such dire straits, we found that some of the people who had been exposed to trauma and thirst became more receptive to our thoughts. The crystals were a bonus, because after their discovery by one of your people, it opened up the gates to mind to mind communication. It is the combination of natural ability, extreme stress, and finally the speaking crystals that open up the communication link.

You mean not everybody can do this?

Not nearly everybody! But you must understand that for every rule, there is the possibility of an exception, rare but possible. Only a few of you have the special qualities needed to sense our speech. Almost all of the children we are bonded with learn a great deal, and they are not even aware that the lessons are coming from us. They grow up knowing about things as if they have always known them. Your people call it instinct.

You mean when I would eat berries and nuts in the woods, it wasn't just that I had always known what was good to eat?

Exactly, and there are far greater things that you have not tapped yet. The bonding lasts until the child reaches their passage ceremony. Then they are bonded with other children.

Mandeler mind-spoke: *Does this mean you will no longer be with me?*

I am afraid so, Mandeler. It is time for me to be bonded with another gifted child.

The other night in the animal shelter, I thought I could hear you speak then. What was happening?

Alheeza answered: *You have such a strong natural ability that we were having thought breakthroughs. Today just enhanced what you already had. Your father was like that too, he was a natural sensate.*

The Gathering

When the little group arrived back at the main lodge the sun was setting and there were a number of other travelers parked in the yard. The twins squealed their announcement that Mandu had returned. A couple of dozen excited people poured out of the lodge to greet them. He was expecting his family and the Cochrals but he was surprised to see other neighbors that he had only met on rare occasions. Herbin held up his arms and the group went quiet. "People, Mandu has passed through the tests of manhood and he will be presented to the group after we have freshened up. Though we were late getting back we will still meet in the greeting circle after dark."

Like most estates there were large cables of iron weed that stretched from the entrance to significant buildings, remnants of this planet's fortifications against previous Raptor attacks. Attached to cables were decorations in preparation for Mandu's passage.

Mandu was led into the lodge and was taken to Herbin's room where a loaf of steaming nut bread awaited him. As he munched he noticed the fresh set of adult clothes laid out for him. He finished the small loaf, washed it down with tea, and then looked over the clothes. He pulled on the form-fitting charcoal pants that went all the way to his ankles with white buttons along the thigh. Then he wriggled into the finely woven green tunic with gold and blue embroidery on the sleeves. It was high collared and his amulet was safely out of view. He strapped the thick plaited belt around his waist. It had a sheath and one of the strong, sharp, hardened glass knives with a carved ironwood handle. He sat on the edge of the bed holding his new light weight stockings while uncle Almar handed him a tall set of polished boots.

The prime hunter drew himself up, unfolding his massive leathery wings. For such large creatures their departure from the darkened cliff was almost soundless. Their black shapes cut across the star field as they made their way towards a small opening in the forest.

Mandu staggered as the room around him dissolved into the dark landscape where four huge creatures took to the sky. As quickly as the apparition appeared, it was gone, leaving him shaking.

His uncle Almar, turned to him asking, “Mandu, you look like you have seen a ghost!”

Mandu looked into his uncle’s concerned eyes. “It’s nothing really, probably just exhaustion from my manhood ceremony today. I’m really tired, that’s all.”

“Alright then, let’s finish getting you dressed because there is a party outside and they all want to meet the young man of the day. After all you will be called Mandeler from now on, and counted among the men in our community.”

Moments later as they stepped out into the early evening, Mandu stopped to look towards the south-eastern horizon. Could there be something terrible coming from that direction? A cold shiver ran down his spine before he turned to follow his uncle.

When Mandu came out of the lodge it was fully dark. He was led around to the gathering area where they took their place in front of the group. The others had brought blankets and were sitting comfortably on the ground. With glow globes around them, Uncle Almar stood on his right with Herbin on his left. Alheeza crouched in front of them. His uncle reached out to take his elbow, drawing him near he whispered, “Kneel to be recognized by your peers.”

Almar cleared his throat, taking in those in front of him. Finally he spoke in a strong voice,, “I stand before you as a witness to Mandu’s sixteenth birthday and his manhood passage. I would like to introduce you to him with his full name. Mandeler Freedahson, son of Mandel and Freedah. Please stand and be recognized by your peers!”

The group all shouted, Mandeler, Mandeler, Mand…that was all that he heard as his world turned upside down: *He could see, as if from a great height a vast landscape dimly lit, yet clearly visible. Wind whistled past his head as he looked below to see a forest passing under them. He looked from side to side taking in his three wing mates. Then in an opening ahead, there were spots of blue light and the silhouettes of the small creatures gathered together. From his throat came a rasping scream as they dived for the kill.*

Mandeler was knocked back by the sheer force of the scream. This was no dream, it was real! Huge dark shapes thrashed against the iron weed cables making them sag and pop. Hooked talons and slathering yellow fangs sought out their victims. Their long black necks reached easily into the panicked group. A glistening black head, with a swept back cranial fin, knocked him aside grasping Almar and shaking him like a rag doll. As Mandeler lay terrified on the ground his nostrils were filled with the stench of the creatures. All around him was chaos as several more of the huge flying creatures reached past the cables, snatching at those gathered. The screams of the victims filled the air. The speed of the attack caught everyone off guard and in the dim light of the remaining globes it was as if some great explosion had knocked the group to the ground. As the Raptors withdrew the air thundered, as their powerful wings hoisted their bleating victims into the dark sky.

As their attackers departed, a momentary quiet was replaced with the sounds of people's pain and anguish. Clutching his new amulet, Mandeler reached out to find Alheeza's mind and instead he felt the pain of a dozen injured people well up inside him. Their screams now beat within his head and the feeling was overwhelming. Then everything went black.

When he awoke, he looked into Alheeza's face and sensed him mind-speak: *Come with me, young Mandeler. People are hurt and you are needed.*

He must have been unconscious for a very short time because the scene in front of him was hardly altered. The iron weed cables were hanging loose, their decorations shredded, and the survivors were milling about. Alheeza led him to his Aunt Mirra and he kneeled down next to her. She had Jaida and Jamis wrapped in her arms and they were all in tears. He placed his hand on his aunt's shoulder and instantly was thrust into her grief. It welled up inside him like a swimmer struggling to the surface, desperate for a breath of air. He shuddered and gradually the intensity settled so that he could make out details. The twins were confused and afraid with the loss of Uncle Almar while Mirra was shaking from witnessing the horror. On top of that one of their denzels had been taken and the other was seriously hurt.

He felt himself being drawn away and found Petulla assisting the injured, one of whom was her husband Herbin. Petulla was a well-known healer in the colony. He asked, "How can I help?" Without looking up she replied, "Fetch my medicinal chest in the lodge near the great cabinet." Not hesitating, he found his way through the chaos and into the great room. People were already coming inside seeking shelter. He found the cabinet and the compact chest near it and returned to the chaos.

Herbin still lay wrapped in his ceremonial cloak and his complexion was ashen, no glow about him at all now. Clutching his amulet under his tunic, Mandeler reached out with his mind feeling Herbin's pain. He sensed the deep gash in the left shoulder, a broken arm, but there was also a great pain in his chest.

Petulla said to him, "I think his arm is broken and he is cut badly. There may be something else inside, but I can't be sure."

Working gently, she drew the bleeding gash together, smearing the edges with a paste. Then she manipulated Herbin's arm, resetting the broken bone. She had set aside a pair of scooped-out melon husks, and placed them on either side of the broken arm bone, binding them with dark leaves and twine. She sprinkled water on the bound leaves, watching them swell. Turning to Mandeler she said, “As it dries the binding will hold its shape, keeping his arm safe. I don’t know what deep internal wounds he might have.”

Mandeler knelt beside her and placed his hand on Herbin’s stomach, still clasping his crystal with the other. In a few heart beats he felt the connection take place. He sensed bleeding and although there were no external signs, the injury was very serious. Without thinking he reached into Petulla’s medicinal case and drew out a clear vial and pulled the stopper out. He asked Herbin to open his mouth and lift his tongue. Then he placed fifteen drops of the clear fluid under the tongue. Placing his hand back on Herbin’s solar plexus, he could feel the elixir spread through Herbin’s body and then the damaged artery seemed to tighten and the bleeding tapered off. Herbin’s breathing became steady as well as his pulse.

Petulla turned, looking at the youth she had known as Mandu, “How did you know how to do that?”

Mandeler just shook his head.

With the help of others, they were able to move all of the injured into the great lodge. In the darkness everyone wanted to be in the safety of the fortified lodge. Three people and one of the denzels had been taken and the injured ranged from those directly hurt by the attackers, to those scuffed up from the scramble to safety. Illumination globes filled the interior space with a soft light and all was quiet except for the low murmurings of the survivors, spread around the room in blankets. Some hid their faces while others watched with all hope drained out of them.

Throughout the evening Mandeler helped Petulla make her rounds and then he sought out his aunt and cousins. He found Jamis and Jaida under a shelf wrapped in Mirra’s arms flanked by Alheeza. He got down and crawled under the shelf with them. It was a family cluster with the two large ones wrapping their arms around the smaller ones. There were tears and whimpers and that was all they could do. How long they had been under there he could not tell, but Alheeza kept between them and the room, stationed like a protector against anything that came their way. Sniffing back the last of his tears he reached out with his mind to the girls and his aunt. He felt pain of loss and fear of the unknown. There were no answers, only questions. For him, the biggest question of all was what had happened just before the attack, when he saw through the Great Raptor's eyes as it flew towards the estate.

He crawled out with the promise to find something for the girls. Mandeler found some sweet cakes and cold tea. None of them were very hungry but the little cakes seemed to relax the girls and Aunt Mirra assured him that they would eventually sleep. Mandeler then turned to find Herbin.

He was laying with his head in Petulla's lap and she was stroking his hair. He sat cross-legged beside them and reached out to Herbin's mind: *What are we going to do now?*

Herbin looked at Mandeler answering in the same soundless speech: *I do not know. I have only seen an attack from a great distance before. I thought we were safe here and that the estate was well protected but I was wrong, so wrong!*

It was not what he was expecting to hear. This man, like his uncle, had always been larger than life and in charge of everything. Now he was broken and disheartened.

It took a few moments to gather his thoughts and then Mandeler mind-spoke: *I don't know if it helps but I felt something just before the attack, something to do with the Raptors coming.*

Herbin looked up into the young man's face: W*hat do you mean you felt something before the attack?*

Mandeler stopped for a moment trying to recall what the feelings were and then he continued: *It was as if I was somewhere else or maybe something else but I am sure that it had to do with the approaching Raptors.* As he conveyed those thoughts, he remembered the night back home and the shadow crossing the stars. Was it all connected?

No one within the brotherhood of mind-speakers has ever had any sort of connection with Raptors. I have no idea what all of this means but I think it is important. Do not say a word about this to the rest! Mandeler nodded slowly.

Alheeza was still parked in front of the girls staring out into the room. Mandeler settled himself on the floor beside his long-time friend and leaned on his shoulder: *Did you pick up what was said between Herbin and me?*

Alheeza responded: *I caught tendrils of it only.*

Mandeler filled him in as best he could since the experiences were so far outside of his knowledge. They sat there well into the night sharing thoughts and finally Mandeler fell into a fitful sleep.

He awoke while it was still dark. A few illumination globes dimly lit the hall with its huddling figures. Only a few slept while others still moaned from their injuries and losses. He walked to the portal and carefully opened the ironwood latches. He stepped out under the star-studded sky, securing the door behind him. Argil was now past full and high in the sky. He searched the star field for a glimpse of a Raptor shadow but all was still. He then reached up under his tunic and clasped his amulet, sending his sense outward. How long he stood there, he could not tell but finally he got just the echo of a great beast gliding far away in the night sky. He tried to imagine what the next days would bring.

The first golden light of dawn caught his cloak. The festival area took shape in the long shadows of the sunrise. Above his head iron weed cables hung in disarray like tattered laundry. As he looked more closely he saw some of the debris was shredded clothing, and along the ground were dark patches that could only be blood stains. He rose and wandered to the edge. Along the trampled perimeter he found rectangular disks. They were shiny black on one side and porous on the other, with a ragged fringe at the narrowest point. As Mandeler held one closer, the rotten smell of the Raptors filled his nostrils. His stomach heaved as he realized what he was holding. This must be a scale chafed off in the struggle against the fortification cables. He dropped it as if it had bitten him.

Afterwards

Much later the next day Mandeler sat on the same rock holding a bowl of cold porridge in his hand reflecting on the past day's events. He had seen Freegate along with the new denzels leave for their homes at first light. They said they would mourn Vernyet in their own way. The rest of the people were reluctant to even come outdoors.

What next? His family was broken. His only uncle was dead leaving Aunt Mirra, who was usually so strong, gaunt, tearful and distant. The children had not only lost their father but their denzel Tuck. Nip was badly hurt and all around them people were crying and moaning. What had seemed like a simple birthday party had turned into a horror story.

As he sat pondering the full implication of the attack, he felt more than heard someone approaching. Petulla came around the corner and sat on a rock next to him. She did not speak for a long time and then turning to him she said, "Our colony is spread out over a large area and we do not see many people from afar. Vernyet and Freegate traveled for five sun cycles to get to this manhood ceremony. I am not part of the male tradition but it doesn't take a genius to figure out that you were the reason they came. After watching you help heal Herbin last night I think you have some special gift. How that will play out in our future I do not know."

Mandeler said nothing for a while and then the older woman placed her hand on his, squeezing it before she rose, and left.

The next day was mostly taken up by tending to the injured and cleaning up after the disaster. The hands-on work kept Mandeler busy enough that he had little time to think about what came next. Herbin called for him in that unspoken way: *Mandeler, there is something pressing that I wish to discuss with you. Most of us cannot telepath over any distance. As you know, Freegate, Charleez, and Vanzooth have gone back to their settlements but there are people to the west and north that have no idea that the Raptors are abroad. Would you consider traveling with Alheeza to the north as far as Portside, telling communities that the Raptors are abroad again?*

At first it sounded too good to be true, an adventure afar and then it hit him, he would be away from his family. A shiver ran down his spine then he telepathed: *Thank you for trusting me but shouldn't this be done by one of the experienced men?*

Herbin shook his head: *You have natural abilities that make you the best pick. We don't want any more people hurt like last night.*

Herbin was up on the second day with his arm in a sling, carefully moving about. His first task was to call everyone together. Standing before them he raised his hand and a silence fell over the group, "People (*and he included the denzels in mind-speak)* we have things to do, but let me say this to you all. As you know in our custom we have no funeral for those taken by the Raptors because no one knows if they are alive or dead. Tomorrow morning at sunrise we will gather and speak their names together for the last time and then go about our way. For the time being our estate will become the temporary home for those that have lost a loved one. We will stay together and see our way through this pain. For now, we will just focus on the next season and make sure we can provide for all the families. Our place is big enough for everyone, and we would love to hear the voices of children in the halls. More urgently, we need to spread the word of this attack so that others do not suffer as we have. To that end, Mandeler has agreed to take the news to the outlying communities. Now let us share our last meal together before tomorrow's parting."

Mandeler stood for some time reflecting on the announcement. His reverie was shattered as Mirra spoke, "So we are to lose the last man of the house."

He looked into his aunt's tired eyes. "Herbin said it was urgent.

I'll take Soom with me for company. We should be able to make a quick passage with the young muzel and a few supplies. With any luck, I will be back before the moon cycle comes around again."

Mirra looked at him for the longest time and then said, "I am going to miss you but I know you are the best choice to go. The girls still have Nip to share between them and he is recovering well. Life without Almar..." She trailed off, and her eyes took on a glassy look as they filled with tears. Mandeler reached towards his aunt and they hugged each other firmly. After a few moments she pushed him away and said, "We'll manage, you go and alert all the others so they don't lose a loved one!" She turned on her heel and set off for the lodge.

The Unknown Trail

Next morning Herbin, who was getting around much better, took Mandeler aside, mind-speaking: *I have been putting a few things together that you may need. Petulla found some traveling clothes. Apparently she throws nothing out and packed clothes of mine from when I was a young man. She added a medicine kit and traveling rations. Here is my heavy traveling cloak, too. It's almost waterproof and you can roll up in it to sleep. Remember, it is best if you keep your crystal hidden at all times. And I have something else…*

He then turned and led the way to one of the back buildings. He reached through the handhold and unlatched the tight fitting door. It took a few moments of rummaging around but he came out with a long contraption that Mandeler had never seen before. He held it between his knees carefully drawing back a pair of stretchy cords that clipped at the end of the long slot. Then he placed a thin stick into the slot. Looking up, he awkwardly held the contraption in one hand pointing it at a stump. *Thwap!* The slender object flew so fast that he could not see it before it was quivering in the dense wooden stump.

Mandeler had never seen a tool like this before and was amazed: *What is that?*

Herbin turned: *It's a projectile weapon and we called them flingers. I have never used it much. It came from a settlement far to the east and it was intended to ward off Raptors although I never used it. I think you may have a better use for it while you travel.* There were a handful of glass-tipped projectiles and a few blunt practice shafts along with the weapon. Herbin handed him the flinger, *Take a couple of practice shots so you can get to know it better.*

It seemed clumsy at first loading the practice arrow into its groove. He held it by the two grips and gently squeezed the trigger. *Thwap!* The shaft thudded off the side of the stump. After a few tries it was easier to point it. With practice he learned that the arrows flew fast, but dropped a little in flight. His last shot was with a glass-tipped arrow. Again it whizzed to the stump but this time it buried itself deeply into the tough wood. He had to split the stump with a wedge and maul to get the two arrows back out.

Mandeler was carefully wrapping the flinger when he heard Herbin pry open a board on the corner of the shed. He withdrew a small object and returned to where Mandeler was kneeling with his gear. Herbin mind-spoke again: *Since you will be traveling into the mountain and beyond, I have something you will need once you leave the expanse of the estates. Remember, we trade here and where you are going you will not have any valid trade vouchers.* He reached out and placed a pouch in the young man's hand.

Mandeler hefted the bag and glanced up saying: *This is heavy. What is it?*

Look for yourself.

He undid the drawstring and stuck his fingers into the little sack. He drew out a slender spiral object with lumps near the end. The weight was surprising for the size of it. He looked at it for a moment admiring the shiny shaft with its precise spirals and found that the lump spun in his fingertips. Then his head jerked up and he looked directly at Herbin: *This can't be a threaded screw with a nut on it can it? These are rare. I have heard of them but I have never handled one. Most of these have been lost since the time of the early colonists. These are very valuable!*

Bring back as many as you can.

There was so much going through Mandeler's mind that he could hardly grasp everything that was happening: his ritual passage, the attack and those taken, and now this hastily prepared journey into who knew what. He mind-spoke: *I am grateful for all of your assistance but I can't help but feel there is more to all of this than just a trip to warn people of the flying menace.*

Herbin replied: *I don't know either. I feel something sinister about this last attack and I just want to err on the side of caution. I feel better since Alheeza will be there to give advice. After all he is old and wise but he cannot communicate with non-telepaths as you can. You must be there to pass the word.*

He had always thought of this delightful young beast as 'Star' because of the beautiful pattern along its pale blue rump. He reached up placing both hands on the broad cheeks and sent a silent thank you to his mount. The young muzel would be his mount for this trip. Mandeler had a gentle touch even as an understudy and the animal had always been drawn to him. He had never ridden a muzel and without Almar to coach him, all he could do was clutch his amulet and reach out with his mind to the creature. It twitched its long ears and blew out a few quick breaths through its brow nostrils, and then it settled. At first the feelings were tentative and then the young muzel put his head down towards Mandeler touching his forehead. In that instant there was a bond between them. He patted the finely scaled cheek and turned to gather his possessions. As he did so Star danced lightly on his long toes flicking his narrow spit tongue and shaking his head.

The morning came quickly enough. Standing by his mount and facing his family, Mandeler crouched down and hugged the girls together, "Little ones, please stay close to your Mom, she needs your hugs more than ever. I love you both and I will see you soon."

As he stood, Mirra reached out hugging him closely. She whispered in his ear, "Come back to us." And before the tears in her eyes gave her away she turned and stepped behind the twins.

Petulla also hugged him, saying, "Take care, my young friend and have a speedy return." Herbin also embraced him awkwardly with his cast adding: *You have everything I can think of. Look into the hearts of others, but only trust your own heart.* Then openly he spoke, "Mandeler take care, may our paths cross soon."

Dressed in Herbin's brown travel clothes and grey cloak, Mandeler prepared to mount the tall muzel. His packs of food, clothing and personal items were slung on either side of Star's neck. Mounting a tall animal like Star would be a challenge to all but Mandeler had seen his uncle do this many times before. At his will, Star settled down on his haunches and brought his body down to Mandeler's level. He sat astride Star hooking his heels into the chest ridges. Then he leaned forward grasping the tall row of supple neck spines to steady himself as Star rose to his feet. The group waved their farewells as the three of them, Mandeler, Alheeza, and Star, trotted down the lane.

The Camp

The flat-topped conifers started to slide by as the young muzel fell into an energetic stride. With a bit of practice Mandeler found a matching rhythm on the animal's back. It was as if he had been riding for years and he felt an instinctive bond with Star. Alheeza loped at an easy lope and after all of the turmoil of the past few days this was a release. To take action was what he needed and it felt right.

The lands to the north of the Cochral estate were mostly forest punctuated with occasional conifers. As they rode along, small hedge hoppers leaped into the low bushes to hide from the riders. Once he heard crashing and got a glimpse of a large shadow moving away through the woods. At this time of year the migratory flyers were off to the north, but still he could see the occasional yellow-backed kite sitting in a tall tree, a sentry watching them as they passed.

Mandeler found his mind coming back to the recent past and the uncertain future. The taking of his Uncle Almar still pulled at his heart, and he was intermixed with fear and uncertainty about the Great Raptor dreams. What lay ahead brought fear and also a sense of excitement. It was Alheeza that broke through his introspection: *We must find a suitable place to camp for the night because we are still another sun cycle from the next village.*

Their immediate needs brought Mandeler to full alert. He had been so wrapped up in his memories and fears that he had not been planning for the upcoming darkness. He mind-spoke: *Of course. What do we need for shelter out here in the forest?*

If we can find a herman nut grove, that should provide two of our basic needs. They have been less numerous since leaving the estate but I think we will still find what we need.

They traveled for another span of time before a nut grove appeared at the edge of a clearing with a small pond. The intertwining branches, with their nut clusters high in the branches, were very distinctive. At the edge, Mandeler willed Star to his haunches and he slid to the ground. It was just as well they had found what they were looking for because he was far more tired than he expected.

They moved effortlessly into their pattern of mind-speaking.

Alheeza: W*hat do we need first?*

From the lessons of the last attack, we need cover from above that is impenetrable to the Raptors. This tree should do that and we can all shelter within it.

Very good, you are on the right track now. How do we use the cover of the herman nut grove to make a shelter?

Mandeler answered: *I think I am starting to understand why your race wanted to bond with us.*

Alheeza almost seemed to smile: *Ah, this has not all been a waste, has it?*

What did you come up with?

I think you are a great teacher and you know so much about the plants and animals, but you can't build anything.

That is very good. Yes, we needed the colonists as much as they needed us. The Raptors started hunting us about the time of your arrival. Our kind were very vulnerable at the time of the great storm and subsequent tragedy. We needed the protection that your fortifications gave. In turn your people needed to find out how to live off the land. I will tell you more about that later, but first let us set about making camp.

As if this revelation was nothing more than an everyday conversation, Mandeler went to his pack and unfolded a few simple tools. He took the saw made from saw-weed and started to cut the lower limbs away from the closest nut tree. As he drew the delicate sawblade back and forth he began to understand the symbiosis of the two races. One was a tool maker and the other knew the local resources. His light-weight saw was made from the braided strands of the saw-weed's long fibrous leaves that grew in bunches at ground level. He had seen the few precious metal tools that were left from the original colonists but this planet had no hard metals of its own. So many things could be made from what was here, if you knew how to find it. The denzels surely were the catalyst that made life possible here.

Mandeler had shed his traveling cloak and brown work tunic and was sweating freely by the time he had cleared an opening into the tangled side of the herman nut grove. Inside there was a small cathedral of woven limbs overhead. It was not weather-proof but it was probably Raptor-proof. He put his tunic back on as the evening chill started to settle in and climbed up into the canopy. A couple of yellow-backed kites were startled making them burst from the upper limbs. He climbed into the branches and using his knife he stripped bunches of nuts and let them drop to the ground. Star had followed him in and was already crunching on the nut clusters, spitting out the tortoise-like shells as he ate.

At the base of the mother tree, the main trunk twisted up and to the side making a natural overhang that was sheltered and dry. Here Mandeler piled his belongings and sat down. Alheeza came to sit beside him mind-saying: *I can smell treecats here. We must be in their territory and we will need a fire tonight to make sure they keep their distance.*

Mandeler replied: *We might as well cook a herman nut stew while we are at it then. Can you take the water bag and fill it while I get the kindling and start a fire?*

The easiest way to make a fire was to use hot coals from a previous night but carrying glowing coals with you had some limitations. On a sunny day Mandeler could use his focusing glass creating a hot point, or he could use his fire bow and tinder to start the evening blaze. He would not use the precious fire sticks unless there was an emergency.

Within the protective arms of the giant herman nut trees, their small fire gave comfort and light. A tea crock sat in the coals alongside a larger cooking crock that bubbled with herman nut stew supplemented with dried fruit from their rations. Mandeler reached for the small crock and drew out a bowl of sweet tea. He blew on the edge and sipped the brew. What little conversation they had shared this day was limited to directions and lessons about their trek through the wilderness. Fatigue was creeping into his every bone. After he and his friend had eaten their fill of the stew and stowed the gear, he mind-called to Star and the big gentle animal came to the edge of the tree base. Here he settled down and placed his head on the ground. Mandeler wrapped himself in the heavy traveling cloak and settled up against Star's side. Unlike at home, Alheeza also came and nestled next to the other two. Drawing from each other's heat they were soon asleep.

The dreams came almost at once.

She swam with all her might reaching for the surface. As her head broke free of the water she took a great breath. Shaking the water from her face she stopped for a moment to take in the beauty of the sun hanging low on the horizon, its brightness catching the wavelets. She drew her leathery wings free of the surface and beat the air with increasingly powerful strokes. With every muscle straining, the last of her body cleared the surface and she climbed up with ever-increasing speed. The wind chased the last of the water droplets along her long olive nose as she rose into the morning sky.

Mandeler opened his eyes expecting to see an expanse of sun-sparkled water but everything was dark. It had seemed so real and it was definitely not his physical body that he had been dreaming about. It had olive green wings and a prominent nose. Where had the dreams come from? He could feel the warm bodies of his companions next to him. As he lay there he became aware of the smells around him: the cool damp air, the decaying leaves, the familiar scent of his companions and the lingering odor of the evening fire. His hand reached under his tunic and clasped the amulet. He almost felt the crystal pulse as he sent out his senses for any trace of the flying terror. There was nothing at first but then he was aware of a dark body pumping massive wings somewhere in the distance. Then the image was gone. He lay there for some time reflecting upon the dream and what he could remember of the actual Raptor attack. He remembered a blunt armored face with a double row of irregular yellow teeth. It had a back swept fin on its head and a smaller one on its jaw as well as penetrating green eyes with a slavering orange tongue. None of his recent dreams had that. Where had it come from?

As he lay there he thought he could hear the distant screech of the Great Raptor. Had he fallen asleep again or was it real, he could not tell. He strained his eyes in the dark but he could not see the stars through the branched canopy above. All was quiet now. He must have fallen asleep again as he woke up in the dim light of the early dawn with icy rain drops landing on his face.

Alheeza stirred and mind-spoke: *Ah, the pleasures of living in the wild. Now aren't you glad we had a hot supper last night?*

Very funny!

Mandeler pushed himself upright and stopped. His whole body ached from yesterday's long ride and the sore spots from the rough ground. He pulled his hood close around this face and heaved himself up. He peered around the side of the tree and there in the branches of the next tree were the saucer-like eyes of a green and yellow striped treecat staring back at him. The cat was about two-thirds the size of Alheeza but could still be very dangerous. It was alone and seemed content to sit and stare. Reaching into his tunic he pulled out the crystal, then stepped forward. The cat backed onto the branch behind it. On impulse he jumped forward and thrusting his arm in the air shouting, "Get out of here!" It turned and leapt out through the branches.

The naming of these creatures had been inspired by the stories of earth's early animals. There were no real cats here on Azimov-4 but the broad flat face, prominent canine teeth and their stealthy way of stalking their prey made it very cat like. The ridges of interlocking scales seemed very natural here as did the vestigial wings that stretched between their legs allowing them to leap great distances from the tree tops.

As the rain intensified Mandeler silently thanked Herbin for helping him pack so well for the trip. The heavy traveling cloak was surprisingly warm and the rain was still beading on the surface. His packs seemed to be made of the same water resistant fabric. He and Alheeza had a cold breakfast of dried fruit and nuts.

Mandeler asked: *How are you going to stay warm in the rain this morning?*

Our scales are hollow and give a good deal of insulation from the cold and wet. I still feel chilled on a rainy day, so let's be off to find a friendly lodge tonight.

Mandeler slung the packs on Star and took off on foot with Alheeza. The denzel seemed to be well acquainted with the trail for he never faltered on the poorly defined path. The rain became a light mist but it hung in the air until late afternoon. The land started to become hilly and it was not until they reached the summit of a larger hill that they could see a small settlement in the valley ahead.

Alheeza telepathed: *Huxbee.*

Huxbee

Mandeler could feel the rush of excitement as they made their way down the slope to the little cluster of buildings. He had only traveled to adjacent estates and never to this village. From the stories told around the dining table, he had heard all about the people that lived to the north. Now he would get to see them first hand.

The village was nestled in the valley with forest on either side. In keeping with the architecture of the highlands, all the buildings had steeply pitched roofs that intersected cleanly with the tapered walls. They had the traditional ironwood-barred windows and flush-fitting doors. The structures were once brightly painted with details in green and yellow but now all were looking shabby. Ten smaller buildings were divided by a central pathway. In the center stood a large structure that Mandeler assumed must be a lodge. As they got closer the path became lumpy and he realized that someone had taken great care to select interlocking fieldstone. Many doors were flung open to the street and there was the sound of craftspeople at work.

Mandeler slid from Star's back and walked towards the first open shed with Alheeza at his side. A man with grey hair was sitting at a bench boring small holes in a length of wood. With well-practiced moves, he placed the small auger at even intervals from the other holes and began to spin the tool. The floor was covered with small shavings from the bright yellow wood. Mandeler carefully said, "Excuse me, sir, can you tell me where I can find the elder of the village?"

As if he had all the time in the world, the craftsman finished his small hole and laid the delicate drill carefully on the bench. His pale blue eyes sought Mandeler's and they lingered there for a moment before he said, "Well young man, what would you be wantin' with him today?"

"I have been sent by Herbin Cochral to warn the people about a Raptor attack at his estate, five sun cycles ago."

"Now that's worth a telling!"

The old man stood, untied his apron and placed it carefully on the bench beside the drill, and beckoned Mandeler to follow him as he set out with a slight limp towards the large building. As they passed other open doors, the old craftsman called to those within to join them for a gathering. One man came out immediately and the elder artisan asked him if he could help tend to the young muzel. Mandeler directed Star to follow and he did.

The doors of the central lodge opened quietly on its ironwood hinges revealing the dimness within. After a day of traveling the warmth of the hall was very inviting. Only a few of the window shutters were open making it hard to see at first but then he could make out a great long table with a fireplace alight at the end of the room. There were two rows of pillars on either side of the central area with curtains drawn over the alcoves.

Alheeza mind-spoke: *I will find a place outside the circle, it is best if you are not seen with me at your side. I will be here for you as needed.*

Thank you, responded Mandeler.

"What is your name, young man?" asked the gray-haired gentleman.

"Mandeler Freedahson, sir."

"Well Master Freedahson at least you have good manners, even though you do not carry good news. Sit. Would you care for a mug of brew while the others assemble?"

Ale had not been a part of Mandeler's boyhood tradition but out of politeness he nodded his head in acceptance. A woman about the same age as his host brought two large mugs of foaming ale. The older man took his and drank deeply then he said, "My name is Sigfree and I am the elder of Huxbee. The rest will join us as soon as they have put their things away." Then he looked down at

Mandeler's mug as if to say, you don't like the beer?

Mandeler put the mug to his lips and drank. He almost gagged on the bitter brew but as he swallowed it warmed his insides. Putting it down, he involuntarily shook his head. The old man was looking over his drink and the lines around his eyes creased into a smile as he said, "As you can see, we brew it strong here."

All Mandeler could do was nod.

The others started to trickle into the building, some accepting the same mugs of ale, others going to the fireplace and coming back with tea. A tall slender woman wearing a long skirt and a baggy turquoise sweater came through the door. Her dark brown hair was tied up on top of her head and she looked directly at Mandeler as she crossed the room. To Mandeler's surprise, he felt a chill run down his spine as he came under the scrutiny of this strange woman. She must be just a few season cycles older than him.

When it seemed that all were there, the older man stood and lifting a hand for silence, said, "This is Mandeler Freedahson and he has come with news from the estates south of here." He looked at Mandeler and gestured for him to stand.

Mandeler had been sipping his ale very slowly but even so he found that he was slightly light-headed as he rose to his feet. He looked around at the dozen people assembled and clearing his throat said, "At dusk, five sun cycles ago the estate of Herbin Cochral was attacked by several Great Raptors. There was a gathering at the time and four were taken along with many injuries. I was told that the communities as far north as the sea are to be warned about the renewed attacks." He felt a strong urge to reach up for his amulet and then he could hear in his head: *Keep your hand away from the stone, you did well so just stand there and answer their questions.*

A broad shouldered man with a touch of grey at his temples spoke up, "I am Burtran. How many of these cursed creatures were there?"

Mandeler blinked a few times and tried to bring back the images of that night: their slashing talons, the little gleaming green eyes and snapping jaws. But how many were there in total? As he started to speak he knew exactly how many, "Four."

The whole room erupted as everyone started to talk at once.

Mandeler sat down taking in the room with its pained faces as the group struggled with the knowledge that the night terrors were abroad again. Sigfree's voice broke through the voices, "Enough!"

Everyone turned to the elder and he spoke again, "Four known Raptors have ravaged a gathering only days away. That does not mean that our village will be hit. Now listen to me. We have the reinforced lodge and from now on nobody leaves it after dark. Now let's prepare for sunset." There was a low murmur of voices but the group started to break up and drift away. The young woman shot him a look that made Mandeler feel like he had deliberately brought bad news to ruin her day. He was still feeling the bite of that look when Sigfree spoke to him, "Gather your things, young man. You can share our evening meal and sleep here in the lodge.

"Thank you, sir."

He left the lodge in search of Star.

Later that evening, Mandeler sat at the end of the long table next to Sigfree. It was the same group as the afternoon meeting but two small faces also came to the table. There was a little boy about five and a girl maybe two season-cycles older. Their denzels were at a low table and Alheeza joined them. Sigfree looked over at the denzels, "Why is the denzel traveling with someone who has passed the manhood?"

He and Alheeza (Soom) had gone over their cover story and he said, "He is also traveling north to be bonded to a boy near the sea." The older man just nodded.

The food was plentiful and tasty enough but nothing could match his Aunt Mirra's cooking. After all it was the northern estates that produced some of the richest food. They traded their food stocks for the handcrafted items that may have come from places like this.

As he was finishing up a slice of winter pie he felt his amulet pulse. He stood and walked to the corner of the room and turned his back to the group. He reached under his tunic to clasp his crystal and instantly he was connected: A *darkened sky and an indistinct landscape. He felt it being drawn to an area ahead. Lower and lower the great creature flew. Mandeler could sense it searching ahead and then…*

The sound of sharp claws scraping on the roof brought him out of his reverie. There were shrieks of horror from the villagers as they scrambled to the edges of the room. The building trembled as something large heaved itself about the coarse shingled roof. The tearing sounds became more intense. Alheeza broke in: *The flinger, can you get the flinger ready?*

That jarred Mandeler into action. He spun and tore open his pack. Quickly in the dim lights of the illumination globes he removed the slender projectile weapon and pulled the elastics back. Shaking he drew out one of the sharp arrows and notched it in the slot. Then he turned and watched the ceiling. The wide rafters were trembling and dust was falling from the interlocking boards in the roof. Alheeza broke in again: *Take a second arrow and hold it in with your extended hand.* Mandeler paused long enough to reach down for a second one. In the time it took to do that there was a crashing sound as a great set of talons broke through the planked roof. They withdrew and were replaced by the most repulsive head of a Raptor. The black armored head rotated as the green eyes searched the room. Sigfree was still trying to make it to the edge of the room as the Raptor struck, it grabbed him by the shoulder and suddenly he was drawn up screaming, and out of the ragged hole in the roof.

Mandeler was stunned by the speed of the attack and he hoisted the projectile weapon to his shoulder and took a breath. A second head appeared in the opening and he pulled the release. There was a shriek as the Raptor recoiled, a small shaft protruding from its cheek just below the vertical fin. He hastily loaded the second arrow and leaning on a pillar, pointed it at the hole. There was a great deal of trampling on the roof and he thought they may be making ready to leave. Instead the same Raptor thrust its head down the hole reaching his head towards Mandeler, mouth agape. Mandeler's nostrils were filled with the putrid breath of the beast and in that last instant he fired the flinger. This time it went deeply into the slit of the crimson eye. The Raptor recoiled thrashing its head back and forth smashing everything within reach. Pieces of wood flew in every direction as the center of the room was demolished by the death throes of the great beast. Then as suddenly as it started it was over and the room was quiet.

Dust and fine debris floated past illumination globes like snow caught in the light. In the eerie silence people stared at the limp Raptor's neck hanging from the ceiling oozing orange blood from his eye and self-inflicted wounds.

Then the tall young woman that had given Mandeler such a hard stare rose from the rubble and said, "Holly Raptor Dung, how did you do that?"

He stood as if in a trance and stared at the great Raptor, its large head resting at an odd angle against a chunk of the table. In a low voice he said, "I don't know, I just pulled the trigger!"

A low whimpering started at one end of the room and was taken up by several others as the survivors started to take inventory of their lives. Not far from him the lady that served his ale started to wail uncontrollably. He felt around for his packs and found them unharmed in the wreckage. The medicinal case was easy to locate so he hefted it under his arm and turned to the distressed woman beside him. There appeared to be no injures but after clutching his crystal he found that she had been the lost man's wife.

He set out across the floor but stopped some distance from the lolling head and watched for any breath or sign of life. Without concern for being seen he grasped his amulet and reached with his mind to the creature. There was not a trace of life in the scaled predator; the Raptor was truly dead. As he stood there he became aware of the awful stink that was permeating the room. These creatures smelled like decades of decay. He let his hand fall to his side and turned to the people behind the pillars.

The slender woman said again, "Who in Azimov's abyss are you?"

Mandeler just stood there dumbfounded.

She repeated, "I said, who you are?"

Slowly he said, "Mandeler Freedahson from Almar's estate to the south. Who are you?"

She said, "I am Gwenelle."

He felt a woman's voice in his head: *And if you're just a farm boy then I have dung for brains.*

The Trail North

Mandeler did not sleep that night nor did the inhabitants of Huxbee. After taking inventory of the slight injuries, everyone wanted to flee the wreckage and stink of the lodge. Mandeler had to agree that lightning and Raptors attacks never seem to strike twice. A meeting was called in one of the work sheds. The man that had first spoken up was called Burtran and the folks naturally listened to his guidance. It was decided that the entire village would take refuge at the next settlement, Melville. Nobody trusted the rotting rafters of the lodge and furthermore there was a dead reeking Raptor stuck in the roof.

In the early hours people stripped the village of anything of value and piled it by the doors. Many buildings were designated store houses and since it was early spring, they were nearly empty. Three carts made similarly to the traveler but taller and wider were heaped with personal possessions and supplies. The village had two aging muzels and Mandeler was asked if Star could be used to pull a cart too.

It was amazing to see how quickly the people had pulled together to prepare for their departure. Almost everyone including the two children had shouldered a pack and had on heavy traveling clothes. They stood at the end of Huxbee and watched as two men with torches went into the lodge and before long, smoke started to trickle through the broken roof. The Raptor lay sprawled to one side with wings askew, its long tail dangled to the ground. The black skin still had a slight purple tint but it seemed dull in the morning light. It was the largest creature Mandeler had ever seen. Then the first flames leapt through the shattered roof.

As one, the group turned their backs on their homes and started down the trail. No one turned to look back at the lodge crackling from the fire. Was it his imagination or was the stink of roasting Raptor filling the air?

The troop made good time down the trail. Burtran knew the way north since it was where they took most of their trade goods. It turned out that they crafted musical instruments and had brought the best of them and their tools. Sigfree's wife, Helgee, was placed in the cart with blankets to keep her warm. She had been inconsolable during the night and now sat staring blankly into the distance.

The smallest of the children walked and took turns being carried but mostly the group trudged on in silence. Star walked along with his burden as if he had done this all his life.

The next village was almost three days away but Burtran had assured Mandeler that he knew of two safe places they could hold up at night. Mandeler had to wonder what Burton's definition of safe might be after seeing how determined a Raptor could be.

Mandeler walked quietly beside Burtran with Alheeza at his side. He started to reflect upon the last day: the strange vision preceding the rooftop attack, Sigfree being taken, firing projectiles at the Raptor's head and killing it, their quickly mounted departure with all of the village's refugees hurrying down the trail. Then there was that unknown telepath.

Alheeza broke into his thoughts: *Your people had a saying, something about, "The best laid plans of mice and men go oft awry."*

And where did you learn about human poetry?

We denzels are an old race. We live several of your lifetimes. At this, Mandeler turned and looked at his companion. Alheeza continued, *I was a companion of Jamie Cambers when we were both young. Since then, I have been bonded to many young people and during that time I sat to the side and listened to their parents tell stories about the early colonists and their home on Earth. Robbie Burns was a very popular Scottish poet and I liked a few of his lines. But my original point was that no matter how we plan a trip, things happen and the plans change. So here we are. Instead of two of us hastening down the trail we are fifteen.*

Mandeler turned and looked back at the group. They were strung out along the narrow trail as it wound its way through the copse of trees. As they traveled downhill the flat topped conifers and herman nut groves gave way to tall twisted trees, still devoid of leaves, that grew in irregular clusters. Flocks of noisy purple kites and small orange headed mockers would burst from the branches as the troop approached.

He thought about the tall outspoken women in the hall the night before. Where he grew up folks were so much more reserved and... he looked for a word: polite. At this he turned and looked back, he saw Gwenelle some way back striding along in bulky walking pants and the same baggy sweater. Her long hair was tied back revealing her high forehead above the piercing blue eyes. Her thumbs were hooked under the straps of her pack and as he watched her gaze came up to meet his creating an unfamiliar stirring within. He turned looking down the trail unable to hold her gaze.

Alheeza mind-spoke: *That is why the bonding ends at the manhood passage. Our council does not include man-woman interaction.*

What are you talking about?

You will see.

Burtran turned and brought the group to a halt. Raising his voice he said, "We are approaching the Gabbing River and the path gets steep." Pointing to three of the stocky villagers he said, "Come and help me restrain the first cart for the decent." As they positioned themselves Helgee slipped from her seat and took a hold too.

He was right because as they emerged from the trees the sound of rushing water came up to meet them. They stood on the edge of a steep bank looking down on a river that wound its way between the shallow hills. The river was jumping and dancing off the multitude of rocks within the stream. The trail down to its edge was much steeper than any hill they had encountered so far. Mandeler joined the others to brake the descending cart. When it came to Star's cart, Mandeler went forward to help guide the young animal. One by one the carts were carefully guided down the path to the river's edge.

Burtran pointed out that this was the ford, a place where the river became wider and shallow for a short distance. Winter was not long past, making the water frigid. Most people took off their socks and pulled up their pants. Mandeler looked down at his manhood boots and wondered just how water proof they were? In the end, he too removed his footwear. With the children hoisted on shoulders, the group cautiously made their way across the ford. After they dried their feet, Burtran led them along the narrow path that hugged the steep canyon wall bordered by the river. When they rounded the second bend they came upon the mouth of the cave.

The Cave

The river had cut a channel through the layers of local rock leaving a steep river bank. The sandstone shelf created a natural facade with the narrow cave opening tucked beneath it. The entrance was oval and about man high but only half that wide. Mandeler climbed the sandy mound to follow Burtran but in the dim light he found it hard to see how far back it went. Gwenelle pushed past him with a pair of illumination globes in her hands and as she did so the darkness shrank away from them, revealing a high ceiling within.

Burtran said, "In the summer we get heavy rain storms along with high river levels. It covers the road into here but the cave has been dry for years. We'll sleep safe from floods and Raptors here tonight."

Others started to carry goods from the carts and in no time everyone was settled around the edge of the large space. Mandeler asked about Star's safety but Burtran assured him that they could settle the muzels under the low overhang along with a cooking fire. The animals had been safe there on other journeys. It was amazing how well these people worked together. Soon the fire was lit and a communal pot settled in the flames to make the evening stew. This team work was new to him as he had always worked in ones or twos with his uncle.

Alheeza telepathed: *Your race had great strengths and weaknesses and what you are looking at right now is the power of a dedicated group getting things done. I am always amazed to see it at work. Why do you think we were drawn to you?*

Mandeler nodded his head and looked at his long-time friend: *You have such a deep knowledge of us. I feel like such a child next to you.*

When you picked up the flinger and challenged the Raptor, I felt helpless next to you. Your race can use tools and I have always been amazed at how quickly you learn.

Mandeler responded: *I thought it was you that had the cool head and had anticipated everything. I was just standing there like a post when you prodded me into taking up the flinger. You even had me place a second arrow where it was quicker to fire a second shot.*

It is always easy to sit back and watch what others are doing. I saw the first flinger being invented and because of that I understood the principle but it is you that shouldered the weapon and fired it directly into the creature's eye. I could never have done that. We cannot make or use tools like you do. You have my admiration my young friend.

And you have my gratitude for teaching me so many things. Now what was this you were saying earlier about man-woman relations?

Alheeza bowed his head: *On that topic you are on your own my friend.* And with that he turned to walk back into the cave.

Mandeler looked up at the sky and could see the first of the evening stars appearing above. He reached under his tunic and clasped the amulet searching for danger, but all was quiet. With that knowledge he entered the cave. It had been transformed with the glow of a dozen illumination globes. People had settled around the perimeter and up the back of the cave. Some were still finishing their bowls of supper, others had drawn their families together and were huddled closely. As he worked his way to the right to join Alheeza, he heard a low tune being drawn from a flute. It was melancholy in nature but as he listened the melody rose and fell in waves. In this remote spot it felt so comforting. As he watched the musician she looked up and the penetrating blue eyes met his. Gwenelle kept the instrument to her lips and without faltering she held Mandeler's gaze. It was only when she drew the tune to a close that she dropped her eyes. He felt that same tingling but tried to hide it as he made a fuss about pulling his cloak up around his neck. One by one the bioluminescent globes were allowed to dim and finally sleep took him.

He slept soundly for some time before the dream took him. *He was near the water again. She turned her head from side to side and just beyond the rhythmic beat of her own wings were other flying creatures. They must be Raptors but not the raptors of his early dreams. These were olive green with lighter underbellies, and softer, rounder faces with ear wings that curved. Set below the rounded nasal brow were clear intelligent eyes. They flew on…* he opened his eyes to the darkness of the cave, sensing that they had been looking back through his dream at him.

Instinctively he reached under his tunic and clasped the stone. He let his senses reach out beyond the cave. Still breathing heavily from the dreams he sought the presence of the great night predators. There was no response and he felt his body relax noticeably. Just as he was about to release the stone he felt a short burst of something, there was another presence reaching out. *Dung this floor is hard!*

Mandeler lay there searching for another glimpse of the phantom telepath. Could it be the tall woman? There was nothing in the darkness, just the sound of people, denzels and the muzels sleeping. It crossed his mind that perhaps they should have posted a lookout but he dismissed that almost immediately because who could actually stop a Raptor? Sure he had killed one by happenstance. Anyway they were well protected above by the overhanging sandstone and the small entrance. Sleep found him again and so did the dream.

He was standing in a crowded market with more people pressed together than he could have imagined. Mandeler scanned the faces seeking a single person. Then he caught a glimpse of the tall slender figure moving through the crowd. She turned her head and as the dark hair swirled out of her face the blue eyes locked onto his and he got that strange feeling again. He awoke again but this time to the smell of porridge!

Light streamed in through the entrance and it gave shape to his world. There was a steaming bowl of fruit porridge on the ground next to him and Helgee was kneeing beside him. Mandeler elbowed his way up and looked at her.

She said, "I have to thank you for killing that thing before it took any more of our loved ones!" There was a look of anger mixed with grief.

He reached out a hand to hers and said, “It was just a lucky shot, nothing more. I just wish it had happened before Sigfree was taken.”

She nodded and this time he could see the tears welling up as she rose to make her way back outside.

Mandeler shared his breakfast with Alheeza and then taking up his gear they went outside. All was busy with the preparations for departure. He helped to direct Star to his station at the second cart. The villagers had fed him well the night before and the young muzel was keen to carry on.

A few moments later they started off with Burtran in the lead. Not far down the trail they came to the path leading up and this time it was not as steep and with some effort all of the carts were soon at the summit.

Mandeler walked near the front of the troop, a few steps behind Burtran. There was almost no conversation that day. It was as if the group of travelers were finally grasping the full impact of grief and loss that drove them north. The trail seemed to be going gradually downhill. The forest started to change with the tall twisted trees being replaced with broad reaching green clad branches with knurled trunks thicker than a man was wide. The overhanging branches were filled with long tailed climbers with bulging eyes that dropped nuts on them as they passed. Flocks of broad snouted kites with black and white markings were quiet as they passed only to start chattering again as soon as the troop had gone by.

He found his mind wondering again. Since the manhood passage it was as if his quiet country existence had been turned upside down. Nothing was sure and the future was a gaping void.

Alheeza broke the silence, mind-speaking: *I need to spend the night with the other denzels. We have much to discuss regarding the recent attack on our races.*

They ate their cold rations while trudging on. Just before sunset Burtran brought them to a halt in front of the tallest stand of trees Mandeler had ever seen. These giants had a root base that spread out like so many fingers rising up to form a single thick trunk. Far above it split into long branches covered with broad serrated green and yellow leaves. These were the first new leaves of spring.

Burtran explained the four giant Manfriend trees would be their shelter for the night. Crossing to one he pointed out that the palisade of roots would be the fortification needed. The trunk was hollow and with the raised dirt between the roots it provided a very safe, dry place to spend the night but there was only room for a few people in each. Again the draft animals would have to stay in the open with a small fire.

As people started to drift off to their trees for the evening he found himself standing with Helgee, Burtran and Gwenelle. Helgee nodded to Burtran and said, "Our village is a family affair and with all of the chaos I had no chance to introduce Burtran as my son." Burtran smiled and looked at his mother with appreciation. They turned and started to take their gear up to the tree lodge.

Gwenelle spoke up, "I am not from here. I came from Portside to apprentice as a flute maker." She stood almost defiantly and Mandeler was not sure what to say next. They stood staring at each other and then he said, "Well, I am definitely not from here either. Where is Portside?"

She let out a long breath and her shoulders slumped visibly, "It is many days to the north. It is a fishing town on the side of the sea."

"How did you end up here making flutes?"

"My father was poor and one day I saw Burtran in the market selling the flutes. Next day I took my father to see them and he struck a bargain with him. I would give a year of my work in return for learning the flute craft. Then three months later you arrived along with those cursed creatures smashing all of my hopes and dreams!"

Mandeler absently mind-spoke: *Yours and a lot of others!*

Her head shot up, and she looked from side to side.

Mandeler slowly said, "Did you hear someone say, yours and a lot of others?"

She looked scared now but she nodded her head in agreement. He went on, "Don't be afraid, that was me and you hear me speak from mind to mind."

Holy Raptor Dung! Can you read my every thought?

Raising his hands slightly Mandeler said openly, "I know it scares you, but just let me explain."

She was shaking her head back and forth slowly and he proceeded with care, "There are some of us that can talk to each other but not everybody can. I cannot read anybody's mind that does not want me to. It is more like talking without moving our lips." He mind-spoke: *Like this.*

They stood there looking at each other and finally she said in mind-speak: *There is more to you than meets the eye, kid.*

He smiled and mind-spoke to her: *There is a great deal more about you than meets the eye, Miss Gwenelle. I assume this is the first time you have talked by mind-speak deliberately to another?*

What do you think! She still looked worried.

She was looking at him with those intense blue eyes and he went on: *As far as I know there are no other people here that can sense us. It might be best if you don't talk to anybody about this because they might not take it well.*

Her confidence seemed to be recovering a little and he went on: *Should we take our things up into the Manfriend tree?*

Melville

Everyone was tired from the two sun cycles of hard walking not to mention their collective grief from the attack. By the sound of things most people wrapped themselves in blankets and cloaks falling quickly to sleep. Mandeler was aware of Gwenelle close by and that strange stirring in his belly but his exhaustion overcame him too. His dreams were fleeting with only glimpses of blue eyes on drifting flute music. Just before he awoke there was a green raptor flying into the sunrise. The image remained clear as his eyes opened to the filtered light of the rising sun. He levered himself up taking in the smells and sounds of the morning.

Gwenelle had already risen and he stood to gather his gear as Helgee and Burtran wrapped their things together. He came out to see an overcast sky and the villagers readying the carts. It appeared that it was a cold breakfast of dried fruit and nuts. Alheeza joined him and mind-spoke, *The other two denzels were telling me that the next settlement is still a hard day's walk from here and the people are anxious to get on. They also believe it will rain again soon.*

Alheeza, one of the villagers appears to have spontaneously turned telepathic. She does not seem to know anything about denzels, mind-speaking or the passage ceremonies. How can that be?

There may be an explanation. When we first made contact it was after the great storm. Some of your people suffering from the trauma started to have breakthrough telepathy. This was enhanced by the chance finding of the first speaking crystal. Perhaps the terror of the last attack was enough to breakdown her barriers?

Mandeler responded, *That might explain a good deal. How much do I tell her about our telepathy guild, the crystals and the role of the denzels?*

For now keep it simple and keep your passage experiences to yourself. Test and exercise her natural abilities and let us see where it goes.

Mandeler nodded and went to prepare Star for the next day's journey. It was apparent that the villagers wanted a hasty departure for they were on the trail quickly. The denzels knew their local weather well because the drizzle started a couple of spans of time later. It turned into a downpour by early afternoon. Rain and mud are depressing and he could feel the mood of the group slumping deeper. Their efforts to make progress were hindered as the trail turned to mud. Several times a cart would get mired down and the villagers would have to put their shoulders to work to free the vehicle. A very bedraggled group entered the village just at sunset.

Melville was larger than Huxbee and even in the gloom of the evening the town looked in better repair. Its paint was brighter and some of the two dozen buildings looked new. He hoped there would be room for everybody. Burtran confidently went to the large lodge, where he beat upon the door. A girl in her early teens opened the heavy wooden portal and looked out. From her face it was easy to see that she had not expected to see a sizable troop of soggy travelers. She disappeared and a grey haired gentleman looked out into the rainy night. He recognized Burtran immediately and waved them all in.

There was a fireplace ablaze at the far end of the great hall. The peaked room must have been five times the height of a man at its center and there were two great tables running down the middle. It was a traditional layout with two rows of posts running down either side of the room. Behind these were heavily curtained personal spaces.

Mandeler's mind was drawn back to their host, as he began to speak. Standing well to the side he instinctively reached under his tunic for the crystal. As soon as he touched it, the scene changed. The head man took on a slight aura and the next thing he noted was that Gwenelle's hair was also radiating. It was the first time since his manhood passage that he had linked the crystal with a guild member. He waited patiently for the head man and Burtran to finish with the introductions and when his name was mentioned he stepped forward and bowed his head slightly saying, "I am Mandeler

Freedahson and I come with news about two Raptor attacks." Then he mind-spoke to the head man, *I have just come from my manhood passage and I sense that you are from our guild.*

The old man's brows twitched slightly and he mind-spoke, *Welcome Mandeler, we will talk later.* Openly he said, "Welcome to our modest home. I will call the others and we will have a sharing of these unwelcome tidings." He lifted his arms and said more loudly to the soggy group, "Please bring your personal things in and place them along the side posts, warm drink will be brought shortly." With that he turned to the same young girl and gave her instructions to fetch the villagers.

Mandeler went out to check on Star and found that the animal shelter had just enough room for the three extra muzels. Apparently there were those that could handle the mules without the full telepathic capabilities that his Uncle Almar had. Looking back, the Huxbee mules were old and there was one woman that tended to them. She did not seem to have any mind-speak tendencies but she handled the animals well enough. Here was the same thing. The handler took their muzels into a shed and gave them rations of a nut he had not seen before.

When he returned to the main lodge, Gwenelle was just coming out from a curtained alcove. She had changed out of her sodden travel attire. Her hair was again twisted into a knot exposing her slim neck. Her long dress was tight at the waist and as she walked the swing of her hips almost took his breath away. She was beautiful and as she walked past him, he was at a loss for words. He heard his name called and he went to the grey haired leader who mind-spoke, *Come with me to change into dry clothes and we will have a word before the sharing time.*

Mandeler nodded and followed him to a back room where the old gentleman closed the door. Once the wooden latch clicked shut, he turned and mind-spoke, *My name is Ilford and I welcome a member of our guild to Melville.*

Thank you sir, my father was Mandell and my uncle was Almar, who was recently taken.

Ilford nodded and continued, *I knew both of your kin and was there for your father's manhood passage. I am not surprised to find that it is you carrying the news along with Alheeza. Before we meet with the rest, tell me briefly what has happened.*

Mandeler began with the attack at his initiation, the loss of his uncle and three other people, and then to the Raptors tearing through the weakened roof of the Huxbee lodge and the loss of Sigfree. It was when he touched on the killing of the Raptor that Ilford stopped him. *You killed a Raptor?*

Yes.

With a single arrow?

Yes.

! How did you do it?

The first arrow hit its cheek but when it came back I shot it in the eye.

So they do have a weakness. Long ago there was another night marauder vanquished but the details have been lost with time. So much was lost in the great storm and afterwards. We had to learn how to store knowledge all over again. He shook his head adding: *Put your dry things on my young friend, and then come out and join the sharing time.*

When he emerged from the back room there were forty or fifty people gathered in the hall. Ilford motioned for him to join Burtran and himself at the head of the table. A mug of ale was passed to Mandeler and this time he just sipped it, knowing what a kick it had.

Ilford stood and called for silence, "People of Melville, we have grave news. Our neighbors to the south, in Huxbee, were attacked three sun cycles ago. Sigfree was taken and the hall damaged to the point that the villagers now fear for their lives." He could hardly go on for the voices raised in alarm. Shouting over them he said, "Quiet, **Quiet**! Now hear the full details from one that has seen the last two attacks!" He turned toward Mandeler motioning him to stand.

Mandeler looked around at the distressed faces in the room and found that his stomach was suddenly churning. The words would not come at first and then he sensed Ilford, *Breathe and then speak as if you are talking to just one person.*

He consciously took in a breath and then he found Gwenelle's face, the anger was gone and she looked back as if urging him to speak. He heard his own voice start, "I am Mandeler Freedahson.

Seven sun cycles ago four Great Raptors attacked the Mulestead estate to the south, four men and a denzel were taken. Three days ago, Raptors tore the roof open at Huxbee and took Sigfree. One of the great ones was killed in the attack. My task has been to warn the people to the north that the night marauders are back and that no one is safe." The room burst into shouts and gestures again. Mandeler eyes stayed on Gwenelle's and she nodded adding: *Well done kid.* Why did she always call him kid, she couldn't be more than a few season-cycles older than he?

Three men came up to Mandeler and wanted to know more about the killing of the Raptor and how it could be repeated. He talked about the flinger and took it from his possessions to show the men. The fact that he had to be so close seemed to destroy any of their hope for a meaningful defense.

It must have been a hand of time before Ilford called for silence once again, "People, we have a crisis to deal with. First Burtran of Huxbee has asked for shelter since their village is uninhabitable. We are in better shape since this building has a new roof and support beams. They have brought some of their provisions and personal items, including valuable musical instruments. I think we can find space for all. Once they get their goods to market they can repay us for our hospitality. What we need to do now is keep the night movements restricted for fear of an attack. Tonight nobody leaves this room until the sun comes up tomorrow. I know this is difficult but it seems prudent to take precautions starting now."

You could hardly call it a feast but loaves of bread, nut butter, dishes of spiced mash and dried fruit were spread on the table. Mandeler ate his fill and found some water to supplement the ale that was flowing freely amongst the group.

There was a sharp cry followed by a smacking sound. Mandeler sensed, *You filthy bastard, you put your hand there once more and I will cut it off!* That mind-speaker he knew, it was Gwenelle. She bolted to her feet and stomped around the room toward Mandeler saying, "I like the company at this end better." As she sat next to him, he noticed her release the handle of a knife and let it slide back into her pocket. "Men… got only one thing on their minds!"

The Trail Ahead

It was another restless night in which Mandeler awoke several times with mixed dreams about Raptors and pursuit. When he was awake it was with a keen sense of awareness that Gwenelle was curled into a ball next to him. She too seemed to be having dreams because she would twitch and whimper from time to time.

At first light, the hall emptied and Mandeler found himself alone with Alheeza. He mind-spoke: *What is the trail ahead like now?*

The old denzel replied: *We have two choices, we can follow the great river Andreas as it winds its way to the high falls and then along the flat lands behind the Blue Mountains. Or we can go over the mountains and straight to the sea. With the first choice we take a small boat, piloted by a local, as far as the falls. We stop at the villages to spread the word as we go. Our second choice is to send a fisherman from Melville to take that route and spread the word for us. That allows us to take a trail over the Blue Mountains and hopefully reach Portside a third of a moon sooner.*

What is on your mind, doesn't it seem obvious that the quicker route is the logical route?

Alheeza went on: *The mountain pass will still have winter snow in the high places thus it increases the risks. I believe there is something more pressing about the Raptor attacks. There seems to be so something else driving them this time. No Raptor has torn open a building to get at the occupants before.*

Are you saying there is urgency about our mission and we need to hurry at all costs?

Yes.

Mandeler paused: *I bow to your greater knowledge and experience.*

Ilford came into the hall mind-speaking to both of them: *Alheeza my old friend, how good it is to see you. I am also glad that you are Mandeler's companion for this journey.*

Alheeza telepathed: *We were just discussing the options for departure. Let me ask you, have you had any word from the traders crossing the Blue Mountains this spring?*

There were a few that came through earlier in the winter but we have not had any since then. I expect there is still a good deal of snow in the pass. Why do you ask?

We are contemplating going that way to get to Portside sooner. Can you fit us out with snow crossing gear?

I will consult with our trade goods handler and see what he has on hand.

Again Alheeza mind-spoke: *As you can tell, there is an urgency about our quest and I would like to leave today.*

Give me a hand of time to prepare.

Mandeler asked: *What will the charge be for the things we need?*

Ilford turned his kind eyes upon the pair of them: *Alheeza was also my bonded denzel as well as your father's and then yours. What I owe him for the knowledge passed down cannot start to be repaid with a few traveling goods.*

With that he turned and left the room.

By the way Ilford was talking he has known you for a long time. How old are you?

I was very young when the Great storm occurred, 413 of your season cycles ago.

Now Mandeler was dumbfounded, *you remember the first of the colonists and their technology?*

Yes. I was there when your ancestor, Jamie Chambers led the survivors to safety. I will tell you more later.

It was nearly lunch time when Mandeler and Alheeza had finished filling their packs. They had been discussing the arduous task ahead and it seemed unlikely that Star would be able to cross the glaciers. Arrangements for him had been made along with the writing of a declaration about the Raptor attacks to be carried down to the river settlements.

He was saying his goodbyes to Burtran and Helgee when Gwenelle breathlessly came up to them, "What is going on, are you leaving us?"

"Yes," Mandeler replied.

"Where are you going?"

"We must carry word about the great night marauders to the coastal settlements as quickly as possible; therefore we are taking the Blue Mountain pass."

"Are you going to Portside?"

"Yes."

She seemed somewhat unsettled and walked away. Why did every encounter with her seem unsettling?

Their departure was without any particular fanfare and the trail to the north was well marked. It was still muddy from the previous rain and Mandeler's boots were smeared with the green clay. Even Alheeza was gradually turning ochre as they splashed along the trail.

As they walked along, Alheeza started to fill the young man in about Mandeler's family history. His father was indeed a natural sensate that started to show telepathic tendencies before his manhood passage, just like Mandeler. He was inquisitive, adventurous and bright. Alheeza enjoyed the bonding with him and kept track of his life after he became a man. The pairing of Mandell and Freedah was a joyous time because everyone felt it was a very good match. It was during the last wave of Raptor attacks that the family, including baby Mandeler, were caught out after dusk traveling between Estates. In the attack, their traveler was overturned, spilling his parents into the waiting jaws of the Great Raptors. Miraculously baby Mandeler and Alheeza were unharmed and the next day Uncle Almar had come to rescue them.

Mandeler thought he could remember groping talons and the

gaping mouth full of yellow teeth, but it was easy to mix his dreams with the early stories.

The trail had been climbing since they left the village and it was hard going. They pressed through low bush punctuated by boulders. Mandeler was starting to wonder if he would ever have the stamina to keep up with a denzel. Given Alheeza's age, how could he have such endurance?

The Manfriend trees were a welcome sight this close to sunset. They climbed up into the sheltered area surrounded by the palisade of roots and were just getting comfortable when sounds of splashing could be heard coming up the trail. Mandeler reached one hand for his knife and the other for his amulet, searching the area for danger. As they peered down the track, a figure in baggy clothes stained with green clay came into view. Her hair was undone and billowing behind her but by the swing of her arms she still appeared to be angry.

He telepathed to her: *Are you looking for us? We are in the great Manfriend tree to your right.*

Oh frap! There you are. And she stomped over to where they took cover.

Mandeler reached through the roots and added: *Hand your things up and join us.*

A bedraggled Gwenelle sat cross-legged on one side of their shelter. She sat there without speaking for a time, and then she reached over and put a hand on the denzel, saying in a soft voice, "Oh gentle one, I wish more people were like you."

At which point Alheeza replied in mind-speak: *Gwenelle, yes we denzels are the gentle ones, but it is time you knew us for who we are. We are the teachers and guardians of knowledge.*

She jumped, trying to press her way through the roots behind her, but finally she settled and said, "Do you all talk in your heads?" adding in mind-speak: *Great thunder, you're all scary!*

Both Alheeza and Mandeler looked at each other and then Mandeler broke into fits of laughter. When he could get his breath he spoke openly, "I have been called a number of things but never scary." He added in mind-speak: *The Great Raptors are scary, but talking with a denzel is more of a marvel, don't you think?*

She looked from one to the other several times and then her shoulders slumped and she let out a great breath saying, “No, I guess you two are not all that scary but it still feels weird.”

They sat in silence for a while and then she went on in words and mind-speak, “I was just starting to learn how to prepare the seasoned wood to make flutes. Then that horrible stinking Raptor came crashing through the roof and I thought we were all dead. After slogging through the trail to Melville, my reward was that groping fool of a carpenter. He was at it again this morning. *He pinned me to a back wall until I pressed my blade into his tender parts. He let me go*. I grabbed my stuff and followed you. Please let me travel with you. I just want to go back to Portside. *I feel safer traveling with a kid and his denzel than staying back there with that fool trying to grab me at every turn.*

Mandeler thought for a few breaths, reviewing the things that he and Alheeza had discussed about the trek over the snow covered mountains. He looked at Alheeza, who nodded imperceptibly. Then he mind-spoke to them both: *Alheeza and I agree to take you with us but we have some concerns.* He drew his pack closer and turning it, showed her a pair of wooden frames with lacing across it. *These are snow walkers and we only have sets for Alheeza and me. What will we do for you?*

Gwenelle seemed to straighten up and she reached for one of the snow walkers. She turned it slowly and then mind-spoke: *This is simple. I can bend some swamp willow and lace it together with strips of its own bark. Let me go cut a few saplings before full dark.*

With that she slipped from the tree and was gone. The light was starting to fade and Mandeler was worried about the coming night. In just a few breaths of time she was back clutching several swamp willow stems. She plopped herself down again and drew out a small illumination globe from her sweater. She shook the orb making the bio-luminescent bugs burst into light. Then she started to strip the branches with her knife.

Mandeler drew out the travel rations and spread spiced mash on slices of flat bread. For Alheeza he tore up the bits of bread and added the mash to a bowl. It was a quiet meal taken with water from the drinking bag. Gwenelle had finished the outside frames and set them aside for the night. Conversation was minimal and soon they were rolled in cloaks and sound asleep.

The dreams came as usual. *He could make out the rough ridge of mountains on the horizon. The colors were muted so that everything looked monochromatic. He strained to see the details below but a large tree came into focus and at the base was something aglow. The Great Raptor circled several times, and then picking the tall stump of a dead Manfriend tree, he came to roost on it. There was no way he could make his way through the tangle of branches to reach his desired prize. Screaming his frustration, he spread his wings and leaped into the air. The branches of the adjacent trees swayed from the downward thrust of his departure.*

Everyone in the tree shelter jumped with the scream. Mandeler's heart was trying to pound its way out of his chest. Gwenelle thrashed beside him. Suddenly the enclosure was lit by her globe.

"What in Azimov's Abyss is happening?" she shouted.

The Storm

There was no more sleep that night. They talked about the Raptors and how they seemed to be hunting more intensely. The tree had given them safe refuge for the night but they would have to take care every night.

At first light, they were on the trail making haste towards the mountains. As they departed Mandeler checked his amulet. The area appeared clear of danger. He kicked himself for not checking before going to sleep but he would be more diligent from now on.

The trail started to climb steeply on the second day and their packs felt even heavier. The muscles in Mandeler's legs burned with fatigue as they climbed. He looked with wonder at Alheeza, who just kept up the same steady pace despite his age. Gwenelle was breathing hard, as well as looking tired from the sleepless night. As they reached the crest of a hill there was a glimpse of the snow covered Blue Mountains. They stopped several times to share travel rations, washed down with spring water. As they climbed, the Manfriend trees gave way to flat top conifers and they gave way to scrub brush with exposed rock. The trail was getting harder for them to see but Alheeza never faltered, leading them ever higher. All were on the lookout for a suitable campsite.

Mandeler asked: *Alheeza, I have seen tracks along the trail that I do not recognize. What are they?*

Mountain Wolf, we call them Wornzels. They are about twice our size and are carnivorous. They prey upon the herds that graze along the base of the mountain. The problem is they eat anything, including us.

That's comforting, added Gwenelle.

They almost missed seeing the cave opening. The sun was low on the horizon and Alheeza had not been this way in a long time. The rocky hill side, with its patches of snow, had a few scrub bushes in sheltered spots and it was behind one of these that they found the little cave.

Mandeler reached under his tunic to check his crystal before entering. He led the way, dropping his pack on the dirt floor. Gwenelle set out a globe to light the space, which had a low entrance that opened up into a long chamber. At the back were traces of other visitors, some human and some not. Alheeza suggested a fire might be in order to ward off the chill and unwelcome visitors. In anticipation of a cold night they had collected a bit of dry kindling, and soon they had a cheery blaze at the entrance. Soon a cooking bowl was pushed into the flames and before long the cave smelled of hot stew and wood smoke. It was a feast compared to their meals the day before. After the meal, it was time to get out the warm clothes for the freezing night and prepare for the cold days to follow. In this area Gwenelle had prepared well, with extra socks, leggings and heavy sweater with a hood. Afterwards, Gwenelle sat in the glow of her globe and finished lacing her snow walkers.

The conversations had been small talk mostly about the trail ahead but as the night deepened Gwenelle said, “How many others are there like you? I mean the mind-speakers, how many are there?”

It was a question that only Alheeza could address: *All denzels have the gift, we've always had. It was after the great storm long ago that we discovered humans with the skill. Not many, but enough that we could teach them some of this world's secrets. It helps us and it helps you.*

How is it that I didn't know about any of this?

Only the gifted are trained by our kind for the mind-speaking guild. The women have their own way of honoring it. I suspect you were never tested and went undetected. Remember that the trauma of the Raptor attack may have opened your telepathic skills. What we need to do is practice with you so that you can tell when you are communicating mind to mind and how to use it in a directional fashion. We can make it very selective. There is no need to shout our thoughts about. You have already done this unintentionally because Mandeler could hear you before I could.

She blinked her surprise, “How did I do that?”

After the attack you were so focused on Mandeler that I could not hear you. Try now.

She looked uncomfortable as she turned towards Mandeler. It was obvious that she was having trouble focusing fully on him. Alheeza broke in: *Who killed the Raptor that night?* Her eyes locked onto Mandeler: *He did.*

If a denzel could smile he did so now: *Did you say something?*

Yes: I said 'He did'.

But I did not hear it and looking at Mandeler I am sure he did.

All Mandeler did was nod his head.

They practiced some more and it was obvious that she was a sensate to the heart.

As usual the dreams came but this time the flying creatures seemed distant and then suddenly there was a new presence. Mandeler awoke in complete darkness. Instinctively he reached for his crystal while easing his knife out with the other hand. Clasping his amulet brought his night vision and there at the entrance stood a long legged mountain wolf with its bristling rows of back spikes. Its eyes burning red and its mouth hung open exposing rows of razor sharp yellow teeth. Mandeler steadied his breath and pulled the crystal free from his cloak. It cast an emerald light in the cave and the creature took a step back. It shifted its weight back and forth on its clawed feet, as if to judge its opponent. Coming to his knees, Mandeler raised the glowing gem into the air, telepathing: *This is my cave! Death awaits you if you enter!* ***Now be gone!***

He had never seen such a large animal turn and run so fast.

Azimov's abyss, what was that? telepathed Gwenelle as she shook a glow globe.

It was a mountain wolf. I think it was just curious, mind-spoke Mandeler.

How could you know it was there?

I saw it standing at the entrance.

After you pulled the green light out?

No, before.

But how? It was as dark as the inside of a muzel.

Alheeza broke in: *My guess is that there is more than he is telling us.*

In the pale light he studied their faces then glanced down where one hand clasped the exposed crystal and the other still held the naked blade. It was all so bewildering because he had acted on instinct. He groped for the words, then mind-spoke, *In my dreams I can see at night, not bright images but details all the same. When I clasp the amulet I have started to see the same way. Then I just felt so protective of you that I pulled out my knife and told it to go away.*

Alheeza said, *I suspect that you told it more than 'just to go away'. As for your crystal enhanced vision, I have only know one other that had that gift, and that was a very long time ago. We will have to study it more.*

Gwenelle was wide-eyed in the ensuing silence. Then she added, *Holy Raptor dung, I'm starting to think you're freaky.*

In the morning there were fresh mountain wolf tracks around the entrance but there was no other trace of the beast. Mandeler took his flinger out of its sling along with the two practice arrows. He spent a hand of time practicing with the weapon. Gwenelle was fascinated by the contraption, so he let her try a few shots and she appeared to be a natural with it. They found themselves grinning at each other as he put the device away.

While trekking up the hill the patches of snow became more frequent, until in the late morning they came to a plateau covered in white. At the end lay a rising snow-clad expanse bound on either side by rocky peaks. This was the glacier with its high summit leading to the coast.

The climb was steep and the two humans were straining to keep up with the denzel. Since the snow had deepened, Gwenelle and Mandeler found it harder to move. They stopped to put on their snow walkers. Even Alheeza had a set of four little round snow walkers to keep him from sinking into the soft footing. Despite the clear sky and bright sun, the air continued to get colder. Alheeza, who had seemed immune to the cold, asked to have his small snug cape put on. It was laced under his chin and behind his forelegs. They also tied a slender line from one to each other. They could see their breath as they set off again up the white slope.

After another hand of time trudging up the endless slope, Alheeza mind-spoke: *We had better hurry because there is a storm coming.*

How did he know that? Gwenelle asked Mandeler.

He knows a great deal about this planet. He has been right about the rain twice on this trip alone.

Their breathing was becoming labored as they strained in the thin mountain air. Alheeza studied them, appraising their endurance at this altitude. Finally he mind-spoke to Mandeler: *It is time to share some of your copeander.*

Without questioning, Mandeler rummaged in his pack and pulled out a section of the dried fruit and passed some to Gwenelle. While chewing his copeander, he watched as she took a tentative bite of hers. The look of disgust turned to amazement. Even in a few mouthfuls she looked invigorated.

They resumed the trek with renewed energy and soon they emerged on a high plateau. As they trudged on, Mandeler became aware that Gwenelle's telepathic was becoming almost instinctive. Throughout the early afternoon they conversed in mind-speak with a sense of familiarity until their attention was drawn to the rapidly changing sky.

Alheeza turned: *We must act quickly before the storm reaches us. Mandeler it is time for a snow shelter or we may all perish.*

Hastily, the humans used their snow walkers to scoop a large pile of the loose snow. As Mandeler remembered, the objective was to carve a cavity within that would protect them from the elements. He got down on his hands and knees to hollow out the interior and then pushing the snow out to Gwenelle, who then built walls to protect the entrance from the storm. The interior was just being finished when the wind hit, making Gwenelle stagger. Moments later the air stung with driven snow that blotted out all detail around her.

She crawled in behind Alheeza to find a snow covered Mandeler shaking a small glow globe to life.

She mind-spoke: *Are you cold?*

Just a bit of snow on the outside, I am really quit warm from the work.

I've never seen a storm like this. A person could get lost just a few strides from safety and never be found until it cleared.

That story has played out many times. Alheeza answered.

It was surprisingly comfortable, if not roomy, within the snow shelter. The sounds of the wind whipping snow into drifts outside made it feel even more snug inside. The storm brought a premature darkness that night. They dined on hard travel loaf and wedges of cold nut butter, washed down with water. Never had a meal been so welcome. Even though it felt safe within, it was still chilly to roll up on ice to sleep. Wrapped in cloaks, they nestled together for the warmth. Alheeza was soon making sleep noises. Mandeler felt a tingle of excitement as Gwenelle pressed up behind him burying her face in his neck, but he could not drift off with the tall woman so close to him. These were all new feelings and none of them were relaxing. Despite all this he did sleep, all be it fitfully.

The Trail to the Sea

He knew it was morning because the roof of their snow hut ceiling began to glow. Shedding the fragments of his dreams he took in his surroundings. All three of them were nestled together. He could feel the unpleasant dampness of the icy floor that had wicked through his cloak but he could also feel the pleasing sensation of Gwenelle snuggled up to his back. Glancing at the entrance he could tell why the air seemed stale, it was blocked with snow. He slipped out from underneath them and pushed up and out of the entrance hole. The thin crust of snow broke as he pressured up, emerging to see an expanse of glittering snow topped by an intense blue sky. The storm had passed, taking with it all traces of yesterday's foot prints.

They ate the last of the traveler's loaf and put on their snow walkers. The texture of the snow was fluffier and they sank in deeper than the previous day. Just after the sun reached its zenith, they found themselves looking down on the descending glacier Far out on the plains they could see the coastal community of Portside. If they could fly it was just a few hands of time away, but that was just in his dreams. It would be a least two more days of hiking to reach the city.

Alheeza cautioned them about the steep descent and made sure the safety lines between them were secure. This side of the glacier was known for its hidden dangers They needed to keep a sharp eye out, and spread themselves as far apart as possible. Alheeza led the way, followed by Gwenelle in the middle.

They were making good time going downhill, in high spirits,

when Mandeler heard a muffled thud from beneath him. In the next instant he was surrounded by crumbling snow, falling into darkness. He seemed to fall forever, only to be jerked painfully to a halt, as the rope around his waist went taut. He heard a distant scream from above. Taking inventory of his dim surroundings, he found that he hung like a rag doll between two glass smooth ice walls. As he struggled for a grip on the surface, every breath hurt. Glancing down did not make him feel better either, for the narrow slit went on for as far as he could see. It started as a quiver to the safety line, and then little by little he felt his weight being hoisted towards the crack of blue above. It seemed to take forever to reach the world above. As he got his hands on the upper ledge, he was able to right himself and eventually help to pull himself over the ledge. There at the end of the rope were Gwenelle and Alheeza, straining against his weight. With their help he scrambled over the edge of the chasm. They all collapsed into the snow, gasping painfully for breath. Only then did he hear in his head: *Frap! You're heavy!*

Alheeza mind-spoke: *Are you hurt?*

All I know is it hurts to breathe.

Alheeza continued: *Let us have a look at you.*

They removed his cloak, pack and safety line and finally with care, his tunic. There were nasty bruises forming along his lower rib cage. Mandeler reached for his emerald crystal looking inward for a few breaths. Nothing was broken, maybe a rib or two cracked, muscles torn and definitely bruised. Gwenelle found the medicinal case, and following his instructions, she drew out a small pot with an odd symbol... Mandeler peeled away the wax lid and started to apply the ointment where he could reach. Gwenelle followed suit and put it on the other spots. The salve felt warm as it soaked in, taking much of the pain with it. A chilly breeze came up and he shivered involuntarily making him reach for his clothes. As Gwenelle was helping him put on his tunic, her eyes settled on the glimmering green jewel that rested upon a beautiful swirling design.

What is this? She mind-spoke, placing an extended finger upon his bare chest.

The finger upon his chest sent an involuntary chill down his spine. He telepathed: *It's a long story. Can I tell you about it later?*

She removed the tingling finger from his chest and as she did so he got a glimpse of her hands, raw from rope burns. After dressing, he took her hands and applied the same healing compound to them. Still holding her hand, he mind-spoke to her: *If you had not been with us I would have perished, taking Alheeza with me. You saved my life.*

She replied the same way, *I am getting used to having you around, what else could I do?*

Then they broke apart. Picking up their gear, they set off once more down the hill. The rest of the trek down the glacier was uneventful. As they neared the bottom, the glacier became broken and steep. At the side the rocky moraine gave them a better trail to descend. It was slow work on the rubble but once they reached the river at its base, they found a path leading down the mountain. There were streams to cross, boulders to avoid and all the while the green vegetation became more plentiful.

An exhausted Mandeler was looking worse for wear. Without Manfriend trees or a known cave they had to seek out some other shelter. Not long after they spotted something on the edge of the small river, where the high water had undercut the bank and the stunted trees had toppled over. It was high and dry and with no rain today it would probably stay dry tonight. Gwenelle took charge of making a fire using one of the precious fire sticks. A short while later a travelers' stew was simmering in its pot.

She helped Mandeler get out of his cloak and tunic, this time the ribs were dark and blotchy with bruising from the fall. Her attention was distracted by the intricate chest tattoo that was punctuated by the crystal that hung on a slender thong. Mandeler caught her staring and mind-spoke: *It's written in the ancient language of Earth, and the stone was a gift for my manhood passage.*

Some gift! That would attract the wrong kind of people in Portside.

Let's keep it secret, please.

Absolutely!

He added: *It also helps the mind-speaking process.*

I have seen you reach into your shirt and clutch it while we were traveling. She tentatively reached out and placed her finger tips on the translucent gem as it lay on his chest. At the same time they were each hit by a vision enhancement and could see a shimmering aura about the other. If he thought there was a tingling sensation when she touched him before it was nothing like the feeling now. They held each other's eyes in unblinking intimacy until Mandeler gently reached his hand up and drew her fingers off the crystal. The glow vanished as the crystal link was broken, but he was left holding her by the fingers. An echo of the tingling link remained and he knew they were brought together on a level that he did not understand.

They sat there on their heels for a few breaths of time until Gwenelle placed her hands on either side of his face and kissed him tenderly on the lips. Then she picked up the salve and started to apply it to his injured chest. Mandeler could still feel the lingering touch of her lips as she finished tending his ribs. He had no experience with women in this way but it certainly felt good.

She broke the silence by mind-speaking to him: *Is that what you get when you touch the crystal?*

More or less but it was different with you, I mean, I have never had the sharing of the sight and feeling before.

She nodded and turned to look for something in her pack.

He would have liked her to kiss him again but he was afraid to ask.

In the shadows, Alheeza watched the exchange with wonder, and a hidden smile.

As full darkness enveloped the river bank, they settled into the cramped space under the cut bank. Much to Mandeler's surprise the tall woman crawled in behind him and nestled up to him, wrapping her arm around him as if it was the most natural thing in the world to do. In a few moments she was sound asleep but he lay there very still, hoping Gwenelle would not take her arm away. Sleep was long in coming with her so close to him.

As they lay together in sleep, her hand came to rest on the lump that was the crystal. Her fingers found it within his shirt so that when the dreams came, it was shared. *It took a moment for the eyes to adjust to the darkness, and then the landscape started to take shape in its shades of grey and brown. The colors of the day were lost in this panoramic view. Wind whistled about his ears as the rhythmic beat of great wings drove the night marauder forward.*

Slowly the head turned and took in the two other Raptors flying at even spaces to the side. The Queen had sent them forward looking for a special one. He knew that the prey was close as they flew up and down the river valley but could not find where they had gone to ground. One last pass and then he turned screaming his outrage as he started to pump for altitude again.

Gwenelle awoke a heartbeat ahead of Mandeler. She felt him jolt awake in her arms and they heard the last distant scream of the departing Raptor. She mind-spoke: *Holy Raptor dung, is this what you go through every night?*

He answered: *Yes, but the last couple of weeks have been worse.*

Were those great cursed things that close to us? It felt like we were being hunted.

I wasn't sure at first, but yes, it seems too much for a coincidence.

Does Alheeza know?

Portside

It had taken two more days to reach the farming area just outside of Portside. Among the open fields were well used paths where people could be seen coming and going. A cart was being pulled by an animal that looked like a small muzel but with thicker legs, longer ears and an even blue grey color. The friendly farmer was on his way to market with a load of last season's hard shelled bread melons. After chatting with him, Gwenelle and Mandeler were invited to join him on his way to Portside. Seated beside him, he spoke about local affairs such as the upcoming mating ceremony for his sister's daughter. From the ease of his manner and the lightness of the conversation they silently agreed that the news of the Raptors had not reached this far yet.

The wind was blowing from the sea bringing with it the smell of the salt marshes. Portside, the town, was right on the shore and compared with the settlements that he had seen to date, it was large. The outskirts of town were made up of small irregular wooden buildings that nestled closely to each other. The cobble stone streets were just wide enough for two carts to pass. There were more people coming and going along the lane than he had ever seen before. It smelled different too, a mixture of the salt air and closely packed humanity. The first dwellings were a bit shabby, but as they got closer to the center of town, more shops appeared with brightly colored signs and sometimes entire walls were painted with scenes of farming or fishing. He had never seen brightly decorated buildings before.

Gwenelle mind-spoke to Mandeler, *When I started out with you, all I wanted was to get back to my home town and see my father but now...*

Mandeler waited a few breaths to hear what she was trying to tell him but when it did not come he mind-spoke, *What do you mean?*

I…I can't say, and with that she reached over kissing him on the lips again. She held the kiss for a moment then she slid from the cart and openly said, "Thanks for the ride and I hope to see you again."

With that she strode off down the street with her satchel over her shoulder.

Mandeler was stunned, he felt as if someone had just slapped him. He had not known her for long but in the short time together he felt something special. Now she just walked away. He wrestled with his rational side reminding himself that she was only traveling with them until they reached Portside and their time had run out.

Alheeza mind-spoke: *Don't ask, even denzels do not understand the inner working of man-woman relations. But we do need to make contact with people from the mind-speaking guild. There is a place not far from here, follow me.*

Mandeler slid down to join his mentor, thanking the farmer before following Alheeza down a narrow alley. As they walked along he could not help but think of the outspoken woman whose lips he could still feel upon his.

In the darkened alley, Alheeza stopped in front of a door that was painted sky blue with a white border. The unlocked door opened into a small room with no furniture. The floor creaked as they entered and inside his head he heard: *Who comes looking for guidance?*

Alheeza responded: *It is Alheeza with Mandeler Freedahson from the southern estates.*

Come up and let us have a look at him.

Apparently knowing his way, Alheeza pushed open a side door and they climbed the steep staircase to the second floor. The room was brilliantly lit with a series of windows along one wall. Resting on a low couch was an elderly denzel with fading body color, and in a rocking chair sat a balding man dressed in an orange robe. As Mandeler and Alheeza moved into the space, neither of the room's occupants moved their eyes to follow them, yet he felt under their scrutiny. He could not tell which one mind-spoke but in his head he heard: *Sit and tell us what brings one of our most gifted here with a novice mind-speaker.*

Alheeza started: *As you know I was bonded to one of the promising offspring of the humans. This is Mandell's son, Mandeler, and he is my companion. We carry news of the latest Raptor attacks. Two solar weeks ago, four winged marauders took four humans and one of ours, and then at Huxbee there was another attack with a single human taken. There was an incident worthy of note at Huxbee because this young human managed to kill a Raptor.*

At this, both of the elders sat upright and turned their unseeing eyes upon Mandeler. He had never felt so uncomfortable in his life. One of them commanded: *Speak of this.*

He drew in a ragged breath and plunged forward: *I was given a projectile flinger by Herbin Cochral and during the attack at Huxbee, Alheeza suggested that I arm myself. The killing arrow was fired at an arm's length into its eye. It thrashed itself to death in the next few breaths. That is all I can tell you.*

Alheeza continued: *Now tell them about your dreams.*

How did you know about the Raptor dreams?

Gwenelle told me.

Mandeler continued: *I have been having the dreams for some time. I just thought they were dreams, but after the attacks and while on the way here, it became clear that I can see through the raptor's eyes from time to time.*

The elderly denzel mind-spoke: *Come close young one and reveal your crystal.*

Mandeler did as he was told. As he did so the two elders reached out, each placing a digit on the emerald stone. In that instant, they were locked together in a glowing aura that forged a link amongst their very being. This was different than sharing with Gwenelle, this was far more intense. Moments later Mandeler collapsed on the floor.

When he awoke, the sun was low on the horizon. The room was filled with the savoury smell of food. There were others in the room now, with denzels and humans all communicating in the wordless speech. A middle aged woman was kneeling next to him with a mug of hot sweet tea.

As he sat up with his mug, the room full of guests turned as one to stare at him.

The old one mind-spoke: *I am Frabeen and this is Stroshine* (indicating the bald man) *we are the keepers of our mind-speaking guild.* He introduced the eight others in the room and continued: *It appears that you were meant to be here at this time. You have a very special gift, that of dream walking with the great ones. What was learned during our mind link with you was that your special talent is communicating with the raptors. The Great Raptors seem to be aware of you and there is a growing fear of you. We believe they have been in pursuit since the attack at the estate, and I expect they will be trying harder now that you are here with us.*

In his heart, Mandeler had come to fear that all these things were true.

Frabeen went on: *Let me tell you something of our history. Before your kind came to our world we, and another race of flyers, were locked in a cycle of death with the Great Raptors. Then just before the time of the great storm the other race disappeared. We suspect your dreams are some sort of contact with the lost race of green raptors.*

As you know it was after the crippling storm that some of your people were hunted as well. Every fifteen season cycles since, the Raptors would cross the great waters to kill at will. They seem to be drawn to groups around a telepath like a homing beacon. This may explain why they are following you. Aside from that, we know surprisingly little about them except that they vanish from our land during the intervals between hunting cycles. Perhaps through you, we will learn more.

He paused for a few moments and then went on: *On a practical side, we have arranged for you to meet with the town fathers to carry your message of warning to the people.*

Outside, the sun went down and darkness spread over the land.

A Dash in the Darkness

Word came back to the guild that the town fathers did indeed want Mandeler's news. He was directed to come immediately to the Portside town hall two hands of time after sunset. Apparently movement about the town at night was still considered safe, but Mandeler had his growing doubts about how long that would last. The guild seemed to be leaning towards Mandeler's fears and wanted an honor guard sent with him. It was to be composed of one elder of the guild and six men in their prime. The men assembled in the alley in front of the blue door. Mandeler was astonished to see them decked out with heavy leather tunics with carved breastplates made of ironwood, ornately carved rock-melon helmets with cheek guards, and shin plates. They carried long staffs with hardened glass blades on the tip and a counterweight stone on the other end. It was the first time he had seen armed men trained to move as one group. They were formidable.

As they readied at the door, Mandeler noticed the sixth man in the group carried a projectile flinger that was drawn and cocked.

It was Alheeza that broke into his thoughts explaining: *I know you fear a Raptor attack, but you will see that Portside at night is a far different place than during the day. In this trading town there are elements at play that are outside the law. These men are members of our guild and we patrol our parts of town after dark. As we travel to and from Portside, they are here to protect us from the thieves that thrive in the darkened streets of Portside, not the Raptors.*

He was starting to understand how Gwenelle was so resilient and self-reliant after growing up here. She had pulled a knife to fend off a would-be assailant as if it was an everyday occurrence. They set off down the narrow street with two guarding the front and the other four taking up the rear guard.

Mandeler had never seen large men walking with so little noise. Once or twice a shadow came out of a darkened doorway, only to fade back as soon as it saw the strength of the company. As they approached a large flat roofed building, with pillars framing its double doors, Mandeler felt a stirring from his crystal causing his vision to falter. *For a moment he was somewhere else flying in a star lit sky, then it cleared.* There were men guarding the doors as he approached. They were dressed similarly but the symbols and shape of the breastplates were different. As they were expected, they were ushered directly inside the well-lit chamber.

The size of the room was impressive but his attention shifted to a raised platform where three people sat in ornately carved chairs. They were flanked by a pair of expressionless guards. Perched on the tallest central chair was a somber old man with a beard and long grey hair gathered in ponytails behind his ears. Around his neck was a thick band of sparkling gems. The purple robe he wore was of the finest material. Its rich fabric was studded with bright stones stitched in a triangle on the chest. On his left was a stern-faced matron, her grey-blond hair was tied into two buns on either side of her head. From her ears hung two large clear stones that sparkled in the globe light. Her burgundy robe was rich in texture as well, but unadorned. A younger man on the right was clean shaven with glistening black hair. On his brow strap stood a single yellow stone, the same color as his long robe.

The group came to a halt in front of the town rulers. From the raised platform the senior stood raising his right hand in greeting. With a deep resonating voice he said, “Welcome to Portside, we understand that one of your members brings grave news from the Estates. Present him at once.”

Mandeler stepped forward but was struck by a sudden weakness. He heard himself speak as if from a distance, “**They are here**!” Then he was taken by the waking dream, *She had sent them to kill and retrieve many. The silent killers plunged towards the coast town. The leader of the hunting pack let them search their own targets, his quest was singular. The others extended their talons searching for prey. Into the narrow streets, they dove where their razor sharp* *talons dug into flesh hoisting their screaming victims into the sky. It was joyful to hear.*

The leader concentrated while circling as he searched for the 'one' that his queen sought above all others. He was drawn near the center of town where a large structure stood out from all the rest. As he approached the feelings grew stronger and finally through the small openings he could see several of their numbers standing near the glowing figure of the 'one' most sought. The opening at the side was guarded by two of the puny creatures. As he approached, they stood their ground. The air thundered as he touched down in a swirling cloud of dust. He flung both creatures aside reaching within as far as his neck would stretch, just short of the 'one'. He was attacked with sharp sticks stinging him but he lashed from side to side knocking them down. A sharp pain in his cheek brought him around to a single creature bending over some device. As he opened his mouth to kill again, a blinding green light flashed in front of him. It came from the 'one' and he had to turn his head to avoid the blinding radiance.

Mandeler had come out of his waking dream to find that he was holding his crystal aloft, filling the hall with intense emerald light. What lay before him was the mirror image of his lucid nightmare. Men were down and scattered all around him. As in the night with the mountain wolf, the world he saw was changed. The telepaths glowed with auras but to his surprise so did the Great Raptor. He focused his will against the winged marauder and sent out: ***Back! Go back you beast of darkness! Go back!*** To his surprise the massive creature paused, turning its ugly fin topped head to the side. Its narrow tongue slavered over the rows of sharp teeth. It seemed frozen in place until a second arrow struck deeply just below its eye. It howled in rage, shaking its head but as it retreated the beast grabbed one of the honor guards before leaving the hall.

As the sounds of its wingbeats dwindled, Mandeler staggered from the exhaustion of the encounter. Screams could still be heard in the distance as the raid continued in other sectors. Gradually the sounds of the attack were replaced by the wailing of the survivors searching for their loved ones. The sky was empty except for the stars and a coastal town started to mourn its losses.

Inside the great hall it was as if an explosion had occurred, scattering the occupants about the room. Blood smeared the floor and pooled near some of the bodies. The survivors looked wide eyed about them taking in the carnage. The pale faces of the town elders peered out from behind their dais. Of the honor guard, three lay unmoving on the floor, one more was bleeding from wounds, and the elder denzel also lay in a pool of amber blood. It was Alheeza who broke the silence: *Quickly let us tend to our wounded and then get back to the guild house as fast as possible.*

Mandeler took his medicinal case from his shoulder pack and stepped toward the first of the injured men. While he set about his work his mind came back to the visions he had of the attack from the eyes of a Raptor. He had seen himself as a Raptor would see him and it made him tremble with fear.

The Quest

In the two days following the attack the town was redefined. No longer were people going about their lives worried about trivial affairs, it was a town united in its fear against the Great Raptors. It had made all men equal overnight. Each night was a time of concealment, for all nocturnal movement had ceased. There were a few that ventured out in the old ways but the skies still held the night marauders and to go out at night was to risk being taken. Three more went missing in this way and all that was heard of them was their departing screams.

The guild house had been hit on the first raid, but they had fared better retreating to the main floor where it was better protected. The town fathers had fled to the countryside leaving the community without leadership. It was the surviving elder, Stroshine, who had been instrumental in organizing members of the guild to help give order to the town. The guild gathered people in the square to make announcements for the care of the injured, sheltering those who had lost the most, and opening of the market square so food stuffs could flow again. It appeared that twenty eight people had been injured, twelve killed and another fourteen taken. It had been an enormous attack by an unknown number of Raptors. People were scared to come out of their homes, even in the daylight, so the mind-speaking guild went from door to door passing the word of progress to date.

For Mandeler every evening was filled with meetings with the senior guild members who had an endless number of questions for him. They speculated about his dream's connection to the Great Raptors but nobody could give him any information about the green raptors that appeared only in daylight.

The next day he found himself standing at the side of the market place watching people coming and going, when he noticed a figure on the far side walking purposefully through the crowd. His heart picked up as he noted the familiar gait but only got a glimpse and could not be sure. There was a tall man apparently walking with her. It was not until they reached an opening by the bread melon stand that she turned and Gwenelle's blue eyes stared directly into his. She picked her way towards him, mind-speaking as she came, *Frap, am I glad to see you.*

It was as if he had seen this before. She wore a loose turquoise blouse gathered at the waist, as well as baggy pants and tall boots. Her hair bounced freely as she moved towards him. With that she threw her arms around him and he was enveloped by her familiar scent. In that moment he realized that he had seen all of this in a dream and now it was playing out in front of him. They held each other in a tight embrace but after a few breaths she pulled back and they looked into each other's tear filled eyes. He telepathed: *I suppose this does not look very manly?* He tried to focus for a minute and added: *Who was that man you were walking with?*

She cuffed him playfully on the shoulder, *Oh that was just one of the men from the dock, he worked with my father. He told me stories about the traders that have ranged far and wide. They're an unruly bunch but I want you to know that I'll take you ahead of that lot any day. Now come with me, I need to talk with you.*

She pulled him along to a darkened tavern a few blocks away and selected a corner table sitting so she could see the door. She threw a couple of trade chits on the table for the proprietor ordering pale ale, flat bread with dumplings, and steamed star clams. She told him about searching for her father when she first got to town, he had been staying at a rooming house near the docks. When the food came she took a big swig of the ale and then noticed Mandeler just staring at the bowl of little red stars floating in hot broth.

Gwenelle mind-spoke: T*hey're star clams. We get them this time of year along the sandy shores. Try one.*

They look extremely odd.

With her fingernails she plucked one from the bowl and popped it in her mouth smiling. Tentatively, he took one of the multi-armed creatures in his spoon, studied it, before slipping it into his mouth. She watched with curiosity as he chewed purposefully and then he swallowed.

It's a bit rubbery but tastes better than I thought it would. He broke into a sheepish smile.

They hungrily tucked into the rest of the food. When all of the plates were empty she put her hands around her mug and looked at him: *I assume you were near the attack?* She went on without expecting an answer. *Did you know they came after me too, the bastards? They smashed the thin door at my father's rooming house and ravaged the place. We got down a trap door under the floor just in time. My father got a few scratches but is alright otherwise. He left on one of the trading vessels this morning and is headed to the Eastern shores. He will be back in a moon cycle. I would have liked you to meet him but it won't happen this time.*

Mandeler did his best to take this all in and then added: *That sounded too close for comfort. All along I thought they were after me and not you. I am glad you got away and your father too. I had something happen that night as well and it has unnerved me. The speaking guild are very concerned but do not know what to do about it.*

She leaned closer: *Tell me what it was?*

I dreamed again, but this time I was not asleep and I could see through the eyes of the Great Raptor. It was searching for me and I saw myself as it attacked those around me. Then I shouted and it stopped or at least faltered in its attack.

Holy raptor dung, you're deep in it this time.

She reached over and placed her hand over his telepathing: *I know you didn't choose this but you're into this now.*

She was his senior by only a few season cycles but her face looked like it carried the burden of the world, she held his gaze and smiled: *What you need is a friend and I'm that friend.*

He let out his breath. He didn't know he had been holding it. All he could do was nod. Finally, he mind-spoke: *I need some time alone with you. There are things that I have to work through and I feel better discussing it with you. I feel that you know me better than the other mind-speakers.*

Alright, where do we go?

They made their way through the narrow streets to the guild house where they retired to a quiet corner in the stone basement. She was lightly dressed so he put his travel cloak about her while they settled down around a single illumination globe. Mandeler started by going over some of his dreams, but before long he could tell that he was not being very accurate in his account of things. Then it occurred to him there was a better way. He took out his amulet while drawing her hand to his around the stone. There was an instant connection between them. It was an intimacy that went to the very heart, filled with reassurance and compassion. *He opened his memories of the early dreams before the manhood passage, and then revealed the history of denzels, Raptors and humans. He went over his dreams about the green raptors, sharing the images of what it was like to fly and how they were day time creatures that never appeared in the attacks on this community. Mandeler then showed her in detail what his memories of the final attack were like. He felt her shudder when the creature entered the town hall, looking at the shimmering Mandeler. Then things shifted so that the scene was now Mandeler clutching his green speaking stone while looking at the shimmering Raptor in front of him. He shouted for it to go and it faltered in midstride.*

They broke apart breathing heavily then Gwenelle mind-spoke: *There must be a reason that you are connected to both the green raptors as well as the great ones. Don't the guild members know anything about the green ones?*

There seem to be distant tales but nothing concrete.

There is a ship that just came back from trading in the farthest reaches of our land. My father said the captain had some strange tales and he might be able to help you.

She started to rise but Mandeler held her in place. *How do I connect with you again?*

I'll come back here before night fall. She reached down and kissed him.

The guild house repairs to the second story were almost complete but the sound of craftsmen could still be heard as Mandeler and

Alheeza retired to the basement. Mandeler telepathed: *It is still confusing to me but I have a mixture of dreams from the future and definitely in the present. I still do not know if I can change anything from the dreams of the future.*

It was your natural ability that made Herbin Cochral choose you for this journey. I admit that neither of us understood what was happening but we gambled that you were linked with the Great Raptor cycle. Now we must take direction from them, but to do that, I want to go over some of the more obscure details. Let's begin with the variation in the flying creatures.

Mandeler's mind was spinning as he tried to pull it all together. The denzels that appeared so omnipotent, had limitations to their ability to communicate. How could he have such a range with the Great Raptors, and then there was his intense connection with Gwenelle?

Alheeza brought him out of his reverie: *Try to open your thoughts to me so that I can better understand the little things that have happened. If it helps, clasp your stone.*

Mandeler reflected on that while he reached into his tunic and drew out his crystal. It was new to him to reveal thoughts rather than words, but he wanted to appear organized in front of his learned teacher. Alheeza watched as Mandeler's face contorted in an effort to release memories as a whole. He shared how the night marauders would cruise the skies in search of the small glowing figures that were denzels and telepathic colonists. It included details of his instinctive use of the crystal to ward off the mountain wolf. Most chilling was how he saw the final attack from the air including how he himself appeared as a brightly glowing object.

When Mandeler shifted to the details of the day raptors, his sense of foreboding left. These creatures were social, aquatic and felt different from their nocturnal counterparts. His mind was filled with questions about how they played out in this story. They must have a part to play but what was it?

Alheeza mind-spoke: *That was extremely detailed, especially the part about the green raptors.*

Do you know anything about the history of the green raptors?

I have not seen them myself but there are legends that have been passed down about water dragons. They are not as big as the great one but they dive into the ocean and feed upon green fins. That is all I know.

In the silence that followed they could hear the last of the workmen leaving. How long they sat there Mandeler could not tell but when he heard familiar footsteps coming across the floor above him, his spirits began to rise. Her hair was dishevelled and she was breathing heavily when she came down the stairs. As she sat on the carpet beside them, it was obvious that she was excited about something and finally she mind-spoke to them: *I found a sailor who has seen them.*

You found someone who has seen one of the green raptors?

Yes!

Fantastic!

Alheeza was leaning forward, his eyes flashing with anticipation: *Who and where is this person?*

Gwenelle replied in kind: *My father met him when they were fixing his boat. His name is Larson and he has traded far and wide beyond our lands. He tells about seeing great green flying creatures that dive into the sea to feed on some large swimming things.*

Mandeler mind-spoke: *Do you think he could take us to them?*

What are you thinking? It was Alheeza.

If these things are in my dreams, then they are there for a reason. I think I should go and seek them out. It's the only way to know for sure.

Gwenelle: *He might take us but it will cost. I mean he is a trader and that means he is a profiteer.*

Mandeler reached under his tunic and drew out the pouch that Herbin had given him. *I have this!*

Alheeza watched as the small heavy bag was passed to Gwenelle. She hefted it in her hand and then untied the draw string. Her eyes widened as she gazed into the little sac: *Frap! You're full of surprises: this is a small fortune.*

Mandeler looked at the other two: *I think I feel a sea voyage coming on. Who is coming with me?*

The Sea Quester

Alheeza, Gwenelle and Mandeler slipped out the next morning to seek Larson at the docks. It took a hand of time to work their way through the narrow streets to the wharf. As they got closer Gwenelle noted that the streets, before the raid, would have been choked with hand carts loaded with field vegetables, sea food and hand crafted specialty items. Now there were only a few on the move. Mandeler's nose wrinkled as a repugnant smelling cart passed piled high with slimy sea creatures.

Larson's boat was the biggest at the stone wharfs. The two local men's fishing boats had a deep belly and a short mast, designed to carry their catch. Larson's boat was a heavy wooden vessel that must have been twelve or fourteen lengths of a man and easily that high again, with two tall masts held in place with great bundles of rope. The name Sea Quester was painted in raised letters on the bow in white and green. A heavyset man was sitting on deck carefully shaping a length of wood with a glass plane. There was no other crew about. Gwenelle seemed to be the self-appointed spokesperson and looking up she called out for Larson. The man sitting in the pile of shavings replied, "The skipper, Captain Larson, is on board but he had a late night and will not be disturbed. Come back later!

This time it was Mandeler who said, "We have some questions about a lengthy passage."

At this the mariner perked up, "What's that you say, you want to book a passage, is that right?"

Mandeler nodded and the man got to his feet and lumbered down a hatchway at the rear. There was some shouting and then he came back up and said, "The Captain said you are to come aboard, he will call for you shortly."

For Mandeler, seeing the sea going vessel was a marvel in complexity. On the estates the vehicles and technology were very simple but someone had put a great deal of effort into creating this boat. For one thing there was not a straight line on it. The hull itself was a broad curved structure with the front and back being higher than the middle. The forward part of the vessel came up into a gently curved point with a great pole extending out from it, and more ropes were tied to it from the hull and masts. The back of the curved hull had a short blunt end and hanging from it was a small row boat. In the middle of the ship was a low narrow house, between the two masts, with a larger boat tied upside down to it. There were ropes everywhere as if the mast might jump out on its own accord if it was not tied down. Near the bottom of each tall pole was a single rail with folded heavy cloth tied to it and the mast. Although the paint was a bit faded, the structure looked well maintained and orderly. All of this must have a purpose, but it failed to come together in Mandeler's mind, yet he marveled at the interconnectedness of the whole thing.

Captain Larson appeared through a narrow door in the rear of the small cabin. He looked to be in his sixties, bare headed with a fringe of grey straggly hair, puffy cheeks and a slight stoop. He stood there in what might have been expensive clothes once, but the short jacket was now a faded blue grey with the buttons undone. He wore breaches but to Mandeler's surprise he was bare foot. He was still a big man with broad shoulders and a slight pot but his eyes were intelligent as they scanned the newcomers on his deck. Finally he said, "What brings you to my ship and where do you want to go?"

"Can we speak of this in private Captain?" Gwenelle asked.

"Ah, yah better come below then."

He led the way down the companionway to his cabin in the rear of the vessel. Compared to the gloomy passageway, it was surprisingly bright with its row of port holes along the stern. A few things were thrown about but there was an underlying sense of order to this room. He motioned that they should sit at his small table.

He sat staring at them with his arms crossed. Mandeler nodded to Gwenelle, and then she said, "We have heard that you have seen the green dragons hunting at sea. Can you take us there?"

"And why would two young people, with their pet, be wantin' to do that?"

This time it was Mandeler that answered, "We have our reasons but it is important that we find them as soon as we can."

"Oh, you have your reasons, do you? Well to answer your first question, yes I have seen the green dragons far out to sea, but I wouldn't get too close if I were you for they are big enough to hunt the likes of you. Furthermore I only sail for profit and how would a young'n like you pay for it all?"

Mandeler answered him, "Young we may be, but we have a purpose for this voyage and as for payment that depends on what your rates are."

Captain Larson studied him, taking in his youth, land man's way of standing with his feet apart, plain clothes, but there was something in his steady gaze that was far beyond his years. Making up his mind, he said, "Many are seeking passage out of this troubled city and that makes my fee even higher!"

With that Mandeler pulled his pouch of hardware from under his tunic and stepped forward. He unlaced the top and poured over half the contents into the captain's hand. Larson had a sharp intake as he stared at the shiny objects. Finally he said, "Well, you are full of surprises this morning. Perhaps we can make a deal."

Larson fingered the precious collection for a moment adding, "Two more and we have a deal." Mandeler plucked two more screws from the pouch and handed them over. Captain Larson slipped them into his jacket pocket and reached out gripping Mandeler's hand saying, "We have a deal young man, transportation for the three of you to the green dragons!"

"My name is Mandeler Freedahson and my companion is Gwenelle."

Larson went on, "Now you'll need some things before we leave. Allenz, the hand on deck, will help you put a list together. I need to get my crew out of the taverns to put a few things aboard before we leave. I expect we can depart at noon tomorrow on the ebb tide. Be here on time or lose your deposit."

Allenz turned out to be a very helpful person. He fetched paper and a writing stick for Mandeler to make a list. Then he sat with them and explained what would be needed. It included foul weather clothing, warm under garments, long lasting rations and blankets.

They had spent a few moments conferring before Alheeza went back to the guild house leaving the young couple to shop alone. As they made their way to the mariner's supply shop they realized that this was more fun than anything in the past weeks. The shop stood at the end of a narrow street with two story buildings wedged closely together on either side. Most of them had display windows but some were empty, while others were boarded over with obvious signs of recent damage. To their relief the marine shop was still open. They stepped by a carved wooden mariner decked out in sailing gear, just inside the doorway. It was a cluttered place with ropes of all sizes coiled in barrels, floats with fishing nets, large stones shaped into anchors, as well as piles of marine boots and clothing.

From behind a cluttered counter the old proprietor studied them. His weathered face gave no sign of emotion as he lowered his generous nose to look over the half rim glasses. Finally he said, "What can I do for a pair of young folks today?"

Gwenelle started off, "We are looking for some rain gear for a trip offshore. Can you help us?"

"Are you looking for working clothes or passenger garb?"

They looked at each other and said at the same time, "Working!"

"Very good, step this way and let's have a look at what fits best."

The heavy weather garments were made of an unfamiliar material. They felt like fabric but there was a greasy feeling to the outside. He was assured that they were the very best rain gear. It included a roomy jacket and a high-waisted pair of trousers. Then there were gloves and three heavy water-resistant blankets for each of them. Payment was settled with a small threaded screw.

They had missed their lunch so they set off for the market to seek out a hot roll and look for a few delicacies for the trip. Gwenelle used her last few trade chits to buy three bottles of stewed golden berries, two blocks of muzel cheese, spiced tea and shelled herman nuts. They also found fresh double-baked nut bread with chopped fruits that the fishermen liked. Mandeler spotted a bottle of potent acava berries on a shelf, quickly adding them to their stores. He paid for the rest with a small metal nut before heading back to join Alheeza.

They got a few odd looks from passersby as they trudged along with their burden but they were in high spirits when they piled their things on the floor of the guild house. Alheeza was delighted with his new blanket and the selection of tasty food items.

That night, at a meal with the elder Stroshine and his helpers, they were told that reports were coming in from other communities where people and denzels were being taken in ever increasing numbers.

Something Ancient

It was with this unsettling news that they retired to the basement to wrap themselves in the new blankets and catch some sleep before the trip. Mandeler was anticipating a night close to Gwenelle and was disappointed when she rolled into her blanket a few hands away. He lay awake thinking about the attacks and tried to distract his thoughts by reminding himself of how nice Gwenelle's arms had been around him. Finally he dropped into an exhausted sleep. As so many times before, the dreams came upon Mandeler soon after falling asleep:

The rising sun appeared as a mirror image in green as it rose from the sea. Its light detailed the large spires of rock reaching from the floor to meet others coming down from the cathedral ceiling. She stretched to shed the night's stiffness and then looked around. Nestled among the slender outcroppings others began to move. The sun was turning amber as it rose tinting the cave with gold. The long necked creature stretched to see the endless expanse of water outside. There was no wind and the sea was glassy smooth, reflecting the few wisps of amber cloud. She felt movement by her side and looked down to see an infant green raptor nestled up to her warm chest. The fragments of yesterday's egg shell were scattered around it. Beside it another egg began to rock, a small hammering came from within and moments later the side cracked. More cracks appeared followed by a small green nose poking out. There was a welling up joy inside her as another of the precious young presented itself.

The scene changed to one of near darkness, this time it felt claustrophobic with the sound of water dripping on stone, mixed with putrid decay. The rough rock wall seemed to press in on her with little room to turn. As she moved, bones on the floor crunched under her foot. She paused for a moment looking into the vacant sockets of one of her victims, the human skull would move no more, nor would the others that joined it on the floor. The great female turned as she heard one of the males come creeping towards the entrance of her sanctuary. He approached on his wing knuckles clutching something in his mouth. Ducking his head in a deferential posture, he reached forward with his offering. The ragged thing in its mouth twitched as it returned to consciousness. As its eyes fluttered open, it took in the darkness and stink. The queen shuffled her bulk forward causing the creature to scream.

Mandeler jolted awake, the last of his scream fading from his lips. In the dark Gwenelle reached out, pulling him close to her. He whimpered "Oh Great Azimov, I saw him… he was still alive… he was still alive!"

She gently asked in mind-speak: *Who did you see?*

He seemed to struggle and then finally he said, "The Great Raptors had Captain Larson."

As if to add to the surreal moment, the cry of a distant Raptor drifted down to them like an echo from the dream.

Give him some copeander fruit. Telepathed Alheeza.

Gwenelle eased Mandeler onto his blanket and shook an illumination globe to life. In its cool glow she searched the packs, finally locating the fruit. She nipped a piece off the side, with her knife, and placed it to Mandeler's lips. He absently chewed at it with red juice dripping from the side of his mouth. It was not long before the color returned to his cheeks and he mind-spoke: *I could not see what it was, but then when it moved I knew it was human. As he opened his eyes I could see that is was Captain Larson. Oh Great Azimov what does this all mean? Could it be one of you I see next time in a dream, or for real?*

As they held each other in a tight embrace, she knew that she was feeling every bit as scared as Mandeler.

He pulled away from her telepathing: *There is no more sleep for me tonight, I need to talk.*

The other two nodded.

He leaned on the wall pulling the blanket around him then he scrutinized his friends. No one spoke until Mandeler broke the silence: *I get all mixed up with time and space. How is it that some of my dreams are of things I have never seen and in one case it happened just as the dream had foretold? Then I get these waking dreams where I can see through the eyes of a Raptor, just as the events are unfolding. I think I am going insane, how can I tell what's real? Oh Frap, I just want to sleep for one night without dreams.*

In unison Gwenelle and Alheeza leaned closer to him. She put a hand on his neck, gently massaging the strained muscles.

Alheeza mind-spoke: *I have gone over some of these things with you. As far as our collective experience goes, you are in new territory. There has never been a mind link with a Great Raptor in our history. We will have to trust our own judgment on that. As for the dreams foretelling the future, that is all debatable. Here is the thing, if you suspect something is going to happen, do your actions change the outcome of the dream? Can you change your future? I don't know, but I think it is worth trying to find out. First, let's find out if Captain Larson is alive and well in the morning.*

What about my sleep? Every night I wake up and it seems I sleep less and less. I can't keep going this way!

For that I have one last thing to try. Gwenelle, reach for that bag at the back. Yes that one. Bring it over here and gently empty it out.

As she tipped the contents onto the floor a shiny object about the size of a hard shelled bread fruit rolled out. It was a curious object, a little more than half of a sphere, extremely thin but still very heavy. She asked: *What is it?*

I suppose the closest name would be a helmet.

A helmet, she said, *But it is so thin and* (she lifted it as if to put it on) *how does it work because it will cover the eyes?*

Alheeza smiled a denzel smile and added: *It is not a warrior's helmet. It is a barrier helmet. Have Mandeler put it on.*

It took a moment to figure out front from back but when he had it settled on his head he looked a bit like a sightless treefrog. He mind-spoke to the pair of them: *This feels weird and it must look ridiculous.* He waited for a response but there was none. *Hey, somebody talk to me!*

It was Gwenelle who finally spoke out loud, "Alheeza told me that if it works, you could not hear us and both of us have been trying to get through to you. Try to answer me in mind-speak only."

What do you think I have been doing? Silence was all he sensed.

He felt hands removing the helmet and then from within his head she said: *Alheeza told me the elders gave this to you. The metal that covers your head is supposed to block mind-speak. They made it centuries ago, after the great storm to experiment with telepathy blocking centuries ago. Apparently it works.*

Mandeler looked at Alheeza: *Do you think it might let me sleep?*

Alheeza answered: *Yes you will be able to sleep with this but remember if we are to unravel these mysteries, you will still have to sleep exposed to the dreams. For now get some sleep.*

He looked relieved for the first time in many solar cycles. *Let me have that thing, it is still a few hands until sunrise.*

He plopped it on his head, wrapped the blanket around himself and lay down. He was asleep in just a few breaths. The other two were left looking at each other. Alheeza opened with: *He needs the rest, help me organize the rest of our gear so we can leave at first light. Then you can catch a little sleep too, I'll stay awake just to be sure.*

Departure

The dawn found them on the dock with packs and bags stacked by them. The Sea Quester swayed gently tugging on her mooring lines. Captain Larson must have scoured all the taverns because a handful of men were adjusting rigging in a purposeful way. Allenz spotted them and soon strong hands were heaving their gear aboard. The deckhand said, "The Captain's compliments, but would you care to take breakfast with him before we catch the noon tide?"

Confidently Mandeler replied, "We would love to but first we need to have a safe place for our denzel to rest out of harm's way."

It was arranged that the denzel could take up a spot just in front of the deck house. Then the young couple was escorted down the companionway to Captain Larson's quarters at the back of the boat. The stern cabin, with its low ceiling, was aglow from the morning light and seemed in much better order than during their last visit. Looking about they took in the rich wooden room with its sturdy round table, secured canvas chairs, storage lockers and side table piled high with papers. They were shown to their seats where they waited for the appearance of the captain.

Mandeler looked around at the odd assortment of things. The table itself was a curiosity because it had a ledge all the way around it and the plates were set into the surface. At a glance it looked as if it was also fixed to the floor. A small table at the side was covered with paper drawings that he assumed were the maps. Placed randomly on these were delicate instruments. The light globes were suspended in webbing to keep them in place around the perimeter. The whole area seemed utilitarian but pleasing just the same. Captain Larson made his entrance through a small door set at the side of the forward wall. He was dressed in a fresh set of clothes similar to yesterday but these were not thread bare. The buttons were still undone and he was bare foot but his presentation was markedly changed. Even his fringe of grey hair was tied back with a black ribbon. His eyes had a sharpness that spoke of near sobriety from the night before.

He dropped into his chair and threw his elbows onto the table, taking in his guests. At that moment a galley hand brought a tray heaped with fresh flat bread, muzel cheese, and spiced tea. Larson leaned back saying, “Dig in. The fresh food will only last a few days out of port.”

The food was simple but good with the surprise being a jar of hard pickled black fruit. These were rich and oily with a distinct taste of the highlands. Conversation was non-existent until the dishes were cleared. Then Larson said, “What you asked for is no small task, but you did come up with a good fee and I promise to take you to the green dragons.”

Mandeler asked, “How far is it and how long will it take to get there?”

“I expect it will take half a moon cycle to make the passage. That is with fair weather and a good deal of luck.”

“Why do you say luck, I would have thought an experienced mariner like yourself would know where he was going and precisely how long it would take?”

“Master Mandeler, you are a bright young man but you have never made an ocean passage. The old lady that creates the weather is as unpredictable as any old hag and she can bring on the most contrary winds, not to mention the rain and mountains of waves.”

After the meal they were shown to a small cabin, just around the corner from the captain’s. By ship standards, they were told they were lucky to have such a luxury but to Mandeler it seemed like an airless broom closet. Gwenelle was delighted to have an area with a closing door that separated them from the men. It had a not too generous bunk, a single porthole, and pegs for their packs to hang on but little room for anything else. In the evening, they expected that Alheeza would take up the floor space if the weather was bad.

The voyage started with the men removing the large ropes that held the ship to the stone pier. Then there was the rustling as the three primary sails were taken up the mast. They billowed out, capturing the light breeze coming from the land side. Soundlessly and gracefully the ship drifted away from the dock, leaving a trail of foam and bubbles in its wake.

In a few hands of time, they rounded a point of land passing into an open area of sea. As the rocky beaches receded, the vast expanse of water opened up in front of them. With it, came a strengthening north easterly wind and increasing waves.

Allenz was their assistant on board the Sea Quester. He answered Mandeler's and Gwenelle's many questions. The ship, as he called it, was a beautifully handcrafted wooden vessel. Mandeler marveled at the intricate connectors that fastened the many ropes to the deck. They appeared to be carved from ironwood, known for its extreme strength once it was shaped and cured. The sails were a particular fascination and he wondered how they would be used to harness the wind since Allenz had told him it was possible to sail into the wind to some extent.

Mandeler was spellbound as they tightened the sails, allowing the ship to slice on an angle towards the wind. It seemed impossible, but seeing was indeed believing. Queasiness started down in his stomach and it got worse as the vessel plunged into the oncoming swells. It only took one glance and Gwenelle knew what was happening to him. She took him by the arm leading him to the downwind side of the ship, just as the spasms hit him. All of his lunch went over the side along with any optimism that he had for the trip.

The bedraggled Mandeler telepathed: *What causes this terrible sickness?*

They call it sea sickness, and the good news is it will pass, if you're lucky it will be soon.

Great Azimov!

It helps to watch the horizon and stay away from heavy meals.

He thought for a moment and then sheepishly added: *I must look a sight and not smell any better than a Portside's refuse pile either?*

I've seen and smelled worse. Now let's get you washed up and find a comfortable place to settle you for the rest of the day.

The rest of the day, Gwenelle and Mandeler sat comfortably in front of the cabin with Alheeza. Mind-speaking to Alheeza had settled his stomach but he was not yet ready to go below. Their conversation came to the point about security. Would Great Raptors track them out on the water and if so, what would happen with an open assault on the ship? How would they bring this up with Captain Larson?

Their opportunity came soon enough. Captain Larson had been very busy with his crew getting the Sea Quester well away from land, before settling on a steady course north north-west. After that he had retired below, leaving Allenz, the second in command, to handle the ship and crew. It was a couple of hands later that a young seaman, named Birdard, came with the captain's invitation to dine just before sunset. He was younger than Mandeler, with no beard and large brown eyes that matched the color of his shaggy head. Still feeling queasy, Mandeler was reluctant to accept but they needed a chance to put their security questions forward, so he accepted the invitation.

To his friends he mind-spoke: *Alheeza I would value your council at this meal. I need both of you to help me feel out a solution with the captain.*

Alheeza looked at each of them adding: *He looks like a cunning old survivor. We'll do our best.*

Gwenelle reached up twisting her hair into a top knot and then wrapped her shoulders with a shawl: *How do I look? Good enough to have dinner with our captain?*

Mandeler broke into a broad grin: *Good enough to have dinner with anyone!*

She playfully swatted him on the shoulder as she got up to leave. Alheeza trotted along behind.

Once they were seated at the small table with Captain Larson, Birdard brought in platters with flat bread, muzel cheese, mashed yellow melon, and a steaming bowl of sea snapper fillets in a dark sauce. There was the usual dark ale plus a flask of clear water. Mandeler had a little bread and water. He watched Gwenelle taste each of the foods but when she got to the hot snapper, her eyes closed and a smile spread across her face. Born by the sea she had an appreciation for the local food. To his surprise he found that he was feeling a good deal better, even though the ship continued in its rhythmic dance through the sea. By the time the evening sky was full dark, most of the food was gone and the mugs were empty.

Over refilled dark ale, Captain Larson said, "There is more to the three of you than meets the eye isn't there."

How was one to respond to that? Gwenelle looked over her beverage and said, "There are always complexities to all people. What does it matter to you?"

"Fair enough, pretty lady. If I am to risk my neck for a few shiny things, I like to know what I am up against."

Gwenelle paused for a moment appraising Larson. He was in his early sixties, still broad in the shoulders but sagging at the waist. He had intelligent eyes that were a bit bloodshot but there was no doubt that he was clever and cunning. She tentatively said, "What if we were just two people seeking the green raptors because we wished only to learn from them?"

"You're hiding something. People who have come of age never travel with a denzel, that is for privileged children only. You hand over a fortune without pause. You ask about green raptors but you never say a word about the big black ones that are destroying the city. I say who are you really?"

Alheeza came to stand between the couple and they all looked intently at the captain. Larson heard Alheeza's thoughts in his head: *We are who she said we are but the three of us are on a quest for the greater good of all beings. We are in great need of your help.*

Larson's last mouthful of ale exploded from him. As he gasped for air, dripping ale from his chin, he looked unbelievingly at his guests. The two people and the denzel had him pinned with unblinking eyes.

Gwenelle spoke openly, "Apparently you can understand the thoughts we direct at you. Don't be scared, there have been people and denzels communicating like this for centuries."

Larson still had not found his voice but nodded his head.

Very good! Mandeler added in mind-speak. *We have been picked by the elders of our group to seek the olive green raptors, but more than that is not for us to share yet. You must trust our intentions and help us if you can.*

Over the next while they tested Larson for his telepathic abilities, finding that he could receive but was unable to project his thoughts in any way. Nevertheless, it changed the dynamics of the evening and they were able to openly discuss important issues.

The Captain said plainly, "What I have been afraid of, and all you have done confirms it, is that you have brought great danger to my ship. I was trading along the Eastern Coast during the last wave of Raptor takings. We were not involved but I did see another vessel that was hit the previous night. They had been very late coming back from fishing and a young person with her denzel was taken while the other two were uninjured. The boat suffered some damage to the rigging but still was water tight. While we were tied up at Portside, there was never an attack on this vessel but I am guessing that you are worried that there will be."

Yes, I have seen several of the takings within arm's reach and I say they very well might come here, answered Mandeler. *The ropes that hold the rigging offer some protection, or shall we say interference to a flying attack, but is it possible to pass a few more of these ropes along areas that are open? It may help in our defense.*

"You were that close without injury?"

Yes.

Gwenelle stopped him by asking, "Tell us truthfully, are you still willing to help us now that you know who we are and what we want?"

"I have no choice since we have left the shore behind. Let's see how this plays out over the next few days."

That will do, answered Mandeler.

The three of them returned to the deck settling on the windward rail. The moons had passed their cycle leaving a rich star filled sky. Larson had promised to join them soon to discuss ways of adding strong lines from the deck to the mast heads that would hamper Raptor flight but allow the sails reasonable mobility.

Gwenelle pulled her small illumination globe from her pocket and gave it to Mandeler. In its dim glow they walked along the rail, Mandeler could not keep from glancing at the dragon constellation. They reached the stern where two men were keeping the ship on course with the long handled rudder. Larson came on deck with four extra hands. After giving explicit instructions, he sent the men aloft to string heavy ropes in the dark. The extra lines were then secured along the edges of the ship, forming a simple palisade of strong cordage. It would deter all but the most persistent of the Great Raptors.

Captain Larson then turned to his guests and said that would have to do for the night. He did not expect any wind changes based on the evening sky so the rest of the hands could get some rest. Tomorrow he would have a second look at what might be done. He bid them a good night and strode below.

The three of them stood there for a few breaths before Alheeza mind-spoke: *We must be ever vigilant. There are many elements at play here. I will stay on deck protected between the mast and the cabin. You two go below and get some rest.*

Mandeler was standing there when Gwenelle reached for his hand in the dimness and softly said, "Come, it is time we went to bed."

The bottom of the companionway was lit by a single illumination globe. The sounds of sleeping crew members drifted down the narrow hallway. Their cabin door squeaked as Gwenelle opened it, dousing the small globe as she entered. Once they were both inside there was little room to maneuver so Mandeler turned and sat on the narrow bed tugging at his sweater. He could hear the rustle of clothing as Gwenelle prepared for bed. Her hands found his cheeks in the darkness and the next thing he knew there were soft moist lips caressing his. His excitement was immediate and as he raised his hands to embrace her, his fingers met the warmth of bare flesh. Her kiss deepened as she reached to finish pulling off his tunic.

Mandeler awoke with some bewilderment, it was dark and he had not been dreaming. This in itself was foreign. Memories of the previous evening started to come back to him. There was a warm body wrapped around his and her delightful scent filled his nostrils. He had something on his head but it took a few breaths to remember the dream blocking helmet. He slid it off to find the morning light streaming in through the porthole. As he reached to place the helmet aside, she moved up against him, causing a tingling of excitement. One of her eyes fluttered open, looking at him: *I'm surprised that you can do that after last night.* She giggled and closed her eye again.

With rosy cheeks, they emerged from their cabin looking somewhat disheveled. They mounted the deck in full daylight and looking up saw a thin film of high cloud that gave the sun a glistening halo. Although the wind seemed the same as the night before, the waves had grown in height, although still rather smooth. Birdard told them to join the Captain in his quarters. As they turned to go back, Alheeza came around the corner of the cabin yawning: *I watched the sky until sunrise. Once I saw a shadow that seemed to cross the stars, probably a scouting Raptor. For some reason they are not coming close and that is good enough for me today. Good night, I will see you in the afternoon*. With that he went below.

They found Captain Larson looking a little bedraggled but clear eyed. He was spooning hot herman nut porridge into his mouth as they came in. "Sit down and take a bowl with me. It will be getting rougher today and we may not get hot food tonight."

"Thank you sir," said Mandeler as they sat down to help themselves.

"I have to say that your news last night kept me awake for some time! What else can you tell me today that will make me feel easier about this quest of yours?"

The Captain had an edginess that was new to them.

Mandeler plunged forward, "I have been traveling for the better part of a moon cycle since the first Raptor raid on the estates. Since then I have witnessed three full attacks plus several sightings. The elders report that this round of takings is much more aggressive than in the past. They also tell us that these attacks come in fifteen year cycles with the takings lasting several moons. This time they are taking more than ever before and we think we might be able to help. For that we need your assistance in finding the green raptors."

Larson pursed his lips thinking and then he said, "How close do you need to get to be effective? The only time I saw them was by accident, and I would not willingly get that close again!"

Mandeler thought for a few breaths and then said, "I would prefer to get close enough to see them. Do you have a plan?"

"I had one when we left. I was going to sail for a few sun cycles and then set you three loose in one of the small boats to find your own way."

"How were you going to fetch us back?"

Larson's eye twitched and he said, "You asked to be taken to the green dragons. You never said anything about getting back."

The only sounds were that of water rushing along the hull and wind humming in the rigging. Holding his own fears down, Mandeler broke the silence: *That was forthright of you. Not comforting but honest. Am I correct in assuming you have modified your plan?*

"I have. I am willing to carry you as far as I have been before. You still may need to take the small boat to view them but I will stand off and wait for you."

That is more than generous. I would greatly appreciate some training in boat handling before we get there.

Captain Larson looked from one to the other, shifted in his chair and said, "I don't know if I would want to play bluff and bet with you. I'll stand by my word: you'll both start the lessons today. Now hear this, you must know the crew are very superstitious and would balk at going to the green dragons. Keep this amongst ourselves, for all our sakes."

As the couple returned on deck, Gwenelle telepathed to Mandeler only: *Did you have any idea we had come that close to being abandoned at sea?*

No, but I was not going to show him any surprise. I suspect our lives may depend on honesty in the right places and a good deal of silence in the rest.

A Sailor in the Making

As they headed back to their cabin Gwenelle added, "My father used to repair boats, but if work was slow he would take a turn hauling in the nets on the water. He often took me out with him so I grew up on the water. This all seems familiar to me."

Is that why the waves didn't affect your stomach?

Pretty much.

Larson was good to his word, because after checking his crew and ship, he spent the rest of the morning instructing Mandeler on the theory of sailing and navigation. He took paper from the side table and using a drawing stick made simple but informative sketches of the wind over sails and movement through the water. Mandeler learned that the bottom of the ship was just as important as the sails in order to make it move, not only downwind but also at an angle toward the wind. It had baffled him on the first day because the ship seemed to move against the laws of nature. It was not until this lecture that he understood what was making this all possible.

When the captain went on deck to check the course and crew it was a perfect time to take Mandeler aside and point out the structures that made up the rigging and hull. The most marvelous device was a thing called a compass. It used very rare metal, left over from the old days, and it could sense north from south. Apparently its value was so great that the Captain would take it with him when he left the ship.

On the captain's instructions, the couple was sent to put their rain gear on. Allenz had introduced Mandeler to the seat of ease on the first day. It was located in a small cabin across from theirs.

Within was a flushing chamber pot with a long operating handle. He had always liked complex contraptions and here was a true gem. It was very efficient in its design and the series of internal parts would flush it clean with sea water after each use. How civilized, compared to an outhouse.

Back on deck the weather was starting to pick up with spray constantly coming over the deck. The crew had reduced the increased heeling, by pulling down the sails one at a time and lacing folds at the bottom so that they were much smaller when set again. The captain also called for a change of course, turning the boat more to the side, so the ship was not laboring in the increasing waves. The forward speed seemed to pick up a bit, but the ship seemed to ride much smoother. Darkness came early as the clouds thickened and then came the rain.

They stood side by side, clinging to the handrail, on the high side by the helmsmen. It was unlike anything that Mandeler could have imagined, the waves building and the wind shrieking in the rigging. At times he thought the air was actually made of solid water. For some reason he did not feel afraid, he felt alive in every way. He could see in Gwenelle's eyes, that same delight in meeting the storm on its own terms.

Almer had control of the deck while the captain was below resting. He instructed the young couple to tie ropes around their waists and then to the mast in case of a wave washing the deck. Even the crew clung to life lines to keep their footing on the slippery surface.

A hand of time later, Captain Larson appeared with one quick look at the sky and the ship, he ordered the crew forward to pull the front sail back against the wind and throw the tiller upwind too. The boat settled into a gentle zigzag pattern, drifting softly downwind, when the other sails were dropped. It was amazing for Mandeler to see how the bucking deck of the ship settled into this easy motion. Larson said, "She is hove-to and that should hold it through the night, now let's go below, get dry and have a mug."

Allenz was left in charge, the last Mandeler saw as he went down the companion way was a crewmember hoisting an illumination globe aloft in the sheets of rain.

The couple pulled off their wet gear and hung it on a peg in the passage way. As they shed their layers of clothing it was apparent that the waxy outer garments only slowed the entrance of the water because it had wicked down from the neck and up the sleeves, leaving them damp from head to foot. Once in the small cabin they continued to pull off the remaining damp garments. Alheeza announced he was going topside. Mandeler thought he could detect a denzel grin on his mentor's face as he slipped out into the hallway.

Mandeler latched the door and turned in the small space. Gwenelle was tugging her sweater over her head. With the dim light from the small window he could just make out the form of her naked torso emerging from the folds of her baggy garment. Great Azimov, he thought to himself, she is beautiful! Pulling it free from her head, she looked across at him breaking into a grin. *Here,* she mind-spoke: *Let's get you out of these wet things too.*

She clasped the bottom of his wet sweater and tugged it up over his outstretched arms. She stood back admiring his tattoo, the emerald crystal lay central upon his chest with the swirling green tattoo radiating outward from it. The color seemed the strongest near the stone. The lettering was in a strange language but at the side was a flying shape she had not seen before. Gwenelle tenderly placed her hand upon the winged creature whispering, "What is this"?

I believe it is one of the Raptors, which kind I do not know, but I hope in the sun cycles to come, all will be revealed.

Gwenelle then wrapped her arms around his shoulders hugging him close. In their embrace they shivered, partially from the cold and damp but mostly from the excitement. She whispered, "It is beautiful and mysterious and so are you, but we don't have much time, the captain is expecting us."

Captain Larson had a knack for sitting comfortably in his chair that was attached to the floor while matching the ships movements, as if it was the most natural thing to do. He clutched a mug of ale in one hand and held a book open on the table with the other. He seemed undisturbed by the sounds of the shrieking wind, waves thudding on the hull, and hammering rain on the deck. As they sat across from the captain, Mandeler felt the first stirrings of queasiness as well as deep fatigue. Larson gave them a steady look and with a practiced move, he reached up taking two mugs from the pegged wall behind him. Then he also took down a leather sack from another peg. He placed the bulk of the bag on his shoulder and flipped open the lid, deftly poured a dark liquid into each of their mugs. "By the looks of you two you could use a shot of this!"

Mandeler almost choked on the first gulp, this was stronger brew by far. It burned most of the way down but it took away his woozy feeling in the process. Captain Larson leered at him and said, "This isn't the weak piss they serve to land men, this is the stuff that sailors drink to keep them going."

Gwenelle obviously had more experience than he did, for she drained her mug in a few gulps, wiping her mouth and grinning at the pair of them. Supper, if you could call it that, was a dense nut loaf, muzel cheese and dark brew. When they made their way back to their cabin Mandeler had to lean heavily on Gwenelle until she led him into bed.

Mandeler was directed to help move the heavy crew boat as it had slipped out of position on the cabin. It had shifted during the storm and repositioning the ten man craft was a laborious task. Several men put their shoulder to it, skidding the inverted boat across part of the cabin. Then Wigins showed him how to use a pointed tool to work the tight knots loose and how to retie them with nonslip ones. They re-secured a number of other items on the deck and then the bowlegged seaman pointed up the mast saying, "Now we go up!"

Mandeler looked up the tall wooden structure, with all of its supporting ropes, and his stomach started to churn.

Wigins slapped his hand on the tall wooden pole saying, "These things are strong but they would snap like a twig if it weren't for these!" He gestured to the side where the heavy triple ropes ran at intervals to the top of the mast. "These are the real strength, they are iron weed, twisted into hard ropes. These take the whole weight of the ship rolling with the wind! Now let's go up the mast and check their holding points. Take off your shoes and use these loops on the side of the mast as a ladder to climb to the top."

It was terrifying for Mandeler to climb the stiffened rope steps up the mast. As he went up the mast the ship's movements were exaggerated, with the swaying back and forth, nearly tearing him from the mast. By the time he got to the first cross bar his legs were shaking and his knuckles were white from strain. From below he heard, "Alright, stand on one foot and lean to the side!"

Oh, that should be easy, I think not. Mandeler thought but he did his best to move over. Wigins climbed past him as if it was the easiest thing in the world. He stopped just above him and hammered his fist against the supporting iron weed ropes. They hummed in response to the strike. The sailor grinned down at him, "That's how it's done laddie, now get your sorry ass down to the deck and don't make a mess by falling!"

He walked unsteadily back towards Gwenelle and Allenz. She had watched the whole performance from the tiller. She mind-spoke to Mandeler: *I'm surprised you went up there so soon after your sea sickness.*

It seemed the best thing to try if I am to be accepted by the crew. On the other hand, I don't think he likes me and wouldn't care if I had fallen.

For the rest of the day Mandeler was taught to haul in the thick ropes controlling the sails, more lessons on knot tying, and finally a hand on the tiller. He was abrupt on his adjustments at first but even he caught onto the principle of steering by the wind.

It was a long day of learning and working the boat. The weather had settled down to a steady breeze with the vessel making good time on course again. They went below to clean up for the usual supper with the captain. They shared what they had learned that day. Mandeler was amazed at what she could do. Suddenly he thought, I have always been amazed by her. He let his memories of their intimacy come back with a smile. When he left the estate there was no way of knowing things would turn out like this.

The fresh water that Mandeler had taken for granted on the estate turned out to be a precious commodity onboard the ship. He and Gwenelle had a cup or two of water in a small bucket to clean up after the storm and the hard day of labour. The up side was that they had to take their clothes off again. There was a good deal of nudging and laughter before they could get their remaining dry clothes on for the evening meal.

By the time they arrived in the skipper's cabin they regained enough composure to engage the captain in a serious discussion. He was at the navigation table working intently on a mathematical calculation. When he looked up he shook his head and said, "The storm put us back by a full day. When I got a look at the sun through my instruments at noon, I knew we were off course. We are farther east than I hoped."

Mandeler mind-spoke, *How can you tell with any accuracy where we are?*

"Not all was lost at the time of the great tragedy. There were learned people who remembered formulas and principles and they wrote them down. It took a generation to reinvent the time piece, but have a look at this." He led them to a large cabinet set in the other corner of his cabin. There was a muted ticking sound coming from the stout wood box. When the lip was tipped open there were three arms of differing lengths marking out a circle. "It is a time piece that records the exact amount of time needed for one Azimov day. See here, it is marked off in twenty hands of time."

The box stood waist high, Larson opened a side panel revealing two weights on iron weed strands. He pulled the uppermost down with a clicking sound and said, "Now with gravity as my aide, this time piece will run for two Azimov days."

He sat back at the table just as Birdard brought in the evening meal. Waving the man away he said, "If I know what time it is at Portside and what time it is when the sun is exactly at its zenith, along with the angle of the sun to the southern horizon, plus what day in the season it is, then I can calculate where we are, within a hand or two of sailing time that is."

Gwenelle inquired: *But if it is cloudy how do you find your way?*

"By guess pretty lady, by guess!"

"Oh!" They said in unison.

Supper was a simple meal of dense nut loaf, muzel cheese, hot melon stew and dark brew mixed with water. After that the pair of them wished the captain good night and were making their way back to the small cabin when Alheeza mind-spoke from the deck: *Come join me on deck for a moment.*

With tired legs they climbed the companion way to seek Alheeza. He was in front of the squat cabin that held the inverted crew boat. Argil was in a new moon phase on the horizon, under most conditions it would have been a wonderful sight.

Alheeza mind-spoke: *We were safe from the flying menace as long as the weather was foul but now I fear that we can be seen again. I will stand watch this night but I ask that you allow the dreams to come as they may. It may help to foretell what will pass.*

As much as his body craved deep sleep, he nodded his agreement adding: *As usual you are wise and I will keep my senses open so we may learn. Good night mentor.*

They made their way back to the cabin but on the stairs they were met by Loppis, who roughly pushed past them. Things did not feel right with the crew. Mandeler shook off the feeling as he followed Gwenelle into the cabin.

Once the door closed she turned and wrapped her arms around him. The day's fatigue seemed to vanish as her warm lips met his. He slid his hand under her sweater feeling the smoothness of her back. Her kiss deepened.

Enemies From Above and Below

They lay comfortably wrapped in each other's arms savoring the closeness after making love. Mandeler fell asleep on his back with Gwenelle pressed closely over one shoulder, her breast against his chest with the green crystal pinned between them. When the dreams came, they were a shared dream, vivid to each of them.

It was the same cave as before, seen with the acquired night vision. There was the clutter of bones on the floor but there was something more. The air had substance, a definite foul odor that penetrated everything. The creature stirred restlessly, moving in a slow circle, bones crunched under heavy feet, the great wings rustled and scraped on rock. She could not settle for something was a burden on her mind and body. Looking down she could see the swollen abdomen distended with this seasons' eggs. They were hers to protect but the tormenting dreams about the little two legged creature with its flaming stone upon a green raptor, made her fearful. How could the queen of the Great Raptors be afraid of something so small? They killed at will, as the bones beneath her feet would testify.

It was the time, in their mating cycle, when the males tended to their queen for the future of all Great Raptors. Every fifteen cycles of seasons, the urge to breed came upon her. This was going to be her last round as queen if things did not go well. How she craved the delicacies that the males brought her with their rich telepathic blood. Gone were the fish eating flying ones, but they still had the denzels, the best food for a brooding queen. The new comers, the little two legged ones were sometimes as good, especially if they glowed well. It had been two days since the last feeding and it had not satisfied her. The searchers had flown from the caves at first dark. Soon they would be in range to strike again. She quivered with anticipation. Maybe tonight they would find the one, after all it was a good night to kill!

Gwenelle stirred in her sleep, troubled by the dream. Mandeler unconsciously hugged her closer and they both fell back into a deep sleep.

It was a different cave but a familiar one. The horizon was barely aglow where the sun had set. The shadow of a large flying creature blotted out the view and the sound of claws scraping on stone announced the arrival of the mate. She looked forward to his arrival, having been worried by the fading light. He rubbed against her neck in passing, before regurgitating a meal for the small ones.

She too had been troubled by dreams of late. There was a small creature in a floating contraption making its way towards them. She felt fear but not mortal fear, just the fear of the unknown. All during the day she had images of the past dreams. Something unusual was about to happen but she could not make the connection.

Still lying in each other's arms with the crystal amulet pressed between their naked bodies, they slept soundly for a few hands of time until the next dream came upon them.

It was the sight of the new moon rising that struck a familiar note. The rippling surface must be a vast body of water, for as the creature flew on, it was a never ending seascape. The hunter sensed his wing mates, knowing they were all driven on by the fear of their Queen. He pumped his wings, longing to find the one that she sought above all others.

Then in the distance there was an object on the water and as they drew near the glow of an ancient one could be seen. This must be what they were searching for. The lead Raptor started to make a large circle to better prepare for the attack. On occasion, they had plucked the new comers from the fragile floating things.

This one was larger, with more things sticking up, but he knew their weakness. Sending his thoughts to the others in turn, he came in from downwind and raked his talons through the fragile material, grasping it by the stick and ropes. As he imagined, his weight leaned the whole affair towards the water, turning the side up and making a perfect place for the others to land.

He watched, as his companions groped for two legged creatures on the deck. Their screams were joyous to hear!

They both sat bolt upright, unable to tell when the dream stopped and the screaming became real. Mandeler yelled, "We have to get to the deck!"

As they untangled themselves Gwenelle raised her illumination globe, just in time to see a naked Mandeler heading out the door, with a flinger in hand.

For Mandeler, the whole ship had been tipped on its side, making it difficult to climb the stairs. As he made his way through the open companionway door, he was greeted by his worst nightmare. On the sloping stern rail, a Great Raptor clung with its wings half folded, allowing the wing knuckles to grip either side of the deck. Captain Larson had been at the tiller and was trying to crawl out of reach, along the lower hand rail. The dark predator spotted him, making ready to grasp at his prone body. At that moment, Alheeza flung himself from the cabin roof, landing on the face of the groping creature. For a moment Alheeza stabbed at the red eyes with his teeth, but was flung abruptly to the deck, as the creature shook his head. It bit down on the old denzel silencing his attack. With one hand Mandeler hoisted his brilliant crystal into the air, washing the deck in emerald light. At the same time he fired the flinger with the other hand. The Raptor recoiled when the small shaft protruded from his cheek. Mandeler heard himself cry, **"Stop! Be gone you foul creature, BE GONE!"**

Time stood still as the young man stared down the huge predator. The night marauder could not look upon the man with the gleaming green crystal, and in the end it snatched the limp Alheeza from the deck with its talons and leapt into the air with a thunderous down wash. Mandeler's heart sank as he saw the dangling Alheeza depart. The ship suddenly righted itself, as the last Raptor departed, sending everything swaying and crashing about.

Gwenelle stepped past him holding a globe in her hand. The deck was lit by its cool light. Mandeler looked around in horror. Larson was sprawled on the deck, bleeding from the head, amidst the broken debris. Overhead ropes and tattered sails hung in disarray. He was standing there, still clutching his amulet, when he felt her hands wrapping his shoulders in a blanket. Captain Larson's eyes popped open and he gasped for breath saying, "The ship, take care of my ship... " Then his eyes rolled up into his head.

It was Gwenelle that stepped past him, to tie a length of rope to the tiller, allowing the ship to heave to. More slapping and banging, but the ship gradually settled. Mandeler looked up and down the deck and saw no one else. Noises were coming from below, and soon the rest of the crew came on deck. They looked about with wide eyes at the wreckage.

It was Wigins that first spoke, "Where is Tweedins? And what in Azimov's hell happened here?"

Mandeler had let the amulet slip back under the folds of his blanket. "The ship has been attacked by three Great Raptors. The Captain is hurt badly and I do not know anything else."

Allenz pushed forward, "You two help me take the captain to his cabin! The rest of you tend to the sails and rigging." There was some grumbling but the men spread out.

Gwenelle whispered in his ear, "You need to get some clothes on."

As Mandeler dressed, his mind went over the dreams and the subsequent attack. When he thought of his long time teacher and friend, his eyes welled up with tears. Even Alheeza could not have survived that mauling. All of his wisdom and knowledge was snubbed out in a second. How was he ever going to go on from here?

Gwenelle pushed the door open and hugged him from behind: *I'll miss that scrawny little guy. I am so sorry Mandeler, what was he trying to do, attacking a Raptor?*

If I was to guess, he was proving that the future, as I see it, can be changed, ***but at what cost?***

Mandeler, I saw the dreams last night too! There was the queen, then the greens, and finally the flight before the attack.

He turned and his blue eyes came up to meet hers. *But how?*

She placed her hand on his chest where the amulet lay and mind-spoke: *We were lying skin to skin with this pressed between us. I must pick it up from you.*

He put a hand over hers. *No one else should have to suffer my dreams. Did you want to get tied up in all of this?*

Did you?

No.

Well then, we are in it together. She kissed him lightly on his forehead. *Let's get your medicinal case and see how the captain is.*

Captain Larson lay in his bunk next to the time piece, his face was pale and there was blood still oozing from a head wound. Allenz was at his side, dabbing at it with a rolled up cloth. Mandeler kneeled down next to him and opened his case saying. "Let me have a look at him please."

Allenz lifted an eye brow and shuffled to the side. He watched as Mandeler placed a hand on the man's head. Unseen was the young man's other hand, slipping under his tunic to clutch his crystal.

Captain Larson had taken a beating. His head wound was not as bad as it appeared, but here were two broken ribs and bruises along his left side. The bleeding could be stopped easily enough, and the chest bound to ease the broken bones. Mandeler reached into his case and drew out the copeander fruit, nipping off a corner with his knife. He rolled it around in his hand to warm it and make it pliable, then slipped it into the captain's cheek. He took a clean cloth from Allenz, prepared it with a salve and wrapped it around the bleeding temple. He ripped a bed sheet into lengths and bound the man's chest, then said, "That is all we can do for him now. Gwenelle can stay with him for he will wake very soon. Allenz you need to tend to the crew."

Mandeler was not sure how he had taken over control, but Allenz lumbered off as directed.

Gwenelle mind-spoke: *I have to tell you, I just came from the deck and what I saw there has me worried. The crew are jumpy. Apparently Tweedins is missing. Either he fell off the ship or was taken by a Raptor. I think there may be trouble.*

Oh Raptor dung, that is all we need now! replied Mandeler with uncharacteristic emphasis.

The captain opened one bloodshot eye and took in his surroundings. He was in his cabin, it was night, and a single globe lit the area. His head hammered like a three day hangover. The young woman was seated near him so he asked, "How did I get down here?"

Gwenelle mind-spoke: *What do you remember about being on the deck this evening?*

Larson's other swollen eye opened a fraction while he tried to bring it all together, then his eyes widened and he said, "Great Azimov, we were hit by Raptors. They were tipping the ship over when that great big bugger came after me. Oh dung, they're big and they stink. Did I see you, or just imagined I had? You seemed bigger and that piercing light... That's all I remember."

Rest, the crew are repairing some of the damage. It is still two hands of time before sun up and then we will see how well you can get about.

She mounted the stairs to join Mandeler on the deck. Several illumination globes washed the crew as they spliced and stitched, bringing the rigging and sails back to working order. She brought him up to speed on the captain's condition. Looking around, she saw the men grumbling as they worked slowly at their tasks. All but a small forward sail was down and the ship rode quietly in the long rolling waves.

After she returned to check Larson, Mandeler approached Allenz and quietly asked, "How bad is it?"

"Looks worse than it is. Two sails are torn, three spreaders broken and a good number of lines aloft have parted. Nothing we can't fix after the sun is up. We are just making sure nothing else comes loose right now."

Mandeler replied, "Good. Any sign of Tweedins?"

"No. His disappearance and the attack by a flight of Raptors has the crew in a nasty mood."

"Anything else I can do right now?"

"No, this is for trained hands. After dawn there will be something to help with."

Mandeler had gone below to go through their things. In particular he wanted to sort out the bag that Alheeza brought from the elders. Tears came to him again at the thought of what had become of his mentor. He undid the draw string and looked inside. Alheeza had never told him about the contents of the bag. It was supposed to be things offered by the elders to help in their quest. It was not hard to recognize the wrapped flinger with its cluster of arrows tied to it. There were several jars wrapped in protective cloth and sealed with wax. Upon inspection, one jar had a fresh supply of fire sticks. He pressed the soft wax back in place and continued. The smaller one had the familiar symbol of a copeander fruit, the elixir that took away pain and fatigue. Stuffed in between the jars was a tiny pouch. He looked inside it only to catch his breath in wonder. He tipped the contents onto his hand. They were heavy, much heavier than the nuts and bolts. They glistened with a yellow glow, could this be the legendary gold that the colonists talked about? Including the mind-speak blocking helmet, they were carrying a fortune in metal goods, a king's ransom according to legend. What had the elders foreseen to send such gifts with an untrained one like him?

He reached out with his mind-seeking and found Gwenelle. He told her about the things in Alheeza's bag, recounting his wonder at finding such gifts. She updated him about Larson, who was in pain, but very lucid. Was there something else that could be done for him? *Cut another piece of the copeander fruit for him to suck on. I'll be there as soon as I finish here.*

The fruit revived Captain Larson wonderfully, for as the sun broke over the horizon, Mandeler helped the captain onto the deck to check his ship personally. All, but one of the crew, were crowded in the bow talking. They made their way back to Allenz, at the tiller, where the captain said, "What's happening up on the bow with the crew?"

Allenz said in a low voice, "Since Tweedins was taken last night the crew are in a foul mood. I don't much like the look of it." He patted the long hardened glass knife in its sheath at his side.

Larson leaned on the compass stand and looked over his shoulder toward the gathered men. His mouth twitched and he winced as if with pain. Then he said, "I agree!"

As they watched, the group broke up with Wigins, Renfrew, and Loppis coming along the right side, while Birdard, Bardick, and Toddfree came back along the other side. They stopped several paces from the Captain. Wigins, acting as the crew's spokesman said, "We want you to turn around and head for port, this here morning!"

Captain Larson looked at each man, taking a measure of his intent, and then he said in a level voice, "You signed up to do my bidding, not to tell me what I should or should not do."

Wigins did not even look at his companions, he just continued, "We intend to turn around with or without your bidding...sir!"

"And if I say no, we are to continue on our course. What then?"

"Then you are no longer our captain and we sail back, see!" Wigins now had his hand upon his knife, as did several others.

"Not while I am still standing you are not!" said Captain Larson standing defiantly.

The blade came from its sheath, in one smooth motion, as Wigins lunged at the captain. He did not take a second step, for a length of glass tipped shaft suddenly blossomed red through his chest. He faltered amid stride, looking bewildered at the bloody arrow protruding from his heart. He fell like a sack of melons to the deck.

Mandeler had his own knife out, as did Allenz on the other side of Larson. The mutineers looked at each other, taking their hands away from their knives. Those at the tiller were the only ones to see Gwenelle load a second arrow from her hiding place in the companion way. Mandeler reached under his tunic clasping his amulet and spoke, "Remove the knife belts and stand to the low side, slowly."

Like children they obeyed. Silently he spoke to the captain: *What now Captain Larson?*

Even Larson had been shocked by the swiftness of the flinger response, he looked his crew up and down saying, "Those that want to stay with me cross to the other side of the deck, those still wanting to go home stay where you are."

Only Birdard crossed the deck.

Gwenelle came from her hiding place, bringing the second flinger to Mandeler, keeping hers aimed at the mutineers.

Captain, we can keep them covered if that helps with your next move, Mandeler said silently to Larson.

"You two come here," Larson said, pointing to two on the left, "And heave this hunk of fish bait into the sea."

Without ceremony, Wigin's bloody body splashed into the ocean.

"Allenz fetch a cask of water and three hard loaves. The rest of you untie the crew boat and prepare to launch it. As you can see you will be watched by these marksmen, so no funny business or else."

The launching of the crew boat was slow and deliberate. No one was allowed to move aside or do anything threatening. When the boat was afloat, and the disgruntled crew aboard, the captain said. "You have food and water for the three sun cycles to sail south. With the quartering wind, land will be easy to find."

The captain then turned to his small crew, "We are shorthanded but we are the best sailors of all. Gwenelle take the till and steer north, northwest. Mandeler you help the other two set the main and mizzen sail.

Without looking astern, the Sea Quester sailed on, toward the green raptors and the unknown.

When the immediate deck work was done, the young couple were able to retire below to their cabin. As the door clicked shut behind them, Gwenelle broke into tears. Mandeler held her in his arms saying nothing.

Finally she whispered, "I've never killed a man before..."

It was that or Captain Larson was a dead man. I didn't have to be a genius to know that with him gone they would have turned on us next.

Gwenelle paused before continuing, I think I sensed that even before I got to the deck. That is why I had the weapons with me. Then I saw the knife come out, and as he lunged I just shot from the hip.

With a shudder, Mandeler continued, I can only guess what you're feeling, but I am glad it was him and not the rest of us.

He reached up taking her hand, placing it on his amulet. As he felt the link take hold, he was filled with the grief that she truly felt for the death of another man.

They held each other for the longest time.

Even in flight the creature had a nauseating smell. Alheeza opened his uninjured eye, just a slit, taking in what he could. The dim moonlight made a silhouette of the Great Raptor as he flew along with his rhythmic wingbeats. Two more shadows of the winged marauders were visible up front. Where the clawed foot grasped him around the torso it was very painful, but he carefully took shallow breaths keeping his movements slight. He hoped the rank predator thought he was dead and he did not want to change that.

He slowly took inventory of his injuries. His back left leg dangled uselessly, most likely a compound fracture, several ribs were broken, the multiple punctures had stopped bleeding, his eye was swollen shut and his head pounded, but he was alive. How much longer he would be alive was another question?

Time passes very slowly when you are being held in the crushing grip of a Great Raptor. The beast seemed to slow and then it was gliding towards some dark shape ahead.

He could hear the thunderous strokes of big wings ahead of them, and then his captor also beat the air in the same way. Claws scraped on rock as they came to a halt on the edge of a cliff. The mouth of a huge cave yawned open in front of them, spewing its stench in greeting. As the Raptor went to shift him to its other foot he took his chance, throwing himself backwards. Bright light flashed in his vision, from the explosion of pain. He ran several paces on his three good legs and launched himself into the emptiness past the cliff's edge as teeth snapped at the tip of his tail.

Out of Reach

With their ship making its way, the remaining crew came together on the tranquil deck to share a meal. It was a time to take nourishment and work out how to sail a ship with a very short handed crew. Allenz and Birdard were uninjured and made up the entire complement of experienced crew. Captain Larson had the knowledge but was handicapped by his broken ribs. Although Mandeler and Gwenelle were eager to help, they could only take on so much with their limited skills. Over a loaf of nut bread and chunks of muzel cheese, Larson set out a plan to keep an experienced person on deck at all times, and with the help of all, they could manage the big craft. Long shifts fell to Allenz but even the captain would take on shorter turns, as he could manage. The hard labor fell to Birdard, assisted by Mandeler. Gwenelle could take the tiller in turns. If they became exhausted, or the weather turned against them again, they could stall the boat sideways to the wind with a backed head sail, enabling them to rest.

In two hands of time later, Larson called the young couple down to his cabin for a private moment. The captain slumped at his table with sunken eyes peering out of his pale wrinkled face, and looked as if he had aged a decade overnight.

Mandeler opened with: *I assume you are worried about what happens when the sun goes down?* He had slipped into mind-speak as if it was common place. The captain just nodded, his eyes staring bleakly at the young man.

Mandeler went on: *There are some things that I know the dark marauders dislike. For one thing they shun the light, even fire is repulsive to them and their night vision is much like what we see during the day. Anything bright blinds them, including this,* he drew out his amulet. Even in the well-lit cabin it seemed to glow. *If we could put a pair of fast-start fire pots on the deck, I think it would help keep them at a distance. I will keep watch, for I now know how to tell when they are near.*

Captain Larson let out a huge breath and said, "That is probably the first good news I have heard today, although having fire pots on my deck is a bit tricky with all that tarred rigging. Leave it to Allenz and me to sort that out."

It was decided that Mandeler would take the first break and try to sleep. He and the captain would stand watch for the night. If Larson's strength gave out, Allenz would be called. With the sails set with a single reef to accommodate changes in the wind, only a crew of two would be needed on deck. Gwenelle was the floater crew, coming and going as she was needed. She also took the first rest period going to join Mandeler in their cabin.

He was on his back, with his mouth open, making sleeping sounds. She crawled in beside him, snuggling up to his side, and drew the blanket over them. Then she slipped her hand under his tunic resting it on the familiar stone. Exhaustion swept over her and sleep soon followed.

Her memory was long and she had seen many season cycles since being a fledgling. She knew the Great Raptors well, the hunters that wreaked havoc on her and her kind before they retreated to the single island. Her ancestral memories marked them as the most hated of creatures, for they attacked at night, killing young and old.

Their island had been a safe haven these past generations but the clan had stopped growing, for now the crowded caves had fewer fledglings each year. The dreams of the two-legged one haunted her. She knew she was being drawn into an unwanted battle, pitting her race against the terrible ones. He was coming and time was running out.

That brought them both awake. It was not one of the terrifying dreams but it was still unsettling in its own way. Given how his other dreams had turned out, they were expected by a creature no one had seen up close in almost four hundred season cycles.

A banging on the door startled them. Allenz wanted them on deck.

It was nearly sunset when they came back on deck. Allenz was at the helm studying a rope contraption harnessing the tiller. He said, "I sent Birdard to wake the captain. After taking a bit of time to think things through I came up with this device." He ran his hand down the rope contraption. "The ship naturally turns up into the wind with a gust, if the sails are set just so. Taking advantage of that, I ran a line through some blocks so that it moves the tiller the other way, taking the ship back down wind. It makes a subtle 'S' course but she averages a steady course without the helmsman having to tend the tiller every moment. It is like an extra couple of seamen!"

As they stood there a puff of wind made the ship heel over fractionally. It responded just as Allenz had predicted. He announced with a beaming smile, "She is balanced to the wind, almost on a perfect course and all we have to do is keep watch in case the wind changes directions. Now the night watch should be as easy as eating fruit pudding."

He then walked forward to a large ceramic pot between the tiller and the mast, where he patted it with some affection, and said, "These here are your fire pots. I've got a rag soaked with some light spirits resting on this pot of heavier oil. Just put a flame to it and you will have a good but controlled fire in a few breaths."

Mandeler looked at Gwenelle smiling, and then back to Allenz saying, "You are the handiest of men Allenz. We would be lost without you."

At that moment, the captain appeared from the companionway, along with Birdard carrying a short chair. Larson swept his eyes over the ship and nodded his appreciation to Allenz. Birdard lashed the chair to the back handrail, next to the swaying row boat that was suspended from the stern. Captain Larson plopped his body into the chair, he was a changed man from the morning. He smiled broadly, inviting Birdard to bring up whatever the evening meal was going to be.

It was watered dark brew, a fresh jar of black fruit, and chunks of hearty nut loaf. They had been eating quietly when Allenz brushed the long lengths of his green-grey hair from his face and said, "Captain, can we speak plainly about what's happening here?"

Larson leaned back saying, "I believe so. Master Mandeler and his good lady Gwenelle have paid for passage to the green raptors island. It is my intention to get as close to the reefs as possible, and after that it is up to Mandeler to get to the island."

It was Birdard who spoke up next, "But why would you want to do that?"

Gwenelle and Mandeler looked at each other, and then he said, "It has to do with the Great Raptors. Somewhere on that island is the secret to stopping their killing. I have to get there."

Birdard continued, "You don't know what you're asking for. The only time we seen them from this ship, one of the big green ones came flying low straight at us and then swooped away. We didn't stay to see more."

"Still that is where we need to go!" Mandeler said.

As morning came, the Great Raptors, from above, had given up trying to reach him in the tiny crevice. For the moment he was safe but he was wedged into the slim defile unable to move. He had blindly thrown himself over the edge and by chance had fallen into this narrow slit in the rock below. If he had gone out any further he probably would have fallen to the rocks far below. Again he took inventory of his state. He was sliced down the side all the way to his hip. As the day crept on the bleeding had stopped, leaving only the throbbing of his battered body. His bed was made from scattered bones, when he opened his good eye it was to stare into the empty eye socket of a long dead denzel. How could it get worse? That is when he felt the first clumps of Raptor dung fall from above.

The sun sank into the crimson ocean leaving an amber glow behind. As it faded, the largest moon of Azimov-4's glowed more brightly. Mandeler stood beside the seated Captain Larson and clasped his exposed crystal. He said, "I can't feel any danger now but I keep searching." The captain relaxed visibly, then Mandeler went to join Gwenelle at the side rail.

As he came to stand at her side, she mind-spoke: *I still can't believe he's gone*.

He stood there for a few deep breaths and then added: *I don't want to believe he is gone either. It is hard to imagine Alheeza surviving such an ordeal but I still feel a bit of hope.*

She linked arms with him. *That will do fine for now!*

It was several hands of time later when he first sensed their approach. As he clutched the crystal he could suddenly see as if through another's eyes: *The hunting pack flew on through the darkness. Over the vast stretch of water the setting moon gleamed in the pattern of waves. Ahead he could see the small dot on the horizon that must be the frail craft that they sought. He was the prime hunter and they had been charged with fetching the 'one' that the queen sought above all others, the small two legged one that glowed the most. He was within their grasp this time.*

Mandeler staggered and then regaining his stance he turned to Gwenelle. *It is time to bring the lamp and light the fire pots.*

The ship had been set with minimal sail for the evening and was making her way slowly in the light breeze. Gwenelle bolted from the companionway with globe in hand. She quickly went about lighting both fire pots and soon had long tongues of amber flame dancing at their rims.

Mandeler had dashed below with a thought. He dug out their flingers and arrows and was sitting on the floor wrapping a rag about the end of a projectile when Gwenelle found him. Looking up he said: *If we dip them in a fire pot we should have fire arrows. I don't think the Raptors will like them at all!*

Gwenelle helped him bind a few more arrows with rags, before gathering the projectiles to follow him back on deck.

The ship had taken on a surreal glow with the blazing fire pots. Mandeler faced the southwest, where he sensed the approaching Raptors. He mind-spoke: *They are very near. Load both flingers and stand by me at the fire pot.*

At that moment the air was split with the scream of a Great Raptor. Mandeler extended his arm and she placed the weapon into his hand. He quickly dipped it in the oil-fired pot and it emerged aflame. Turning, he let his heart guide his movements so that when the arrow was released it arched high in the sky, causing a scream, as it sunk into the chest of the lead Raptor. She dipped the next one for him and exchanged flingers. He twisted around, letting this one track high, this time it snuffed out as it passed through the wing of the second Raptor. The air thundered above them as the agitated Raptors circled. He fired nine more fire arrows, each one striking somewhere on a Great Raptor, leaving a fire trail before being snuffed out at impact. Their screams filled the air and then as suddenly as it started the sky grew quiet. Holding the crystal aloft, it burst forth with a radiating green light. He heard a voice come from his throat that was not his, it cracked the air, **"*Be gone you foul creatures! Be gone*!"**

Whether it was the fire pots, his flaming arrows or his bold command, he could not tell, but the sky above no longer held any winged terrors. All that could be heard was the sound of water passing down the hull and wind whispering in the rigging.

How was he to tell the queen of his failure? First there was the open fires on the weak one's craft, the bolts of fire that thrust up stinging his scaled body, and then the blinding green light that seared his eyes. The haunting challenge from the small one still echoed in his head. Now he must face an even worse fate, his queen.

On the second night Mandeler could sense the Raptors looking for him but something held them back. What it was he could not tell.

He was sleeping during the day shift, without Gwenelle, hoping that his dream cycles were only a nightly event. When the dream came it was vivid. *The queen of the Great Raptors was enraged, she turned on the leader of the pack, slashing him down the side. This male had failed her again, not only did he fail to bring her the 'one' she sought, above all others, but now the fragile craft was out of their flying range. Added to this, his previous flight had lost the ancient denzel at their cave entrance. Now that hated creature lay in a crack, reminding her of the incompetence of her hunters. She howled her rage, striking out once more. This time she opened his neck so wide that his life blood poured out. The queen watched, without feeling, as the pack leader died before her. She called to her second, take him away and make a meal of him. He is good for nothing else! she screamed.*

She felt a deep stabbing pain within her, if she did not get what she needed, the next generation would be in jeopardy. She must protect herself in the interest of those yet to come.

Mandeler burst awake, breathing heavily. He was drenched in sweat like so many times before, but this time he knew what he saw was real. Alheeza might still be alive. What am I going to do?

He ran up to the deck. She was sitting cross-legged splicing a coiled line. Mandeler spoke, "He is alive!"

Looking up, she mind-spoke: *Who?*

Alheeza, I saw the queen in a dream, he jumped off the cliff in front of her cave. She seems to think he is still alive.

Great Azimov! Now what?

I can only see things in my dreams, it doesn't tell me what I should do.

They talked for some time about the dream details. She stood and hugged him closely before they turned to seek the captain.

Captain Larson was working out their position when Mandeler came to join him in the cabin. He looked up and said to the young man, "Tomorrow we should be there. Start to watch the sky to the south. We might spot the first of them today."

Mandeler mind-spoke: *And not a moment too soon! Alheeza might still be alive. All I know is that the green raptors are a key to all of this. I know this sounds outlandish and I still have no real plan, but I wish I had some kind of a weapon that gave us an edge.*

Larson had a distant look as he absorbed this news. Then he ran his finger through his fringe of greasy grey hair and said. "First, let me say that it is hard to imagine being taken by one of those creatures and surviving. He must be one tough little beggar. On the other hand, there may be something you could use," as he got out of his chair and rummaged in a small chest. He pulled out two small jars, cracking the seals and sniffing them. "Yah, I think this might be of interest."

He passed the first jar to Mandeler, who held it to his nose and sniffed. "What is this?" he said with a wrinkled nose.

"The yellow ones are burning stones."

And the other one?

"That there is exploding powder, the only sample I've ever seen."

Mandeler tipped the yellow pebbles into his hand and examined them carefully. Then he handed them to Gwenelle. Her reaction was different, like she was seeing right through them, with a glazed look.

Gwenelle felt an odd tingle run up her spine and for a moment she saw a stooped, grey-haired crone with layers of shawls. Just as fast as the image came it was gone again.

When Mandeler handed her the jar with the dark powder the same old crone appeared again in her mind. She was gone in an instant, but Gwenelle was left feeling the two jars were a key part to their puzzle.

Mandeler looked at her quizzically. *What's going on?*

The spell broke and she was standing on the deck, in the full sun, with a breeze in her hair.

I don't know… I'll tell you what I can later.

Captain Larson started to tell them what he knew about the two little pots. Apparently the yellow rocks were used in making the valuable fire sticks. They were extremely expensive because the stinking stones were hard to come by. As for the exploding powder, he added, "I met an old woman in a coastal fishing village that passed this along to me earlier this year. She didn't say much about exploding powder except it was very rare and I would have need of it in the coming season. I got the burning stones from her as well. She told me to keep them safe and a day would come when their true value would make itself known."

"Just out of curiosity, what did the old woman look like?" asked Gwenelle.

"She was a tiny thing, a bit stooped, long grey hair tied back, and layers of shawls around her shoulders. Why, do you think you know her?"

"Maybe. But continue what you were saying." Gwenelle shivered.

Without noticing her reaction, the captain dug into another chest and motioned them to follow him on deck. As they gathered around Larson, he put a piece of yellow rock on the plate and using his magnifying glass, placed a hot spot of light on the stinking stone. A few breaths later a curl of smoke rose from the yellow crystals, then it burst into a blue flame. The swirling smoke made them cough, so they drew to the upwind side of the deck. With watering eyes Mandeler said, “Great Azimov, that's foul stuff!”

Larson broke out into a crooked toothed smile adding, “Yah, ain't it just!”

“How much of this do you have?”

“Sorry laddie, that is all I've got but I've heard where there's more.”

“OK, where, how long, and do I dare ask how much?”

“Ah, now you've hurt my feelings. It's not far, just a few days over the horizon, and a bit of climbing.”

Mandeler said, “And the fee?”

“We'll get back to that in a minute, just watch this now.”

The captain now took out a tempered pot and a block of dark wood. He made a small pile of the explosive powder on the block, with a little trail of it off the edge. Then he placed the pot over it. Taking his glass, he focused a point of hot light on the little trail of powder. Suddenly it hissed to life and flashed under the pot. In that instant there was a loud bang and the pot was hurled into the air, followed by a trail of white smoke.

Larson's sooty face beamed his delight, “Now isn't that something? I am sure you could use some of that too!”

“Where can we get that?”

“Now that's where I have a problem, this little pot is all I got, and I don't know where to get more or how to make it.”

As Gwenelle watched the two men talking she was taken by a feeling that she could almost remember something. It was just out of reach, like the name of a casual acquaintance, forgotten at a party, but the face looked familiar. The two pots felt a little like that but she did not know why.

Larson was speaking again, “Now as for the fee, I've decided that I'll take no more of your precious metal. After you saved me from that creature the other night I figure it is personal from here on.”

The Island

She had been out hunting and her mate was with the fledglings. Her dreams had bothered her. The sense that something was coming grew stronger. So she ranged farther to the south in search of a school of green fins. It was then that she spotted the strange craft that floated on the water with the tall white wings. The distance was still great, but with her long vision, she could make out tiny creatures on the surface of it. Then she sensed him; he was looking for her too.

On Sea Quester, Mandeler came on deck looking for Gwenelle. She was at her favorite spot, leaning against the handrail by the bow. The waves were almost hypnotic as they were split by the slender bow. He quietly came up beside her, reaching around to place a hand on her hip. She leaned gently into him as they took comfort in each other.

They stood there for some time, looking into the distance before he mind-spoke: *She is looking for us too. It will happen soon.*

Standing there, the first sign of her approach was a sense of his heart taking up a quicker pace. Then in the distance he could see a spot that had to be a flying creature and even from this distance it had to be large. They could feel the growing excitement because it could only be one of the green raptors. Nothing else was that big, flying in daylight and this far from land. The tiny dot grew larger until they could clearly see the olive raptor approaching on swept back wings. It was far more delicate in its lines, compared to the night marauders but there were similarities. Both flew on long curved wings that were attached to the hind legs. The appendages moved in unison for flight. That is where the similarities ended. As Mandeler watched her approach, then circle high above the ship, it was plain that she was smaller than the Great Raptors but still very large compared to him. She made three orbits about their vessel, apparently studying them, and then flew off in the direction she had come from.

Captain Larson shouted from the helm, "Now that was interesting. I would say it wants us to follow that course!"

From a distance, the mountain looked like a single peak, but as they approached the other two peaks emerged. It had rocky crags and steep cliffs all around. There were traces of green at lower levels but mostly it was bare rock. It looked like an impenetrable fortress. The sun was getting low on the horizon as the ship approached the island. More raptors could be seen coming and going from the island, but none of them had approached the ship.

Birdard was high in the rigging looking ahead to see if there were any sunken dangers. He called down to the deck, "Captain, I see breakers ahead. They stretch as far as I can see in either direction."

Captain Larson said to Mandeler and Gwenelle, "I think it may be some type of reef that rings the island. I have seen this in a couple of other places. We could take a day to sail around to see if there is an opening through the reef."

Mandeler felt a growing urgency to get to the island and he asked, "Can a small boat get over the reef?"

"If handled properly it could."

"Then I want to try taking it in today. I feel that time is wasting and I must get to that island as soon as possible."

Gwenelle mind-spoke to him: *I'm coming with you!*

He replied in kind: *I don't want to put you in danger.*

Oh raptor dung, you can be stupid some times. Of course I am coming, that's why I'm here.

In less than a hand of time, they had selected the best gear to take and the row boat was lowered from the stern into the choppy water. As Mandeler stepped near the side of the little craft it lurched under his weight. It felt unstable after the large deck of the ship. Gwenelle mind-spoke: *Sit in the stern land man, I'll drive!*

Like a seasoned sailor, Gwenelle took the oars and steered them towards the row of crashing waves. Their little boat bobbed up and down as it approached the thundering breakers. His stomach churned as he saw how angry the waves looked ahead.

Soon they were dashing down the face of a steep wave as it climbed up behind them. The edge of it was foaming and the noise deafening. Then the bow buried itself into the next wave while the stern was hoisted high, with the wave behind it. It happened so fast that all he could see was a wall of water crashing down on them and then it was quiet.

On the estates, he had learned to swim in the calm ponds but nothing had prepared him for being slammed into the ocean like a swatted night bug. Which was up or down he could not tell. He reached out with his mind, *Gwenelle! Oh Gwenelle, where are you?*

I'm beside the boat, but where are you?

In the water, somewhere deep!

Swim for the light!

Before Gwenelle could dive, a massive green streak exploded into the water next to her. Mandeler felt the impact, followed by a dark shape sweeping past him. In the next moment he was being pushed from beneath towards the brightness. As he broke through the surface, he gulped in great lungs full of air. Treading water, he turned coming face to face with an olive green raptor. She had a bulging forehead with the typical brow nostrils. On the sides of her head were swept back ears that looked more like little wings, and her snout was curved into a smile-like line. A pair of saucer sized violet eyes, split vertically by a narrow black pupil, stared back at him. There was no doubt about the intelligence behind them.

Clinging from the partially submerged boat, Gwenelle shouted, "Holy Raptor Dung! Are you alright?"

Mandeler responded to her: *I couldn't be better and look who found us!*

Maybe it was pure thought, because it was not like when Gwenelle mind-spoke to him, but the thoughts were there nevertheless. *I am*

Labeena the Leader of the green raptor clan. I have foreseen your coming. Take hold of my neck so that we can rise together.

Mandeler kicked towards the outstretched neck, grasping onto the row of soft ridge spines. Unlike the denzels and Great Raptors, with their interlocking plates, she had smooth warm skin that was a deep olive green. Almost like riding Star, he straddled the partially submerged shoulders. Labeena drew her great wings, dripping from the ocean, and beat the air with them. He hung on for his life as she lifted from the water to climb into the sky. Never had he felt such exhilaration, then he heard Gwenelle in his head: *Great Azimov,* (and a few moments later) *you lucky bastard.*

Somewhere from his dreams he knew what to do. He dug his heels into the creases on her chest and leaned into the wind. Through time and space the dreams had already created a bond with these two. He pressed his cheek against the soft neck while squinting into the wind. His eyes watered but he could see the great mountains to his right and the ring of reefs protecting the inner circle. It was calm beyond the breakers. Labeena turned back towards the place where she had plucked him from the sea. There was their boat floating right side up but filled with water. Gwenelle was struggling to bail the water as they flew low over her. Labeena made a wide turn, ending with a skidding halt on the smooth water using her webbed feet like skis. She settled next to the soggy boat.

What Gwenelle saw was Mandeler sitting astride a massive olive green raptor, his face split with a broad grin. Tufts of hair stuck out where the wind had whipped the salty strands back.

Lifting his arms into the air he mind-spoke: *Can you believe this!*

Labeena turned to catch a glimpse of her passenger.

He went on: *Can I help you pretty lady?*

Gwenelle turned to look at them, mind-speaking: *Where are your manners, we must introduce ourselves.*

Mandeler flushed, but mind-spoke clearly: *This is Gwenelle, my most trusted companion. My name is…*

Your name is Mandeler. I know this from my dreams. Then Labeena added: *Is the craft of importance to you?*

Gwenelle mind-spoke: *Yes, it is the last one we have, and I have to get the water out of it so it will float.*

Labeena moved closer, she ducked her head into the little row boat and sucked. As she lifted her great head the boat floated higher by a couple of hands. She turned and spewed water like a fountain and then repeated the same thing twice more leaving the boat floating freely on the surface. Gwenelle levered herself over the edge like a seasoned mariner mind-speaking: *Aren't you just the handiest friend to have.*

She looked up into the violet eyes and marveled at her beautiful lines, even her ear wings swept gracefully back to match the gentle slope of her face. Labeena was floating about one third out of the water, wings tucked forward while using her webbed feet to move in the water. Labeena seemed to be able to use pure thought for she sent the concept wordlessly: *Follow where I go and we will meet you on the pebble beach.*

Gwenelle watched in wonder as Labeena lifted her dripping wings high in the air with Mandeler still clinging to her. In a downwash of wind, she rose into the sky heading towards a grey patch of shore line.

Gwenelle mind-spoke to Mandeler: *This is unbelievable!*

Just like in my dreams! You should see what it looks like from up here! He answered.

Coming back to the task at hand Gwenelle took in the disarray of her boat. Allenz was wise in tying all of their gear and oars to the boat; otherwise everything would have been lost. Gwenelle readjusted things, and then put her back into pulling the boat toward the narrow shore. Her head was filled with wonder about the meeting with the raptors. No amount of planning could have prepared them for this.

It felt like an out of body experience for Mandeler as he leaned into the oncoming wind feeling Labeena's body flex under his thighs as she pumped her great wings in flight. For all of his dreams, he never allowed himself to believe he could fly with one of these wonders. She had taken off into the wind, climbing over the breakers again. Labeena banked into a steep turn and came back down just above the water. As the shoreline approached she banked again, just above the beach, while cupping her wings and settling into a delicate touchdown at the water's edge. Her feet touched lightly to the ground, with her wing knuckles coming down to steady her stance.

Labeena lowered her torso allowing Mandeler to slide to the ground. As he came to stand next to her she telepathed: *Show me the stone.*

Without hesitation, he reached into his tunic and drew out the emerald crystal. As he held it in his hand, it made Labeena shimmer slightly, in much the same way the denzels had appeared different after the crystal.

Labeena: *Beautiful, it is beautiful.*

He mind-spoke: *It was you that I was riding in my dreams. It is like I've known you my whole life.* In that moment he knew they had been moving towards each other all of his life.

She telephathed: *I too have been aware of you for some time. You are welcome here and so is your mate.*

He mind-spoke: *Do you know why I am here?*

I believe I do, but we must not deal with that now. First you and your mate must be presented to the Clan.

Rocks grated under the keel of the row boat while Gwenelle brought the oars inboard. She was still dripping wet from the capsizing and her usual baggy outfit clung tightly to her body. Mandeler was running to meet her on the beach as she tugged the small craft farther up the shore. Mandeler had reached her just as she turned. He swept her up in his arms and spun her about mind-speaking: *Look what you have helped me do, we have found them. It is a dream come true, I would not be here if not for you!*

She looked down into his beaming face then kissed him on the lips adding: *I love you too!*

Isn't this amazing! I have so much to tell you. Oh I can't even imagine where to start.

Then just tell me what is going to happen next.

Labeena wants to present us to the Clan.

Gwenelle reached into the boat and shouldered one of their packs, handing a second one to Mandeler. It was the sound of a second raptor coming to the pebble beach that made them turn. Labeena beckoned them forward, where introductions were needed.

It might have been the wet clothes or being in the presence of the olive raptors, but Gwenelle felt a chill run up her spine as she walked forward hand in hand with Mandeler. She felt small as they approached the pair of greens.

Labeena requested: *Your full names.*

Mandeler Freedahson, from the southern Mulestead Estate.

Gwenelle, daughter of Petter Shipwright, from Portside.

Labeena mind-spoke, *Mandeler Freedahson, Gwenelle of Petter Shipwright you are welcome here. This is my mate, Rachaner. He has come to carry your mate to the clan cave above.*

Mandeler mind-spoke to Gwenelle: *You have just shared a few of my dreams with a glimpse of flight with these magnificent raptors. Let me help you get astride Rachaner.*

He was not used to seeing her look alarmed, so he put a hand around her waist and whispered, "It is easy if you relax. Come let me give you a hand up." Then he cupped his hand saying, "Put your foot in my hand, I'll be your step ladder."

She steadied herself with a hand on his shoulder and one on Rachaner. It was easy to get up. He then took her feet and placed them into the ridges of the raptor's chest. "Now lean forward and grasp the neck spines with one hand while wrapping the other arm around his neck. Tuck your face in beside his neck and hang on."

To her surprise Rachaner's skin was smooth and warm. Rachaner turned his head to watch as she settled in place, he mind-spoke: *I have never carried one of your kind, but fear not. I will not let you fall.*

Labeena hunched forward and Mandeler leapt into place. There was the thunder of large wings beating the air as the two olive colored raptors slowly climbed into the air. They took a great circular path, out over the bay, where the Sea Quester was sailing, parallel to the shore.

For Gwenelle, the initial terror of flight gave way to a sense of wonder as she held tightly to the sinewy neck of Rachaner, feeling the bunched muscles of his chest working the immense wings. He was marvelous! The view was unimaginably beautiful and she could see down into the shallow turquoise water, where rocks came close to the surface of the lagoon. The reef, with the foaming breakers, marked the beginning of the intense blue water where, she assumed, it plunged to some unknown depth.

As they went high above the sailing ship Mandeler called down a greeting, but was not sure his voice carried that far. They headed back towards the mountain where other raptors could be seen coming and going from a cave, about one third of the way up, on the west side.

As they approached the cave entrance, it was obvious that only a small area on the rocky ledge would serve as a landing space. Labeena and Mandeler swept up just above it, where she beat the air and lightly stepped on the ledge. She folded her wings and using her wing knuckles like hands, she moved to the side just as Rachaner touched down. He hunched forward and Gwenelle slid off. Keeping a hand on his neck, she mind-spoke: *Oh, that was amazing and you are magnificent.* His mouth curled into that familiar denzel-like smile.

Mandeler came and embraced her, mind-speaking: *Look where we are! Can you believe this?*

From their perch high on the mountain face they had a raptor's view of the world below. The Sea Quester could be seen, with its shortened white sails, slowly making way offshore. He grasped the crystal and sent his mind to the captain: *We are safe, we are with the olive raptors. I will tell you more tomorrow.*

On board Sea Quester, Captain Larson heard the thoughts in his head. He nodded and said to Allenz, "It seems our young couple have made it. Let's hold this position until tomorrow and see what news there is."

The Clan

The sun was about a hand of time from setting, as a chilled Gwenelle and Mandeler turned to face the cave opening. Dozens of green raptors, of all sizes, were pressed at the entrance gawking at the new comers. Goose bumps rose as Gwenelle shivered in the wind, even Mandeler looked miserably cold.

Labeena mind-spoke: *Tell me what is wrong, you are obviously suffering.*

We are cold from being soaked with sea water, and now the wind is making our wet clothing even colder, replied Gwenelle.

Labeena continued: *Do you mean that your wrinkled skin is not a true skin, but just a cover?*

Yes, we cover our skin with layers of cloth to keep us warm, but when it gets wet it makes us cold instead.

Then remove them so you can dry off in the sun, telepathed Labeena.

Mandeler felt the flush rise up his neck and momentarily warm his face. He had only just gotten used to taking his clothing off with Gwenelle in the privacy of their little cabin. Now he squirmed with discomfort, thinking of disrobing in front of the clan.

Gwenelle looked down at his wet things, mind-speaking: *She's got a point!*

Off came the wet sweater over her head. The goose bumps stood out all over her as she tugged at the bottom of her damp under shirt.

Despite his shivering, Mandeler could have watched her undress all day, but he was brought back to the task at hand. He could not look up while he undid the belt about his waist, and then he hitched the tunic over his head. In a few more practiced moves, he was standing naked on a rock shelf with a goose bumped Gwenelle at his elbow. The wind slowly lost its chill as the descending sun warmed their bodies. They turned their backs on the clan to warm the other side and that was when Gwenelle broke into the giggles first. Mandeler found it infectious and soon they were doubled over laughing until the tears rolled down their faces. It was all very warming.

Labeena inquired: *Are you in pain?*

While still gasping for air Mandeler mind-spoke: *I'm sorry Labeena, in our race we have an outlet for tension and it is called laughter. It may look like pain but I assure you it feels very good. Thank you for your insight into our chilled condition.*

That is how Mandeler Freedahson and Gwenelle of Petter Shipwright were introduced to many of the green raptor clan, standing side by side in their nakedness, where they tried their very best to remember the names and who was related to whom. The sun was setting by the time the introductions were done.

When Gwenelle had stripped off her wet clothing she had spread them on the rocks, along with their blankets from the packs. She now gathered the damp garments. The blankets were woven from the hairy nut tree fiber and were warm even when damp. She pulled one tight around her shoulders and handed the other one to Mandeler.

Labeena mind-spoke: *The Clan is still very excited, but they will settle to their niches soon. Tell me clearly what you need for comfort this night?*

It was Gwenelle that replied: *We have food with us, but we need a place to lay down with our blankets to sleep.*

Labeena answered: *Come and share our family corner.*

She must have known the cave by instinct, because it was dark soon after entering the cave. Mandeler shared his crystal with Gwenelle, allowing her to see the shapes within the blackness. It was the excited movement of the fledglings that caught their attention. Like excited children, they greeted Rachaner and

Labeena by bobbing their little necks up and down. As the newcomers approached, they went still. Their parents nudged them comfortingly, while making a gentle purring noise from deep in their throats. If a baby raptor could be cute, these were, with their large eyes, no teeth, tiny ears and abbreviated wings on a bulbous body.

The humans found a relatively flat spot to plant themselves wrapped in blankets. They watched in fascination as Rachaner regurgitated a meal of fish bits for the young ones. All around them other raptors were settling in with little room to move between them. The place smelled surprisingly sweet, especially when compared to the foul-smelling great ones.

Sometime later Labeena questioned: *Do you know why you are here?*

Yes, we are seeking a way to bring the reign of terror from the Great Raptors to an end, explained Mandeler.

I have dreaded your arrival because it draws me into a struggle that I have tried to avoid, replied Labeena.

The dreams have drawn us together. Not only the ones we have shared, but my dreams of the dark ones as well. The world I see through the Dark Queen's eyes is a terrible place indeed. Mandeler felt Labeena shudder at his thoughts.

Breaths of time passed, then she mind-spoke: *Sleep and we will confer in the morning.*

Mandeler mind-spoke to Gwenelle: *What is there to eat?*

A typical man, thinking with his stomach.

She slipped the wax seal off the top of a jar and the smell of black fruit wafted up, making him salivate. They ate their fill and then they lay snuggled together wrapped in their blankets. The smell of her hair was familiar and exciting. He could feel the hard crystal amulet pressed between them. If it was only a little more private he thought. Drained by the day's excitement, sleep came faster than Mandeler could have imagined. It was several hands of time later that the dreams came to them both.

All was dark deep within the mountain. The hissing breath of the Great Queen filled the dank air. She brooded about their dilemma.

She knew the Great Raptors were in danger. She was old, older than the oldest on the planet. How many generations of black raptors had she spawned since the coming of the two legged ones. It was about that time the olive raptors fled the land, taking with them a rich source of telepathic blood. She had grown dependent on this special blood to give her extended life, thus allowing her to bring forth their next generation. They still had the denzels and even the two-legged ones, but ever since they had banded together, it was harder to get enough of the precious blood to stimulate the nesting instinct. This was the cycle that made her push all of the hunters to their limits. They brought back many of the two legged ones but most of the time they were the undesirables, with no rich blood. Only she and the prime leaders of the hunting packs could see the true glow of the telepaths. Somewhere in the ocean was the 'one' that was so potent that his blood alone would turn the tide of their future. She howled in frustration, knowing what she needed and struggling with the fear of not getting it. She had to risk all to find him or the race would die out anyway. She raked the claws of her wing knuckles, scarring the rock wall, hissing her distain.

They sat up so suddenly that they bumped their heads in the dark. Hardly feeling the pain they reeled from the shared nightmare. In that instant they both knew that Mandeler was the focus of their hunt, while at the same time being their bane. It was dark as they rocked back and forth in each other's arms. Gwenelle was shivering, but not from the cold. She mind-spoke: *Great Azimov, they're after you, just you! They might kill the rest of us, but you are the one they are after. Raptor Dung! No wonder we have seen so many attacks!*

Mandeler struggled for clarity. Finally he mind-spoke: *I'd like to stay here, out of their range, but that will never do! The Queen will still savage the land and it is my home too. I am starting to think it is up to me to figure this out.* He paused for a few breaths, searching his heart. *She must be stopped or this will never end. I am going to ask Labeena to help me find their lair.* He felt her pull back at that statement, trembling, and he added: *Just to reconnoiter the place, without that information we are strapped for a real plan.*

By yourself?

That's what my heart says. Believe me, I don't want to go either but the dreams are clear, it was just Labeena and me flying in a deep gorge near their lair.

They sat quietly for some time. Then Mandeler reached out to her in the darkness. He felt her arm reach up to embrace him and they clung to each other. She whispered in his ear, "You foolish young man, I didn't want to love you, but I sure as heck don't want to lose you either! Why can't I come too?"

I don't know why but I think there is a higher task for you to pursue too, I just don't know what it is yet.

They clung to each other for a while and then in the quiet of the cave they slid farther down into their blankets. Their intimacy with its heavy breathing roused no concern in the cave that night. After all they were guests and could do whatever they wanted.

Departure

Gwenelle did not sleep anymore that night as images of the Great Raptors filled her mind. She knew that Mandeler had been tormented by the dreams with an ever-increasing intensity. As he lay sleeping in her arms, she was grateful that he could doze off and get a little rest because the next days would test him and Labeena to their limits. Lying there she thought of her young man going off to the killer's lair, even if it was to look from a distance, and it scared her terribly. His familiar scent gave her some comfort and she drew him closer.

Mandeler awoke enfolded within her arms as the pre-dawn glow crept into the cave. Wrapped in their blankets, they quietly rose to pick their way through the clan. Once outside they were thankful to find their clothes had mostly dried in the night breeze. The world brightened as the sun rose on the far side of the island, first turning the horizon pink, then amber and finally a full blue mirrored in blue.

For such a large animal, Labeena moved with almost no noise as she came to settle next to them. Mandeler mind-spoke to her: *Do you know what is happening between us?*

Yes, you have come to ask me to join you to turn the tide against the Queen and her scourge. It was never clear how this would happen but fate has crossed our paths and now I must face this with you. After all, it was she that plundered our race, driving the survivors to this small island.

You have many more sun cycles of experience than me and are wiser by far. I feel inadequate to suggest what should happen next.

It is vague in detail, but we see each other in our dreams and here we stand. Let the dreams lead us. You sought me out and now you can lead us from here.

Mandeler hesitated, then he went on: *Before we get into the bigger plan let me show you something. Captain Larson has given me samples of these.* He pulled two small jars from his pack and selected a kernel of the yellow sulfur.

Labeena sniffed it, replying: *I have smelled this in the air when the wind blew from the west. We call the place this comes from the Smoking Mountain.*

Next he showed her the black granules of the exploding powder. Labeena sniffed these as well. *Strange,* she mind-spoke: *There is something familiar about this but I cannot place it.*

Mandeler looked into her eyes while mind-speaking: *They were sent to us by a wise elder with the hope that using them would help in our quest.*

Let time pass and see what comes of it.

Alright, but the bigger question is, where do we find the Queen's lair?

This time Labeena seemed to look off into the distance and after a while she telepathed: *None of my race have wanted to seek it out, but from my ancestral memories there was an area west of the mainland with mountains. Our clan was forbidden to go near it. I can only assume that is where we find the Great Raptors.*

How far, or should I say, how long would it take to get there?

It is two sun cycles from here. By day we are safe but at night we are very much at risk. How do you propose overcoming that?

Mandeler shuffled his feet while he looked out toward the distant horizon. Then he mind-spoke: *The dreams have only shown me glimpses…* He trailed off still staring into the distance. *I know you don't need, or want any of this, but if you will carry me there, I will do everything I can to anticipate them and give us a chance to get through. As for the night, I have one safe place that may serve us well enough.*

Labeena seemed to sigh. *I knew it would come to this. We will leave as the sun shows itself tomorrow.*

Through all of this, Gwenelle sat like stone beside him, taking in the intensity and the oddness of the situation. Here in front of her was a young man that just a moon cycle ago was a stranger, now he was precious. Across from him crouched an enormous olive green creature that spoke in pure thought. They were about to leave her, flying directly to the cave of horrors. A shiver of dread ran up her spine.

As if he sensed her feelings, Mandeler turned and took her face in his hands mind-speaking: *I know you worry about me and you want to come too, but only Labeena will fly out with me. She cannot carry us both without making this even more dangerous. Stay with Larson, I still think you are part of a greater puzzle here. Trust me, and look for me on the fourth day.* He kissed her lightly on the lips. She threw her arms around him and started to weep.

It was just like living within his flying dreams as he squinted into the wind, looking past the dome shaped head, with it sweptback flying ears. Her neck flexed to the pulse of every wingbeat. Despite the wonder of it all, there was a chill in the morning air but the heat radiating from Labeena helped to offset it.

Labeena rarely spoke in his head as they flew together. It was uncanny how comfortable he felt, allowing his body to flex with the movement of her in the rhythmic cycles of her flight. He was under no illusions as to who was doing the flying. He was a welcome passenger trying to anticipate her moves so they could fly as one. They circled the island as the golden orb broke the horizon. Gwenelle took the row boat along the lagoon to a narrow opening in the reef. He was able to keep a mind link long after losing sight of her. She was safely on board and reported that Captain Larson was recovering well from his injuries. Even the shorthanded crew were managing well enough.

He tried to reassure himself that while they got the ship in order he and Labeena could reconnoiter the Great Raptors territory, learn what they could and come back. It was a plan of sorts, built from glimpses of dreams, but he still could not clearly see what lay ahead and that made him tremble.

Labeena sensed his tremor, mind-speaking: *Is it the height?*

He pressed his face against her neck replying: *No, it's just the unknown.*

They flew for a hand or two of time with the great expanse of rippled blue water passing below them. He tried to think of all the things that could go wrong with the landing spot he had chosen, but his mind kept coming back to Gwenelle. He closed his eyes, sensing the deep emerald crystal that pressed against his tattooed chest, while sending out his thoughts to her. He did not know what range he had with her but was relieved to feel her spirit. Detailed thought would not come, but he could sense her. That alone was reassuring.

Mandeler had formed his body to the curves of Labeena's back, squinting into the oncoming wind. He had strapped his two slim packs along his sides so they conformed to her shape as well as possible. The feel of her powerful chest pumping her great wings had become a constant as they sped toward the southern shore. The green raptor's endurance was amazing as the expanse of sea passed below them. There were low flying flocks of white flyers skimming the wave tops, occasionally a lone shape would leap out of the water only to disappear into the depths again. Labeena answered his questions about the sea life as they passed. When he saw a herd of large, long necked swimmers with broad flippers breaching, he asked what they were. Labeena told him that the Clan called them the 'Sure Death', because no green raptor that encountered them ever flew home again. They must have been huge because they looked large even from this height. As he watched, the herd dove, and moments later one of them surfaced with a multi-limbed pink creature trapped in its jaws. The rest came to join it, tearing the captive to shreds. He could see why Labeena was reluctant to spend a night floating in the open ocean with voracious predators like that roaming free.

Hands of time passed, with the sun crossing the sky, before the first hint of land could be seen. They were the Blue Mountains, standing up out of a light mist, their unmistakable white peaks contrasting with the blue sky. Labeena agreed that the first landfall should be one that was familiar and safe. She needed her rest and feeding if possible. Mandeler had planned a familiar stop over, but was unsure of how and when Labeena could find food. He should not have worried because very soon she mind-spoke: *I can see a school of green fins ahead. Stay tight to my body and I will look after you.*

Mandeler scanned the area but saw nothing. He was thinking that her eye sight must have been much keener than his, as she tucked her wings and they dropped toward the water. His eyes streamed tears as the speed built. Just when he thought they would crash into the ocean, she cupped her wings pulling abruptly out of the dive. Mandeler seemed to be squashed onto her back with the force of her manoeuver. *Great Azimov that was thrilling.*

Labeena flew close to the water's surface with her wings spread wide, bleeding off her speed. Mandeler caught his first glimpse of the green fins leaping ahead of them. As they flew over the school of gleamers, she deftly snatched with her hooked foot. Mandeler felt the tug through her body as something was dragged splashing from the water. She pumped hard, gaining altitude, and levelled off. Just as he was relaxing, she pulled up into a short climb and at the summit, she reached down towards her feet with her long neck. In that moment, while they hung in the air, she plucked the wiggling green fin from her claws. As they dropped, she stretched out finishing the short dive, then pulled back level at full flying speed.

Mandeler marveled at how dexterous this large flying creature could be. She had the delicacy of a dancer in the air. Her ability to chew down a large gleamer, while flying, was another feat altogether.

As the last of the green fin slid down her long throat, she turned her head, and their eyes met. *Now we can find this safe haven you have been telling me about.*

Even though they were flying high, they skirted around Portside to avoid any confusion between them and the Great Raptors. Their destination was about as far as they could fly in the daylight left to them. Remembering the trek they had taken across the mountains, he looked for landmarks to make sure he knew where he was. With his landmarks established, he was in constant contact with Labeena, aiding her in their passage. When they descended the north side of the Blue Mountains he could just make out the great river. Smoke rose from Melville as they passed overhead. With less than a hand of time left, Labeena stretched out toward the high estates. The sun set in the west not long after they passed the darkened village of Huxbee. Mandeler felt the crystal amulet pressing into his chest and searched for the presence of the Great Raptors. They were stirring for the evening hunt, but he felt there was still time to reach their destination.

As the sun set, Mandeler felt Labeena's strength wavering, she was near exhaustion as she cleared the herman nut groves. Below, the country was being engulfed in deep shadow. One circle around the familiar estate and she cupped her wings beating the air until they landed, in a cloud of dust, between the lodge and the animal shelter. Labeena folded her wings, pressing her wing knuckles into the dirt to steady herself. In one day, they had covered the same distance that it had taken Mandeler a full moon cycle. Now they sat in the dim yard of his childhood residence in total silence. He winced in pain from his stiff muscles, but managed to get to the ground with his dignity intact.

Homecoming

He was looking towards the animal shelter when he heard a high pitched human scream that came from the main lodge behind them. He was not expecting to find anyone here because his aunt was supposed to stay with the Cochrals. He could hear Labeena turning while he stared at the darkened lodge. He called out, "Who's there?"

The silence deepened, and then he heard from behind barred doors, "Who are you that comes on a Great Raptor?"

It was shrill but it was definitely his Aunt Mirra's voice and he shouted back, "I'm Mandeler and it is not a Great Raptor!"

"Mandu is that you?"

"Aunt Mirra?"

"What in Azimov's creation are you doing flying on that thing?" Mirra's voice was almost hysterical.

"This is Labeena. She is one of the olive raptors from the southern ocean. They fear the Great Raptors too. She is my friend!" he said to her.

While this was happening, Labeena reached her head down to Mandeler where he wrapped an arm around her neck. It seemed like a hand of time but the portal cracked open and a dim blue glow silhouetted the figure in the door.

"Do you carry the guild's crystal?" Mirra asked in a shaky voice.

He pulled it out, holding it aloft, where it began to glow with its emerald light.

"You are real," Mirra said with relief. An illumination globe appeared from behind her and two small figures could be seen. "Mandu?" called Jaida & Jamis together.

He ran towards them as they piled out of the doorway. In an instant he was on his knees hugging the little girls. He felt Mirra kiss him on the top of his head and then she said, “We were sure you were dead. There was never any word from you after you left. Then word came that Huxbee was burned and abandoned.”

“I am home again Aunt Mirra but it is a very long tale. I need to shelter Labeena before we talk.”

By the light of the globe Mandeler could see the scratches on the side of the doorway. It told of an attack by the dark ones. He asked, “Did they breach the building?”

“No, but there has been damage to the roof and the last attack left us more vulnerable.”

It was then that the image, of a dark hunter seeking them, came into his mind. “We don’t have much time and we all need shelter. Are the summer doors functional?”

“They were last year but your uncle was the one to undo the security bolts. Why?” asked Mirra.

“We are having a guest tonight in our hall!”

It took only a short while, by the light of three globes, to undo the security latches and the double wide north doors swung open. He beckoned to Labeena to join him and soon the doors were thumping shut again to lock out the night’s terrors.

Just like when Labeena slept at the Clan’s Cave, she put her head on her back, tucked her wings in and wrapped her long thin tail around herself in the confined space. The building had a high peeked roof with a row of posts supporting it on both sides. There were several small rooms off to the sides. Mandeler had hastily pushed the central table and small furnishings to the end of the room. Labeena filled much of the central space. Even turning around might prove difficult for her.

Getting her into safety was so rushed that there had been no introductions. The two small girls, Jaida and Jamis, peaked wide eyed around the corner of the fireplace. Mandeler took his aunt’s perspiring hand and stepped closer to Labeena as she uncoiled to look at them.

Formally he mind-spoke to Labeena: *This is my kin, Mirra Mulestead, mate to my paternal uncle Almar who was taken over a moon cycle ago. When I was small, my mother Freedah, and father Mandell, were also taken. Mirra has been a surrogate mother ever since and I hold her in great esteem.*

Labeena nodded her great head reaching toward Mirra. Mandeler placed his aunt's hand upon the brow of the olive raptor. He could see Mirra visibly relax as Labeena mind-spoke: *My name is Labeena, Leader of the Olive Raptor Clan. I am honored to Mandeler's kin. Your kin are now part of our Clan.*

There was a squeal from behind them as the twins emerged from their hiding place. "We heard that, we heard that."

"Gently little ones, come, of course you can touch her too," said Mandeler while taking in the fact that the twins could hear Labeena's mind-speech. He whispered to his aunt, "Could you detect any message from Labeena?"

Mirra answered, "You know that is funny, but I thought I sensed her making me welcome and that she is a great leader among her kind." She looked into the eyes of her nephew who seemed taller, broader and a bit weather beaten. His yellow beard had grown, as had his tussled blond hair, but the blue eyes were the same. A boy had left and now a man returned, riding upon the most unusual being she could have imagined.

Jaida and Jamis had come and placed their hands on Labeena's snout. The great head came down to their level, her large violet eyes, with the vertical slit, took in the children. One at a time, she rubbed her cheek gently on the little girls' shoulders. With obvious trust they flung their arms around her neck. Moments later there was the deep throated purr that Mandeler had heard when she settled her own nestlings.

Nip was the last to be introduced. The exchange was formal, but it was plain that the denzels and Olive Raptors had always had a historical respect for each other, despite the centuries of noncontact. The children stayed snuggled up in the curve of Labeena's neck. Turning to his aunt he said, "Give me a moment with Nip and then we will talk further."

Settling in a corner Mandeler mind-spoke to Nip: *I have sad new about Alheeza. He was taken during an attack. He may have escaped near the Great Raptors lair but there has been no contact since.*

That is very sad news. As you saw, when you got here, there have been repeated attacks. Many more have been taken since you left.

I was afraid of that. How much of your real role does Mirra know?

I suspect she has guessed more than most but I have never formally revealed any of the Guild's secrets to her. Obviously she can receive thoughts from our guest, as can the children.

At that point Mirra came to sit with Mandeler. He turned to meet the tired face of his aunt. *Dearest Aunt, can you hear me?*

She stiffened but she maintained her eye contact with Mandeler. He went on, *Our family comes from a line of telepaths, including my father and mother, Uncle Almar, the twins, and apparently you too.*

Now she looked uncomfortable and said, "You're talking in my head aren't you?"

Yes!

"So it is not my imagination, you are a telepath."

Nip telepathed directly to her: *My full name is Jaran. Nip is the name the children gave me. I am here as a teacher to the children until they come of age, just like Mandeler and his family.*

Mirra slumped down the wall, then reached out and took Mandeler's hand saying, "That explains a good deal of the mystery around here."

Aunt Mirra I want to hear all the news, but you must know that I am only here tonight and we leave at first light tomorrow morning. I need a bowl of water for Labeena and something to eat myself. Then we can talk and you can tell how you ended up back here with just the girls.

Mirra reached over and hugged Mandeler to her. They held each other for a few breaths and then she disengaged saying, "I have some herman nut stew on the hearth and we can open a jar of preserves to go with it. Come, we have a barrel of water to draw from as well."

Later he was washed and eating a bowl of warm nut stew while leaning against a sleeping raptor with the girls on either side of him. The incongruity of the situation almost made him laugh out loud. He left here just over a moon cycle ago and in that time his whole world had been transformed. The people did not even know about the olive raptors and now there was one filling the gathering space of his childhood home. As far as moments went this was pretty good. All it was missing was Gwenelle. He reached into his clean tunic touching his fingers to the burgundy stone. His intention was to search for Gwenelle in the distance, but what came to him instead was the sense of three Great Raptors winging their way straight towards him and his loved ones. He kept the fingers in place long enough to take their measure and then he rose to his feet and found Mirra. Leaning down he whispered, "Tell me of the other attacks."

He saw in her face nights of sleepless exhaustion, but her eyes were still clear and she said, "They have been hunting us ever since you left. Herb brought us back here to get supplies when they hit again that night. They struck the buildings, trying to break in, but so far your uncle's building still stands against them. Some of the roof is damaged and they clawed open a section of the animal shelter getting at the muzels. Herb wanted to go back to his estate at once, but I chose to stay here in my home and keep the doors barred. Your Uncle Almar had built such a stout building and if any could withstand their attack, this one could. They have been here three more times. You could see the claw marks around the side portal when you arrived. We are still well stocked with staple supplies, but I do not know how we will manage if this keeps up. "

Mandeler reached to the side and pulled open one of his slim packs drawing out the flinger. There were only three arrows left and he fingered the slender shafts saying, "They are coming tonight, three of them. What do you need to do to prepare?"

"I can take the girls into the cellar, under the back floor and bolt the hatch. What are you planning to do?"

Obviously Labeena must stay where she is while I will stand guard with these, but I could use some help setting things up.

Mirra touched one of the arrow shafts, "When I was looking for supplies I came across more of these in a back shed. Could you use them?"

Absolutely!

"When did you say they would be here, and I won't even ask how you know that?"

"We have a hand of time."

They were returning from the shed, with the precious bundle, when they heard the first distant scream of night marauders. The latches were bolted tight, and the entire perimeter was secure, when the first Great Raptor landed on the roof. Talons scraped on the roof's hardwood panels, followed by the thumping, as if it was testing for a soft spot. Another could be heard outside the portal. There was a scuffling blow to the door but it held as the claws scratched across it. At the back of the house there was more thumping.

Mandeler passed Labeena on his way to his old bedroom. She was fully alert with fear showing in her eyes for the first time. He had the loaded flinger in his hand as he entered the room. There was a good deal of thumping and scraping at the wall and barred window. Mandeler had looked out this window so many times to welcome the rising sun, but now he unlatched the inside shutter with caution. The ironwood bars were well made and had stood up to the Raptors so far. He placed the tip of the flinger on the window sill. In his right hand he pressed the amulet between his thumb and the handle of the flinger, thus allowing it to bring him his night vision.

It was an unorganized attack at the dwelling. The dark creature that he could see was throwing itself randomly at the side wall. Mandeler called out, **"I am here, come and get me!"**

He willed himself to be calm inside by steadying his breath. Now the creature turned, examining the wall, looking for the source of the voice. A large red eye appeared at the window and without thought, Mandeler squeezed the trigger. The scream of rage was deafening as the Great Raptor flailed back in pain. Despite its thrashing, he could make out the shaft of his arrow protruding from the bleeding eye. It did not seem to be the death strike, like the first time, but it was still a cruel blow.

Just when he thought there was pause in the overall attack another Great Raptor landed just in front of the window. It raked the barred opening with the claws of its wing knuckles, making the window casement shudder. Mandeler reached down and reloaded his weapon. When the beast opened its mouth to scream its revenge he fired an arrow into its throat. This time there was a choking scream as the night marauder recoiled from the window, foaming yellow blood coming from its mouth, as it staggered back.

Mandeler held the brilliant emerald crystal aloft and lit the yard with its green light. He gathered his strength and shouted in mind-speak: ***I may be small but I sting. Any of your kind hunting me or mine will feel my sting again.***

Whether it was the crystal's shining light, his skillful use of the flinger, or his challenge, he could not tell, but the great predators rose into the sky and left.

She had never dreamed like this before meeting Mandeler. *An old woman with long grey hair turned as she dropped her shawl to reveal her bare back. Crawling up her torso and ending on her neck was the tattoo of a dark green raptor. Its wings wrapped around her ribs and the mouth gaped open under her ear. As she stared, the crone turned, revealing a glowing amber crystal between the withered breasts. She held out a hand and sprinkled something dark into the fire, then vanished in a flash of flame and smoke.*

The Frontier

Sunrise was such a welcome sight with its long morning shadows. Mandeler clung to Labeena's neck as she pumped to gain altitude leaving the estate behind them. It had been a frightening night but the raptors had been dispersed for now and his family was still safe behind unbroken walls. His quest may have been that of a messenger when he first left home but now it was personal. The only real family he had was in a state of siege, holding out night after night against a foe that was relentless.

Aunt Mirra had brought out a large jug of herman nut oil and that had been a very welcome breakfast for Labeena. The morning departure was very sullen, with tearful hugs and whispered good byes.

Today he and Labeena were heading into the complete unknown. It felt good to be in the cool morning air after the closeness of the lodge last night. He was not sure about how to handle any encounter with future raptors but he knew in his heart that the next test was coming soon.

It came much sooner than even he had expected. Labeena had been pumping to gain altitude, after leaving the estate, when Mandeler felt the faint presence of a Great Raptor ahead. It was not the usual intense feeling of a pursuing carnivore but more like a faint life sign. Searching the forest ahead, he spotted a dark shape crumpled on the ground. It lay in a meadow surrounded by herman nut trees. As they descended towards it, Mandeler felt a chill creep up his spine. One wing was spread out while the other was crumpled under its side. He pressed the amulet to his chest searching for signs of danger. At first he thought he had lost all contact but then he felt a faint heartbeat of the Great Raptor.

They circled the Raptor getting lower with each pass. He felt

Labeena's reluctance to approach even a downed raptor, but she complied with his wishes. They landed as far across the meadow as possible. Even at the edge of the meadow, the creature reeked of death and decay. Swallowing down his revulsion, Mandeler loaded his flinger and set off on foot through the waist high reeds to assess the downed hunter. About twenty paces from the animal he stopped. The gouged turf told of the raptor's hard landing. The head was still partially hidden in the slender foliage but he could see the chest still moving slightly. Bones protruded from the shoulder where one wing had failed in the attempted landing. This creature would never fly again.

Mandeler continued to study the downed Raptor from a distance, still unsure if this was a trap. The long thin tail lay on the ground not far from him. He took the chance and crept up to it. He had been clutching his crystal all the while, now he lay down his flinger and crouched next to the tail. The smell of this beast made his eyes water, but still he reached out and placed a hand upon its tail.

He was immediately connected to the great beast. In that instant, it recognized him causing a shudder to pass along its body. Mandeler could feel that it was dying and time was short. He stood, and walked around to the long neck with its shark finned head. In the crash landing its protruding tusk-like teeth had dug a trench in the ground. From its mouth oozed a pool of congealing yellow blood. Its long neck was twisted at an abnormal angle. Mandeler tentatively placed his hand on its black scaled spine. He did not know what he was searching for or how to ask for what he needed.

A few moments passed, and then the images started to unfold. *The Great Raptor Queen raged before him, compelling him to seek the one. In that instant Mandeler knew it was he that she sought above all others. The death of this hunter meant nothing to her for others would soon be sent to hunt him.*

Mandeler shuddered as the reality of this sunk in. He felt the creature slipping into darkness and he desperately searched for any signs of its origin. *There were blurred images at first, a small cave in the hills south of their estate, the Queen ordering it evacuated, and all the hunters called back to her lair. Large black shadows flew over a great body of water, making their way towards a range of mountains. At its center was a single great snow-capped peak. His view became closer and a gaping cave appeared above a jagged cliff. Night marauders swarmed around the cave opening.*

The images flashed into his brain so fast that it was hard to take it all in, and then all was quiet. He felt a sudden shudder and ragged exhalation. Death had come to the hunter and all was still.

As he walked back to Labeena the difference in their size became apparent. She had seemed so big when he flew with her but he estimated she was barely half the size of the dead night hunter. Her smooth olive-colored skin was also a contrast with the armor-plated giant. She had distinctive swept back wings with smaller knuckle claws and her two hind feet were webbed while the other had grasping talons, she had rows of small even teeth and the great ones had irregular razor teeth. Maybe they had a common ancestor, at the beginning of time, but they had evolved into something very different. He reached her and put his arms around her neck.

Labeena mind-spoke: *They stink too!*

Mandeler's mind was struggling to bring the images forward that had been flashed to him by the dying Raptor, while Labeena had climbed steadily. Doing some simple navigation like that taught to him by Captain Larson, he had imagined a straight line from the estate to the downed Raptor and then projected where that might take them beyond the mountain range to the east. Labeena had a flawless sense of direction and once Mandeler had made it clear where they should go she had stayed on a steady course.

Sometime later, beyond the Coastal Mountains, Mandeler could see another expanse of ocean with a cloud bank in the distance. Emerging out of it was the large jagged mountain. The morning sun glistened off the snow covered peak. As they flew on other minor peaks could be seen poking out of the clouds. From the images the dying Raptor gave him the centre of the Great Raptor's world was a deep cave on the face of one of the lesser mountains. Only when they got closer would he know where it was.

He clasped his crystal asking the greater question, what was he doing here? The response was unexpected.

Alheeza came out of his self-induced hibernation. It took some time for his blood pressure to come up high enough for him to recall the events that brought him to this narrow slit in the rock face, down in front of the Great Raptor's lair. He tried to shift his body but it was held by a covering of Raptor dung. If denzels could laugh this was the time, because the disgruntled creature that had defecated on him had inadvertently saved his life. It had warmed his battered body and kept him from drying out as the sun cycles passed. The cuts on his back had healed enough, the broken leg would be useless the way it was but he was alive and that meant hope. Much to his surprise he felt Mandeler's presence. How that could be, he had no idea but there was no doubt that it was Mandeler's thought signature that he felt.

The shock of sensing Alheeza's presence unsettled Mandeler, but then he realized that his mentor lay ahead of them and was alive. Hope soared in that moment. He did not know what could be done but Alheeza was alive and that was all that mattered at the time.

The sun was not at its highest point yet, maybe another two hands of time to go. He concentrated on the image of the Raptor's cave along with the surrounding mountains, then closed his eyes and sent the images to Labeena. Conversation had come easily, but trying to convey something as complex as another's visual memories taxed him to the limit.

Labeena responded: *That was hard, I know, but now I can see where we are going.*

Mandeler mind-spoke: *If they stay in their cave when the sun is out, could we reconnoiter the area and get back out again without an attack?*

No one has ever tried to do that but in theory it might work.

Let's have a closer look then.

The audacity of flying to the great hunter's lair was thrilling and a calculated gamble, but what could they do when they got there?

Mandeler worried that he was missing something but he could not pin it down.

Labeena must have been thinking along those lines because she asked: *What if there is something we do not know about?*

From what I learned this morning this one is the main cave with the Queen. They seem to always come back here or at least that's what keeps coming up in my dreams. Also they seem to fear the light and hunt only after dark.

They flew along in silence watching the distant mountains growing bigger all the time. The low fog had burned off revealing a coastline that had a long high plain separating the steep cliffs along the shore, with the abruptly rising mountain range. Behind the rocky palisade stood a row of storm clouds, building quickly as the day heated up.

Labeena had been descending slowly and from this vantage point Mandeler could see the winding river with its deep cut gorge approaching. He froze when he recognized the river that had cut the canyon walls; it was the one from his dreams. He had been drawn to this location all along and if he had learned anything from his dreams, something was going to happen here and it made his skin crawl.

Labeena flew on and soon the mouth of the great cave could be seen as the mountains rose quickly to the sky. It was just a dot at first, but as his olive raptor pumped her wings it slowly got bigger and bigger. It must be enormous to be seen so far away. Shadows marched down the mountain as the clouds engulfed the western peaks.

Mandeler was suddenly filled with foreboding. *The Queen knew he was near for she had stirred the nest into frenzy. Her hunters were pushing towards the entrance, despite the blazing sun shining at the opening. This was unprecedented because they avoided the direct sun above all things. Even with their eyes shut the power of the sun struck deeply into their nerves. Going blinded into the torturing sun was less daunting than facing the outraged queen within.*

Alheeza heard the commotion above and struggled to free himself from the dung heap. It had dried over the days enabling him to push his shoulder up crumbling the edge of the pile. Soon he was able to drag his body along the crevice using his three good legs. He could hear a great commotion from above, something had stirred the nest of Raptors and their screams were shaking the rocks themselves. If he could just make it around the corner, perhaps there was a way down.

Mandeler struggled with the choices ahead. Originally he was planning just to find the Great Raptor's lair but now there was the faint hope that Alheeza could be found. They were getting very near to the cave and he could see the writhing hunters spread out along the cliff face. There must be a dozen or more making it look like the legendary snakes in Medusa's hair as their necks swayed back and forth.

It was then that he sensed Alheeza painfully crawling along the bottom of the rock slit.

There was light just ahead as Alheeza squeezed his slender body along the narrow slit. He put his snout into the sunlight and shuddered at the view below. Along the precipice there were several boulders descending towards another narrow ledge, with a great drop beyond that. The plains stretched out beyond the foot of the mountain towards the sea. A greenish flying creature was heading straight towards him, but what was bewildering was that Mandeler's thought signature seemed to be coming from that direction too.

The hissing heads above him drove Alheeza to risk descending the rough boulders to the next ledge. It taxed him of all his strength, but he knew in his heart this was it or nothing.

As they approached, Labeena and Mandeler saw Alheeza drop from the last rough stone onto the ledge. The writhing Raptors above made a terrific din, but they seemed rooted to the spot so he urged Labeena on. She landed on the narrow cliff ledge next to his injured mentor. It was a very delicate bit of flying for the olive raptor to sweep up, touching down just at the right moment to land with her chest and face against the bare rock. Mandeler slid down and embraced Alheeza mind-speaking: *We have no time, let's go!*

The commotion from above became more intense as Mandeler slung the reeking Alheeza around his neck, like a fermented winter stole. Labeena had managed to work herself almost sideways on the narrow space. Mandeler climbed onto her back, draping the denzel across his lap. At that moment two things happened, the storm spilled over the mountain blotting out the sun and there came a great shriek from above.

Labeena launched herself into a dive from the tall cliff. It was shocking how quickly the land was cast into shadows by the building storm. Through the squall, tears streamed from his eyes as he squinted to see what lay ahead. They had never reached this velocity before as Labeena plummeted with her wings folded down towards the cliff base. He stole a glance behind and the impossible was in the air behind them. A Great Raptor had launched itself into a dive off the cliff, despite it being midday. Could the dark clouds block enough of the sun so they could fly? The pursuer was not far behind with mouth agape and yellow fangs snapping. It was all happening so fast, and it was a do or die race for both of them.

The prime hunter had his eyes shut into slits but the muted light still seared into his head. He flew by instinct with only a little of his usual vision. The one that was most sought was just a few wingbeats ahead and that miserable denzel was with him. He knew he would catch them because this was his territory and just the smell of them was all he needed for guidance. As for the hills and valleys, he knew them as well as the edge of his own wings. To kill the green interloper and the puny one was the way it should be. If not, his life was forfeited anyway.

Mandeler almost lost his grip as he sensed what his pursuer felt. This hunter was so determined to catch him that it bore the pain of dimmed daylight, determined to kill him or die trying.

Alheeza had lost a great deal of weight so it was easy for Mandeler to hug their shapes closely to Labeena's neck and shoulders. He passed what he knew about their attacker to Labeena and urged her toward the canyon below.

Just as in the dream, Mandeler could see the muted colors of the canyon walls approaching. The wind roared in his ears, and the tears streamed from his eyes as he tried to focus on vague details of the rapidly approaching gorge. He was diving from a great height because the trees were just coming into focus. Sensing the approaching landscape, he willed them out of the dive. His cheeks sagged with the force of pulling into level flight. Then in an instant he was clipping over the last of the dark trees and all that lay before him was the desolation of the canyon below. As he swooped low over a flat topped hillock, he caught a glimpse of the converging winged shadow. He glanced over his shoulder just as the Raptor screamed its attack. In that moment, they broke out from under the cloud, and the sun burst forth with its full power. The pursuer screamed in agony as the bright light pierced deeply into its neural fibers. It faltered just slightly catching a wing tip on the next hill. Mandeler felt its shock as the great predator shattered its left wing tip. Suddenly it was spinning out of control so that when it hit the ground both wings crumbled, sending it head over tail breaking its neck before skidding to a stop in a shallow ravine. Mandeler shuddered when the mind link was broken with his pursuer. Far behind them, a shaft of sunlight that lit the cloud of settling dust around the battered body of what moments before had been a powerful hunter.

A wave of relief washed over Mandeler with the realization that they had narrowly escaped a terrible death. There seemed to be no others following, but Mandeler clasped his amulet searching with his mind. Yes, there was a terrible ruckus at the cave but no others had dared to leave the ledge blind. He tried to reassure Labeena and Alheeza that they were safe for the time being.

Time dragged, as he longed for the canyon walls to part revealing the open ocean where no threat could pounce unseen from above. Finally the rock walls dropped away and the shimmering sea lay before them. Labeena was exhausted from the pursuit, and skimming above the waves with her wingtips almost touching. Here she could slow her pace and almost rest in flight. As everyone became more relaxed Mandeler became aware of the most terrible smell coming from his companion. He mind-spoke: *What happened? You smell truly awful.*

Alheeza mind-spoke to them both for the first time: *First let me thank you for a very daring rescue. As for the smell, I was buried up to my neck in raptor dung. The stuff Gwenelle is always expounding about.*

You are welcome for the rescue, but you really stink my friend, added Mandeler.

With spans of distance passing under them and no apparent pursuit, Mandeler took his time going through the formal introductions of his two friends to each other. Alheeza might be exhausted, but it did not keep him from asking about all the news since their separation on the Sea Quester. Finally, he mind-spoke, *Compared to lying at the bottom of a cliff covered in raptor dung, this is a holiday.*

It was apparent that they could not make it back to the estate, Labeena was too tired. They would have to seek a coastal refuge with shelter and food for all. Alheeza was a sorry sight after his ordeal with his left eye still swollen almost shut, as well as cuts and scrapes covering most of his desiccated body. The right hind leg hung uselessly and the smell of him made Mandeler's eyes water. How he had survived was beyond reason but here he was, his good eye shining. After a small sip of water along with the last of copeander fruit, he brightened considerably. Then he suggested they turn west along the coast because he remembered a fishing village east of Portside.

Mandeler could not help wonder how to approach a settlement with a smelly denzel and an olive raptor without causing alarm.

Mandeler had time to reflect upon the past days, and try to make sense of what he learned. First of all, his dreams were not ordinary dreams but some sort of exchange between him and others, mostly the raptors. They appeared to be hunting those with the greatest telepathic powers and that put him where? Obviously, they were seeking him out and as he had learned in Portside, Gwenelle too.

From the denzel histories, the cycle of killings and taking had been going on for over four hundred season cycles. Questions, so many questions, he was overwhelmed with questions. How did the crystal amulet and its powers to communicate tie in with the Raptors? And finally how was one small human supposed to change this cycle of death. Was he supposed to kill the Great Queen? How unlikely that was. Even with the coaching of the elders, and mystery substances from Larson, what were their chances? He was exhausted, and his thoughts looped over and over around these unanswered questions.

The rest of the afternoon was uneventful. The sun was getting low on the horizon by the time they spotted the weather beaten village tucked into a small bay with a protective bluff to seaward covered by stunted trees. There were no boats coming or going or any people at the dock. If they landed out of sight from the settlement perhaps Mandeler and Alheeza could walk over the hill and see what could be had.

Earlsbee

As with all plans, they sound good until you actually head off into the unknown. It was easy for Mandeler to climb to the top of the hill, carrying the weakened Alheeza. Labeena crawled along between the stunted trees, and waited on the lip of the hill. She was camouflaged in the trees but to stay in the open would be suicidal after dark. They had a hand or more of time before sunset, so Mandeler hastened down the rocky slope.

Earlsbee

He stopped at the water's edge and gently lowered Alheeza to the pebble beach saying, "I know this is going to be cold but nobody will let us in if we smell this bad." From one of his packs he drew out his only other tunic and pants. Then he stripped and stepped into the icy water. Goosebumps rose all over his skin but he plunged in head first and came up a moment later, streaming with salt water. He purposely strode to shore and picked up his friend. Being as gentle as he could, he bathed Alheeza in the cold water. He rubbed the thin scaled skin with his hands hoping to rid him of the perfidious odor. The light sea breeze was chilling, so Mandeler dried himself and Alheeza with his light blanket and dressed in his remaining clothes. Soon they were on their way again, both smelled a good deal better. A small pile of putrid clothes remained on the beach as they walked away.

It was hard to get any idea of the size of the village, but there were a couple of big buildings near the centre that looked a bit like the lodges of home, but with much steeper roofs. Along the shore were two tall buildings, with short docks protruding from them into the dark water. Several small boats were drawn up on the rocky beach. Scattered about the perimeter of the village were irregular sized buildings with no chimneys or visible windows. Nobody was walking around the village so there was only one thing to do, head toward the biggest one with smoke coming from the chimney.

He readjusted Alheeza around his shoulders, and felt for the two slim packs slung at his back. The flinger had been loaded and placed near the top of the right case, for ready access. He also loosened his knife in the sheath; a moon cycle ago he would never have been so cautious.

The windows were already shuttered for the coming night and the sound of voices could be heard from within as he approached the steep roofed hall. He rapped his knuckles upon the thick door, and when there was no reply he slipped his hand into the wooden latch easing the door open. As he peered through the opening, a hush fell over the room as faces turned towards him. A big man with a bulbous nose, grey hair in a ponytail and a weather beaten face, rose saying, "What brings a stranger into our midst in these troubled times?"

"My name is Mandeler Freedahson from the upper estates and this is the denzel Alheeza."

Before the big man could answer, a scrawny fellow at the back jumped up yelling, "Them's the ones that caused all the trouble, him and that denzel. Them's the ones that made us lose the Sea Quester. He's to blame!" He jumped up from his bench, with a knife in his hand, and launched himself toward the newcomers.

Time seemed to stand still because in one fluid movement Mandeler slid Alheeza and his pack to the floor. His accuser came raging around the group with his exposed blade, slashing the air. No one else moved as Mandeler drew the long weapon free, bringing it to bear on his assailant. The thin man skidded to a halt in front of Mandeler's glass tipped arrow.

Mandeler said, "Toddfree isn't it, the mutineer?"

Toddfree was swaying, spittle hung from his lip, his bleary eyes fixed upon the deadly weapon. Mandeler brought his gaze to the big spokesman, frozen part way out of his chair and said, "This man, Toddfree, was cast off with his other mutinous companions after they tried to take command of the Sea Quester by force. I, too come from that ship. She was still being commanded by Captain Larson and the remaining faithful crew. What has this man told of the events?"

Toddfree was about to speak, but Mandeler twitched the flinger making him rethink his options. It was the big man that spoke, "We don't abide any violence in my hall. Toddfree, step back slowly and give your knife over to Fellgar." Without taking his eyes off the newcomers, he motioned with his chin and a wide shouldered youth rose and purposefully stepped behind the little seaman, pinning his wrists in his vice-like hands. Mandeler lowered the flinger. A little shake from Fellgar made the knife clatter to the floor. Toddfree was then spun around and placed on a chair at the end of the table. Fellgar stood with arms folded behind him. "Now Master Mandeler, please put away your weapon and take a chair across the table from your accuser."

About a dozen and half men and women were seated at the long table. The hall was warm and well lit, with a fire in the large hearth, as well as many illumination globes about the tall space. Mandeler had seen that all the windows and doors were shuttered, as if for a storm, when he approached. The smell of hot food and ale made his mouth water. Mandeler walked towards the chair, with Alheeza limping at his side, and took his place in a chair across from his accuser.

The big man said, "I am Kenward, the leader of this village. We will have a truth search to settle this." He waved to someone at the back of the hall and they ducked into a curtained room. Shortly afterwards an elderly wheezing woman, with a hunched back and frizzy white hair, shuffled into the room. She wore several tattered dark brown shawls and despite her appearance, the villagers seemed to show great respect as she passed. As she got closer, Mandeler could see her aged face had many deep wrinkles but it was the penetrating blue eyes that held him motionless.

She came up beside Toddfree, who seemed to turn away from her, shaking like a frightened animal. She laid her hand upon his head, while clutching something at her frail chest. It only took a few breaths, and then she opened her eyes frowning. The old woman made her way around to Mandeler where she also stood behind him and placed her knobby fingers in his thick blond hair. For Mandeler there was a brief flash of white light followed by the fading image of an amber crystal. He heard the sound of a ragged breath taken in and then she spoke in a crackling voice, "This one speaks the truth," but in his head he heard: *I am one of your kind, you are welcome here. You carry a great burden of responsibility for us all. I sense also that you have a strange traveling companion that you need to conceal. Time is running out…*

Kenward nodded to the crone then turned toward Toddfree, "Your welcome has ended. At dawn you are to leave Earlsbee, never to return." He looked up at Fellgar adding, "Put him in the side room and latch the door."

Then to Mandeler he said, "Enough of this scoundrel, tell me how you got to this desolate bit of coastline."

"There is a great deal to tell but first can we have a private moment to speak?"

Kenward's brows furrowed as he took in the young man. The gnarled old woman, Norwata, simply nodded to him and he rose saying, "Come with me."

Kenward, Norwata, Mandeler and Alheeza made their way to a room behind the great fireplace. After the door was closed he said to Norwata, "What goes on here?"

She replied, "Leader, this one heads the struggle against the dark hunters. He needs our help in order to carry the fight to their mountain. His stay will be short, but his need is great. Danger follows close behind him."

Mandeler made eye contact with the leader saying, "I have an unusual companion waiting on the hill outside of town. I ask that you help find shelter for her before darkness falls. She is not one of us and is very large. If I had just brought her into town, it would have brought alarm to the whole village."

"What manner of companion is this?"

"Her name is Labeena. She is leader of the Olive Raptor Clan and an ally to our race. We are in great need of your help!"

Norwata sat down breathing heavily but she managed to say, "Open a fresh keg of strong ale and have Fellgar go with Mandeler. A fit of coughing took hold of her and when it passed she said, "You lift a mug or two while Fellgar helps Mandeler with his companion. When Fellgar returns, you should go to the boat house to meet our new ally." She slumped down looking exhausted.

Kenward shrugged adding, "Alright Norwata, Mandeler come with me."

As they left the room Norwata mind-spoke to Alheeza: *So we meet again ancient one. Let me have a look at that leg of yours.*

The ridge was silhouetted by the setting sun as Fellgar and Mandeler made their way to the steep roofed boat house. Part of the building hung over the rocky shore with a short jetty sticking out into the dark water. Like the lodge, the windows were barred and shuttered. Mandeler imagined it might hold a sizable vessel. As they walked from the main lodge, Mandeler had tried to size up Fellgar. The young, red haired villager seemed about his age and height, but far broader in the shoulders. Mandeler continued, "We have been chased by the Great Raptors and my friend needs a place to shelter for the night. She is not one of us, but is a great friend to our cause. Please do not be afraid when I call her to come to the dock."

The smile faded from Fellgar's face but he held his ground on the dock as Mandeler went on, "She is one of the olive green raptors that live far to the north. Her name is Labeena. Now open the building while I walk out and call her to the dock."

Mandeler walked out to the end of the planked jetty while reaching into his tunic to clasp the amulet. At the same time he sent out his thoughts to Labeena: *Come to me, I have found safe refuge for the night.*

Along the ridge Labeena rose onto her hind legs, spreading her leathery wings. To the uninitiated her silhouette could have been mistaken for one of the Great Raptors but her swept back wings, rounded head and curved ear wings were distinct. She took a few powerful strokes, which sent her over the stunted trees and down the slope. She came across the water, gliding toward the dock, only to pull up at the last moment beating the air with thunderous strokes, which let her land delicately on the narrow dock. Fellgar, who had been standing at the side of the large doors, looked as if he had seen a ghost, or at least a flying legend. He shook himself back into the moment and heaved the great door open. With Mandeler in the lead, she lumbered along the wharf and into the dark interior of the building.

With the last light of the evening, Mandeler could make out the shape of a sailing vessel between the two wide walkways. Fellgar closed the doors and shook two illumination globes to life. The tiny light emitting insects brought a soft blue light to the interior. The building was constructed around a tiny inlet. It was meant to serve as shelter from the winter storms but also a place to refit and store goods. There was room enough for Labeena to settle along its side.

Mandeler took Fellgar's arm and led him to Labeena. There he introduced them with mind-speak overlapped with spoken words. The look of awe spread over the young man's face. He then left, and not long after Kenward came in through a side door. Mandeler repeated the introduction process after which Kenward turned toward the boat and said, "This is my vessel the 'Strong Heart', she is the best fishing boat this side of Portside. The boathouse has stood here since my father's day withstanding all the storms that winter can bring. If there is any place that can offer strong shelter, this is it."

Mandeler was now looking very tired and he replied, "Labeena has carried me a great distance in the past two sun cycles but she is weary now needing food and rest. Where she comes from they dive for red fins and other marine life, but I do not know what to do here."

"The answer might be closer than you think." Kenward walked over to a stack of barrels in the corner of the building and added, "Help me take one of these down."

Moments later they rolled a sizable wooden barrel up to Labeena. Then Kenward picked up a punch and mallet from the workbench and in one strike he had the lid open and the smell of gleamers filled the air.

When the door of the main lodge opened this time the air was filled with laughter and animated people. Obviously the keg of strong ale had its desired effect. Kenward led his guest to a place at the table across from Fellgar. A wave of his hand brought a beautiful young woman bearing food and drink. She looked at Mandeler with unmasked admiration. He blushed as he took the food. He had not realized how hungry he was until he saw the platter heaped with simmered gleamers, boiled red root and pickled coastlings, along with a generous mug of ale. His host was polite enough to let him eat his fill, before asking about his journey. When he did bring up the subject he did point out that Captain Larson was no stranger to the coast and a true telling of the story would be most welcome. Everyone had crowded around the end of the long table. More had come in the hall to hear the story from the stranger.

Mandeler looked at the rosy cheeks of these honest fisherman and wondered where to start. He was so tired that he wobbled when he rose. As he looked around the room, his gaze fell upon the attractive girl that had served him. He tore his eyes away from her and took a breath saying, "Over a moon cycle ago the Great Raptors attacked us at a high estate, up on the plateau, behind the Coastal Mountains. Several were taken at the time, and since then I have traveled across the Blue Mountains to Portside, then on a long sea voyage to meet unlikely allies in the north. We were trying to find a way to bring an end to the Raptor attacks. Our quest took us looking for the legendary olive green raptor that lived far into the north ocean. We were followed by the night marauders and attacked several times, including once while on the Sea Quester. Following that, Toddfree and his friends tried to take over the ship. One of theirs was killed in the attempt, but Captain Larson decided to set them free in a well-stocked boat, while we continued on. Apparently, they made it here in the ship's cutter, telling a far different tale. What is more important is that today, we took this denzel, Alheeza from under the noses of the Great Raptors and escaped with our lives. The three of us arrived here as a most unusual set of companions: a man, a denzel and a green raptor. I now ask that you offer protection to my brave companions. To answer the rest of your questions I give you back to your elder, Kenward, for he has met Labeena, leader of the Olive Green Raptor Clan. As for me, these have been sleepless nights and your warm food and drink make me want to find my bed.

Please excuse me for I must retire."

The whole place was a buzz as he wobbled away toward the room Alheeza was in. Part way, he felt an arm slip around his and to his surprise the attractive girl had joined him. She beamed at him with total awe saying, "Let me help you get settled. I know how to make a man comfortable." He faltered in his stride and turned to look into her eyes with their open invitation. The memory of Gwenelle's last touch fortified him and he carefully removed her arm from his saying, "I am very tired and must be alone. Good night."

As he entered the small room Norwata looked up at him from the side of the sleeping Alheeza. She looked even more tired than he felt. She mind-spoke: *So you have encountered Rosella, and her charms did not sway you?* Without waiting for an answer she turned back to Alheeza and continued: *I have reset his leg. Because of the pain I gave him an herbal sedative. He will not wake until tomorrow but his leg will heal eventually. Know this: he cannot travel any further in his condition. Let him stay with us. He will be cared for with respect.*

There is something else you should know. From my talks with Alheeza, you travel with an uninitiated woman who shows great gifts of insight and telepathy. She reached into the fold of her blouse drawing out a smooth amber crystal. *I believe Gwenelle and I have seen each other in the dreams and she will need this. Take this with you, for it will help to unlock some of the mysteries. My time is short here and I must pass on the memories of our sisterhood.*

He took the luminescent stone from her delicate hands and slipped the braided loop over his head, where it rested next to his own amulet. He could feel a warmth radiating from it. It reminded him of the comforting touch of Gwenelle.

Norwata reached into a basket and took out three small jars sealed with wax and handed them to him. In one he could see dark granules shifting inside and in the other were white, almost translucent crystals. *Your Captain Larson was given the one like this last year. It is the last of the exploding powder. Give these to your mate. She is the only one left that can solve the puzzle.*

Mandeler asked: *You know about our quest to find some equalizer to help fight the great ones?*

Of course I do, what do you think the crystals and the dreams are all about? Now quickly there is something you must commit to memory before you go. In the last jar is tattoo paint for Gwenelle.

Norwata turned as she loosened her many layers of clothing. Before his eyes, Mandeler saw the naked back of the old healer appear in the dim light of his room. Running up the side of her back, and along her neck was the tattooed form of an olive green raptor. She looked over her shoulder mind-speaking: *Look well and remember that she will need these markings to set herself free.*

In her dream the crone sat with her naked back exposed. The dim light of the room revealed a dark green raptor up her spine and ribs with its head nestled on her neck. She turned as if looking directly at Gwenelle and lifted a glowing amber stone into the air. The image changed and within the cavern, a rock wall glimmered with white crystals. The unsettling part was the sound of the voices that filled the chamber. It was the song of the crystals and it was beautiful.

Gwenelle awoke with the dream still haunting her. It was so real she could have touched it and the sound of the cave still reverberated in her ears. It was the first of the out-of-body dreams without Mandeler and his crystal. She shivered from the sheer thrill of it.

Norwata mind-spoke: *Sleep while you can, I will watch for you.*

Mandeler slipped on his sleeping helmet and fell instantly into a deep sleep. His dreams must have come from within, for they were only fleeting dreams of a tall woman with her dark wavy hair, streaming in the wind. She stood in front of green raptor with a hand lightly resting on its head. Her piercing blue eyes seemed to look right through him while she clutched an amber crystal to her breast. The amber crystal glowed on his breast as the images streamed past.

Mandeler felt the hand on his shoulder. It was Norwata. In the dim light he could see the look of fear in her face, then she spoke, "They are here, we let you sleep as long as we dared but the full force of the dark ones will soon be upon us." Thumping could be heard from above.

No sooner had he emerged from the small room than the air was filled with the screams of the night marauders. The main lodge shuddered as great bodies were slammed into the timbers. Dust was illuminated as it fell in from the quaking rafters. Terrified people stared up from the shadows around the perimeter of the meeting room. Time seemed to slow so that even his heart beat came in measured thumps in his chest. Mandeler cast a wary glance about the place, and wondered how long the structure would take this pounding before something gave way. Armored heads with yellow fangs would seek out the exposed bodies, tearing them from what little shelter remained, only to carry them back to that reeking cave to be devoured.

He assumed that this assault was retaliatory, after his confrontation near the great one's cave, because this sounded far more intense than any other attack. Something had to be done, but what. Movement in the corner brought his attention to Kenward who was beckoning to him from behind a pillar. Mandeler walked purposefully towards him. As he approached the elder, he could see others, including the pretty young serving girl in the shadows. They looked as if they were in a waking nightmare with faces pale and eyes bulging.

Kenward spoke, "In our early days as a fishing village there were some pirates at large and we had an escape route to avoid them. It has not been used in decades, but there was a tunnel to the boat house so we could make an escape. Would that help you in any way? Far be it for me to accuse you of bringing this attack on us, but I cannot help but feel that, after your story, they might be a bit vengeful!"

The hammering on the roof intensified as Mandeler chewed his lower lip considering his options. Then he said, "Show me the passage way."

Kenward simply tapped his foot on the flat stone beneath his feet. They both got down on hands and knees to get fingers along the edge of the rock. Despite their best grip, it did not move. Mandeler drew out his knife, and using the ironwood handle he managed to get it under the lip of the stone. The small lever was enough to create a crack along the floor and soon they had their fingers under it and the heavy slab was tipped up and over. In the dim light wooden steps could be seen descending into the dark.

Kenward shoved an illumination globe into his hands. Its message was clear: Get going and do it now. Mandeler put a foot on the dusty step. It creaked but felt solid. It only took a few more steps and he found himself looking down a long low passage way that seemed to be going downhill. The sound of the stone closing behind him was a final goodbye.

Before he reached the end of the passageway, he could feel Labeena's terror as huge bodies slamming into the boat house. At the end of the tunnel, he pushed up on the planks above and found himself in the darkened work area. His small globe lit the side of the building and Labeena's bulk was pressed up against the side of the fishing boat. He reached out with his mind to her, *I am here.*

How are we going to survive this? Came her response.

Mandeler's mind spun as he grappled with the impossible situation. On the boat with Gwenelle, he had repelled the Raptors but here there was no preparation. Nor were there any fire pots to set a flame, and more than anything he missed Gwenelle with her steady hand and confidence. They were pinned in a boat house, with a number of Great Raptors hurling themselves at the buildings with no regard for their own safety. This was an attack that went beyond any of his experience. All he knew was they shunned light, feared fire, couldn't swim and were almost impermeable to any kind of counterattack. In his haste to leave, he had forgotten the extra arrows in Alheeza's room. What was he going to do?

In his quandary, he paced about and then leaned against the fishing vessel. It moved! Suddenly he had an idea, there might be a way!

He dug into his slim pack and pulled out his last precious fire stick. Tossing the globe onto the deck of the boat he looked for flammable liquids in the work area and was rewarded with a couple of bottles of mineral spirits. Mounting the deck, he found the sails were furled into neat rolls along the mast. He sprinkled these liberally with the fuel and then jumped down to release each of the mooring lines. Mandeler dashed towards the double doors mind-speaking to Labeena: *Get to the other end of the boat and when you see the fire start, push the boat towards the doors.*

He tugged the two braces free on the wide doors and sprang onto the deck of the fishing boat, with a fire stick dragging it along the rough timber. In an instant, there was a spark, followed by flames that spread along the rolled sails. The door pushed open as Labeena gave a great shove and the boat slid into the night air. Mandeler jumped onto Labeena from the bow. They hit the water together and the shocking cold made him lose his breath.

The pack leader was circling the tall building by the water. He felt the pain of smashing into these structures, but soon they would have an opening and then the Queen would get her satisfaction on the 'one' she sought above all others. He called all of his hunters to attack but then something bright burst from the building. His eyes hurt from the searing flames and it was impossible to see clearly. As the fire grew, he backed away into the sky. The sense of the 'one' suddenly vanished as if he no longer existed. How could that have happened?

It was amazing how the fishing boat burst into flame. Labeena tucked into the shadow low under the stern. The water was so cold it almost took his breath away. If it had not been for the fear of the Great Raptors from above he would never have ventured into the chilled water at night. Above them, the inferno was quickly consuming the deck and rigging of the 'Strong Heart'.

How long they were in the frigid sea he could not tell. Mandeler clutched his amulet to search the sky with all of his senses, but he was losing contact with the raptors above. He assumed they were trying to avoid the spark filled column of smoke. It seemed to confirm his notion that fire drove them away, if only for a short while. There was something else at play here, for he truly felt disconnected from them for the first time. The water was numbingly cold, so cold.

The pack leader tried to search for the skinny little one but the flames burned the back of his eyes. Ever since the floating fire had entered the bay, they had all felt the searing pain. Now there was no trace of the one. How could he have just disappeared? Without being able to sense his prey he was lost as to what to do. This was unlike anything he had prepared for and he would have to retreat to the wrath of his Queen.

Mandeler shivered while he stared at the darkened sky. He mind-spoke to Labeena: *I think they are retreating but I can't be sure of where they are. I think it is safe to leave the boat. You should know that I am cold.*

No sooner had he thought that when he heard shouts from the great lodge. They had come out after the attack was halted. Now what would happen, with them having put the torch to Kenward's favorite boat?

He pushed off, hoping to swim back to shore, only to find that his limbs would not move from the cold. As he sank below the surface he could not help but feel the moment was ironical. He had survived several Raptor attacks only to drown in the icy bay of Earlsbee.

Then he felt Labeena's head press up from under him, just like the first time they met. As he broke the surface, he gulped in several grateful breaths, then wrapped his numb arms around her long neck again, and let her swim him to shore.

All he could do was crawl on his hands and knees up the beach. Several men carrying globes had started down the hill, but upon seeing Labeena they stopped. Kenward kept coming, waving his arms he shouted, "Are you mad, that boat was worth a fortune to me. Do you have any idea what you have done?"

It happened too fast for him to react, Labeena thrust forward knocking Kenward onto his back. A low growl that sounded like boulders moving in a river came from her throat. Nobody moved, especially Kenward. From under the olive raptor's shadow Mandeler spoke, "Labeena, let him up, he will not hurt me. He is just upset by me burning his boat."

As she withdrew, a not too steady Kenward rose to his feet and after some hesitation he said, "You're so right about that!" A low growl came from Labeena and he added, "But you did scare away the Raptors. Let's retire to the lodge and have a drink to warm you."

The men turned and made their way back up the hill, with Labeena and a wobbly Mandeler leaning on her, in the rear. Every now and then she would look up into the sky as if expecting to see dark shadows blotting out the stars. Upon Mandeler's instructions, the door was left open so she could see within. From inside Labeena could make out a number of Mandeler's kind gawking at her. It made no difference. She would stand on guard to protect him as long as needed.

Mandeler could not believe how painful it was to warm up again. Once he had been helped up to the building it was discovered how close he had come to dying in the bay. It would not have taken much time for his chill to be irreversible. Now he sat with his feet in a pan of water that felt like burning coals. His painful fingers were wrapped around a mug of hot ale and he was shivering again. The coarse warm blanket against his skin was not enough to stop the shaking.

Kenward sat on a stool, staring at him with eyes that mixed with anger and dismay. By the hunched shoulders, Mandeler thought it may be a while before any real forgiveness came his way. As he was thinking along those lines, Norwata appeared from the side room and painfully made her way towards him. Her cracked voice came clearly across the room, "Young Mandeler, I did not think I would see you again. It appears that our unwanted visitors have also left. How did this come about?"

Kenward bolted to his feet and spun around to meet the wise one saying, "He burned my ship to save his own life!"

"Interesting. Look how well that worked and none of the villagers were hurt either."

"No!"

"I would say that was quite a remarkable feat, would you not?" She mind-spoke to Mandeler only: *Leave him to me, your fight is over tonight.*

"But what about my ship and who is going to pay for that?"

Kenward was shaking again.

"There are ways that are hidden to you leader, have patience." As she said this she took Kenward by the wrist, it was as if a small child was being guided by a parent, for she turned him back to his stool, and he sat seemingly satisfied.

She turned to Mandeler and mind-spoke again: *What is more important is the question: what was learned tonight?*

Mandeler's mind seemed to be foggy from the freezing water, but the question stuck and he knew she had seen something more important than the boat burning. What could it be? The attack had been launched by many Great Raptors, and they had been relentless in their attempts to break into the lodge. When he changed locations, they too seemed to have altered their focus of the attack, as if they sensed him changing buildings, but how? And then the bigger question struck him, what had caused them to give up the hunt suddenly. One minute the air was filled with screaming Raptors, and the next they simply flew away. Why?

It was almost as if she could read his mind because Norwata started to nod her head and she said, "That is the bigger question isn't it, why did they suddenly give up after fighting so hard to reach you? What changed?"

It was as if he woke up after a very long sleep. The water, the cold water. As soon as he and Labeena were fully immersed in the icy water, the attack had lost all of its force. He knew they were hunting him but it was as if he had become suddenly invisible. He said aloud, **"It was the frigid water. They could not see me once I was immersed in the ice water!"**

Aren't you the smart one!

Things happened quickly after that. In the hand of time before sunrise, Mandeler went to his packs and selected a solid looking coin made from the precious golden metal. He placed it in Kenward's hand and left the grey haired man staring into his palm. A fresh set of water resistant clothes was offered to Mandeler and when he was dressed with his traveling cases over his shoulder, he made his farewells to Norwata and Alheeza. Both looked exhausted, but wished him blessings and all the luck possible on his mission.

Mandeler stood on the jetty with Labeena as the sun broke over the horizon. The villagers had spilled out of the lodge, but stayed in a tight cluster, warily watching the preparations for departure.

Despite the short rest before the attack, Labeena seemed eager for the long flight ahead. She ducked her shoulders down and he swung up into place, settled his light gear and wrapped his arms about her neck. In just a few strong strokes, they were out over the bay picking up speed. She climbed to clear the seaward ridge and the open ocean spread out before them. They both felt hope rising as they left the land behind and stretched out toward the remote raptor's island and Gwenelle. They flew towards the building storm.

Reunion

Gwenelle awoke in their cabin. She pulled his pillow close to her face taking in the scent of the blond young man. A shiver ran up her spine as she wondered what fate had befallen him. Could she sense him from this great distance? The bond between them had grown in the past weeks. She was sure he still lived but there was still foreboding.

To avoid the feelings of dread, she had been trying to stay busy on the boat by tending to the bandages around Captain Larson's ribs and helping with the repairs aboard their little ship. The Sea Quester was getting back into sailing order and Larson was breathing easier but what was this uneasiness that crept into her bones. Her last dreams stayed with her throughout the day with a crispness that haunted her still. The crone with the raptor on her back seemed to be with her as she clambered from their bed.

Slowly she climbed the companionway emerging onto the sunny deck. The day was already warm and the fresh breeze smelled crisp and clean. The wind blew steadily out of the east turning their boat so the stern faced the reef and Raptor Island. On the ledge high above the sun reflected off the fine scales of the green raptors as they took off from the mouth of the cave. A few circled high above but most headed out to sea. One of them started to circle down towards the ship and as he passed abeam she could make out the fine features of the big male. Then Rachaner mind-spoke to her: *I greet you with the warmth of the morning sun, Gwenelle, mate of Mandeler.*

The title still gave her pause but she sent back to him: *Greetings great one. Do you have any contact with Labeena and Mandeler?*

She is beyond my senses, but my heart is full with the feeling she is safe.

All of this took place as Rachaner circled low about Sea Quester. Suddenly Gwenelle could hold back no longer. *Would you please take me back to your cave? I need to look for something.*

I would be honored.

On the next *pass* Rachaner cupped his wings and beat the air, driving up a cloud of spray, as he settled onto the water. She did not hear Larson come up behind her but he said, "What are you up to here?"

"I'm going to go back to the island, I can't tell why but there is something I must search for."

Larson replied, "I suppose you will be wantin' the row boat again?"

Thank you no, I will fly to the island with Rachaner. I will get my things.

With that she bolted below and quickly pulled off her sweater and long baggy pants stuffing them into her pack along with travel rations, blanket and a water flask. She tied the water tight pack closed and headed for the deck again. In her under garments she strode past Larson, climbed the rail and dove into the sea. Rachaner floated low in the water and it only took a few strokes to reach him. His intelligent eyes never left her until he felt her purposefully grasp his neck ridge and fit her feet onto his chest ribs. Gwenelle felt him fill his lungs and then his body arched as he dragged his wings clear of the water. With his great strength the air thundered as he pulled them above the surface. Gwenelle clung to his neck with all her might as the powerful creature heaved up and forward. They picked up speed quickly as he skimmed the water and then he started to climb. He settled into a gentle rhythm of flight and all too soon they were gliding towards the cave entrance.

Tears streamed as she squinted toward the raptor's cave. A shiver ran up her whole body as the wind chilled her wet body. Soon Rachaner was rearing up while scooping the air to touch down lightly on the lip of the cliff. As she slid down, a number of the smaller clan came out to greet them. There was much bobbing of heads and a sense of excitement. He turned his head towards her mind-speaking, *The young ones ask if they can touch you. Is it acceptable in your tribe to allow their touch? Their curiosity is such that they want to know more about you and your kind.*

What could she say? Gwenelle stepped forward extending her hands. The juveniles approached cautiously extending their thin necks. Soon a dozen little raptors of varying sizes were sniffing and touching her fingers. It tickled and a shiver of a different kind ran up her spine. As they surrounded her, she started to get fragments of their thoughts. Rachaner and Labeena seemed to pass their thoughts so clearly it was almost like talking to people, but these little fellows seemed to convey more emotions than pure thought. They were excited, a little bit scared, fascinated and baffled by her alien features. Soon they started to press in close and she became alarmed. Rachaner broke in with his thoughts: *Little ones, step back, you are being very impolite. Let our guest have room to walk freely again.*

Like a group of giggling children, they retreated on their short knuckled wings waving their tails and chirping loudly.

As if he read her mind, Rachaner mind-spoke: *We can leave you in peace. There was something you wanted to look for. If I can help in any way all you have to do is mind-reach for me and I will come.* With that he spread his great wings and swooped down from the cliff and out over the water. The chirping entourage had retreated respectfully into the cave.

She was still chilled, and remembering their first visit here she started to strip off her damp garments placing them on stones facing the sun. She pulled out her blanket and dried herself off. It only took a short time in the warm sun to dry off and then Gwenelle dressed in her dry clothing. Gwenelle found a large flat rock that was already warmed by the morning sun and sat cross-legged looking out to sea. Feeling warmer now, she spread out her blanket to let it dry as well. It was time to reflect on all that had happened. Almost without knowing, she drew the pack towards herself and extracted her traveling flute and thin sandals.

How long had it been since she put her flute to her lips? It was the night of the first Great Raptor attack. Since then it had been a whirlwind of travel, terror and love, with all of it unexpected. Now she needed to draw some of the loose ends together and try to make sense of it. She put the wooden instrument to her lips and let her fingers dance on their own. The melody that came forth was nothing she had ever learned from her tutors. At first she did not recognize it but then the sounds from her dream came forward and she knew this was the calling of some shiny crystals locked away in an unknown place. What purpose they held was still not known.

Gwenelle was lost in the rhythm of the moment and was not aware of the small raptor that had carefully crept from the cave. As she took the flute from her lips the little flyer came up respectfully at her side. Gwenelle mind-spoke to it, *My name is G W E N E L L E, what do they call you little one?*

Kateena.

Well Kateena, I am pleased to meet you.

H o n o u r e d, as well.

What can I do for you?

How do you make those s o u n d s?

With that Gwenelle put the wooden instrument to her lips a second time. The same strange melody came forth. She turned to see her companion swaying in time to the music.

Gwenelle paused and asked: *How is it that you move to this music?*

I have heard it often. Other things around also sing to me. Can you not hear them?

I heard it in a dream is all. Where do you hear it Kateena?

This one is quite close.

Can you show me where that is?

Without answering, Kateena turned and limped off, to the side away from the cave entrance. Gwenelle put on her sandals and followed.

Mandeler was leaning comfortably forward on Labeena's neck as she settled into her distance eating rhythm. His mind kept coming back to Nowata's amulet, her tattoo and the message to Gwenelle. He had so little experience with people outside his small family and then on this journey there was Gwenelle and the growing attachment to her. Through all of this was the image of the raptor tattoo and some deeper meaning that came with it. He hardly noticed the darkening sky ahead as they flew on.

It had been days since he had any amount of sleep and the deep fatigue he felt was starting to take its toll. His head started to droop but he caught himself before he could nod off. Before long he drifted off with his body slung over Labeena's neck and torso. Falling asleep on the back of a flying raptor has its drawbacks, for one thing it is a long way down, but sleep he did. Slumber in the full light of day was blissful for it came without tormenting dreams. His only images were that of Gwenelle seated on a rock playing the most unusual music.

The first drops of rain brought Mandeler fully awake. He was startled when he realized that he had fallen asleep in flight. He mind-spoke to his flying companion, *How did I keep from falling off?*

I can sense your every move and all I had to do was to shift my stride in flight to keep you in balance. You were never in danger of falling off and you needed the rest so badly.

The rain was starting to fall in earnest, so he pulled up his hood tightening it around his neck, as he hunkered down as close to Labeena's neck as possible. Even with his water repellent clothes trickles of icy water made their way up his sleeves. A deep chill was setting in as he squinted ahead.

Gwenelle found it surprising to see how agile the little raptor was as she climbed along the rocky crag. It was not long before they reached a narrow slit in the rock face. Without hesitation Kateena slipped sideways through the opening. Gwenelle took care as she followed because some of these rocks were very abrasive. As she entered, the light vanished quickly. Gwenelle stood still for moment allowing her eyes to adjust to the blackness in front of her. Slowly the scene took on some depth. Kateena had stopped not far in front of her and was gazing up into a tall cathedral which now was illuminated by the gently glowing wall. As she stared it became clear that the wall had long spires of granular stone that emitted the low levels of light. She stepped forward and placed her hand on the nearest outcrop. It felt different than cold stone but she could not quite make out what it was. Then her memories of the dream came to her and the place took on a feeling of familiarity.

Kateena mind-spoke, *Can you hear them?*

No, what should I hear?

It is the sound of the crystals singing to us, just like the tune you played.

The cold rain stung like icy needles as Labeena flew into the storm. Mandeler pressed his face into her neck to keep the worst of the piercing rain out of his face. How could Labeena see where they were going? All he could sense was that she was being pressed to her limits of strength. Mandeler focused on just hanging on, hoping that his grip would hold until the squall passed. Time dragged on as he willed the sky to open up before them. Ice water had crept under most of his clothing and the chill he felt was making him feel weak and light headed. Then they suddenly burst out from under the cloud and the sun greeted them. It was the most wonderful sight in the world.

Mandeler asked, *How far is it to the island?*

Still several hands of time.

Shaking with cold he tried to focus his thoughts forward and reached out with his mind.

Gwenelle was just coming back out into the light when she felt it. *Mandeler was reaching out to her,* she could feel it. He was in some kind of trouble but they were getting nearer. In fits and starts she saw that he was wet, cold and feared that Labeena was growing too tired for the last part of the trip.

Labeena's exhaustion was beyond memory. She flew as low to the water as she dared because down here close to the water it was easier to fly. Her wing tips touched the sea as she pumped on. Each stroke took her closer to her beloved island and the clan.

Several had flown out to meet her but it was Rachaner that came the closest touching her with his mind. She would not be able to climb high enough to reach the clan cave. To make it to the beach was the best that she could hope for. Soon she could make out the details of the shore just beyond the breakers. Just a few more strokes! When the water smoothed out in the lagoon she gave in letting her chest touch the water. She skidded in a thin spray of water, coming to rest in the shallow water skirting the beach.

Labeena lay there breathing heavily and could feel Mandeler slide from her back. He paused with his arms around her neck saying, *I owe you my life, you amazing being.*

Then arms were around him and he knew she was there. The rest was a blur but he awoke to a crackling fire wrapped in a blanket.

Tattoo

Mandeler was warm and dry within a blanket. He could not remember getting here and then he felt the hand on his chest move and realized that he was being held and a warm body was wrapped around his back. Gwenelle spoke softly, “You’re awake. You slept almost all night. The sun will be coming up very soon.”

He was naked within his coarse blanket and the fire was the only source of light. Darkness engulfed the world beyond its flickering flames. The campsite looked as if a giant had scooped out the living rock making a warm dry place for just them. The fire felt warm on his face and for the first time in weeks he felt safe from harm.

Gwenelle continued, “You were so cold and tired that all I could think of was to dry you off and use my body heat to help revive you. It was a bit like hugging a cold gleamer but I think you were worth it!” She giggled, something he had hardly ever heard.

Mandeler went to answer her but his throat suddenly tightened and he could not speak. He froze for a few heart beats and then willed his voice to say, “I thought I would never see you again.”

In response she hugged him close saying, “I was scared for you the whole time you were away.”

He turned his head towards her and tried to answer but the words would not come. He rolled to be able to face her in the blankets.

“Gwenelle, I... I mean...It just...oh dung!”

“You need food and more sleep. From what Labeena could share, you’ve been to a terrible darkness and back again. Just shut your eyes and let the sleep come again.”

It sounded like the most difficult thing to do but in just a few breaths he was sound asleep.

This time when he awoke it was full day and Gwenelle was crouching over a fire where a fragrant smell of sweet nut stew made his mouth water. She looked up smiling at him in that special way.

Mandeler sat up and the two crystals about his neck rattled against each other. *I have something for you,* he mind-spoke, as he lifted the amber stone free from around his neck.

I was wondering where the new stone came from, Gwenelle answered.

Norwata sent you this gift. He went on to describe the old healer.

Gwenelle got a funny look on her face and then asked: *Was there a raptor tattoo on her neck and back?*

Yes, how did you know?

She has been visiting my dreams.

Mandeler held it out to her adding: *Norwata is a great healer in her community and she told me to give this to you. It was hers but she said the time had come to pass it on to you.* He held the amber crystal out to her. She came forward ducked her head and he placed the finely braided cord and its shimmering stone around her neck.

As the stone slid between her breasts, it was if she saw the world through Mandeler's crystal, only brighter and it sounded better too. The world beyond took on a new vibrancy with shimmering color that sprang from the rocks and sand. It was almost as if she could hear the very sand that she stood on humming to her.

Mandeler pressed his own amulet against his chest. Gwenelle seemed to grow not in stature but in brilliance. A shiver ran up his spine just watching her.

She took in the fresh feeling of her surroundings. The very air about her seemed to come alive with color as it shimmered and vibrated.

Suddenly she sat down in the sand in front of him. It looked as if she was overwhelmed with the feelings, then she reached out, taking his face in her hands, and kissed him. Oh, wow could this woman kiss, but it was more than just a kiss!

In that moment they could both feel the bond take hold and his memories of the flight to the Great Raptor's cave and back came flooding into her mind. She felt the cold fingers of fear that Mandeler had when they escaped the Great Raptor cave with Alheeza, as well as his sense of relief upon reaching Earlsbee. Then there was the betrayal of Toddfree, followed by the night attack, and the burning ship. She faltered when she came to the encounters with Norwata for she looked exactly like her dreams.

As she drew back she could see that Mandeler had seen her dreams of Norwata too. Gwenelle sat there breathing heavily. She reached down and pulled the crystal away from her skin and the world came back to what it had been. It was just a cooking fire on a lonely beach with the warm sun beating down on them. The whole experience was overwhelming. If this is what Mandeler felt every time he clasped his amulet then she understood the joy and torment that came with it.

She lifted her eyes, taking in this young man, and wondered how she had been drawn into it all. As if he sensed her questions he spoke softly, "I was with a group of like-minded men when I first saw the other dimension. It was quite startling to see other telepaths revealed."

She just nodded and they sat there in silence, then he remembered the jar and the instructions that Norwata had given him. Pulling up his blanket, Mandeler searched for his pack and found it drying with the rest of his clothes.

He came back to the fire side and showed it to Gwenelle saying, "This was given to me by Norwata. She wants you to carry not only her crystal, but the markings as well."

Using his thumbnail he released the sealed lid on the small jar. The pungent smell of the salve made his nose wrinkle but he held it up and mind-spoke: *Norwata had me memorize the pattern of the raptor tattoo. I believe it marks you as part of her sister-hood but there must be more. Please let me try to paint it the way I saw it on her.*

There was a short pause and then Gwenelle nodded. She simply crossed her arms and grasped the bottom of her tunic. As she pulled the garment over her head, Mandeler was struck by the absolute beauty of this woman. She turned and sat cross-legged in front of him. He took the jar in his left hand and put a dab of the cream on his little finger. He closed his eyes for a moment bringing the shape of the twisting raptor back to his mind.

He had become so familiar with these amazing creatures that the subtle differences between the greens and the blacks stood out in bold contrast. The smaller ones were softer in their lines, more rounded at the edges. At first it was just the olive color compared to the almost black of the great ones that was distinctive but the greens had small even teeth unlike the yellow fangs of their larger cousins. Their tiny scales were soft to the touch, much like real skin. Also their intelligent violet eyes and gentle nature set them apart. The blacks were far more powerful but they seemed less independent in their thinking and roles. Their scales were larger and more like armor. They were obviously similar but still very different.

It was an olive green raptor that snaked along Norwata's back. Not sure where he was going to pull his drawing skills from, he placed his finger tip on Gwenelle's shoulder blade. He held it there for a moment hesitating. She sensed something was needed and taking up her amulet she held it in her hand. As she squeezed the stone Mandeler could almost see where he needed to place the salve. He picked up a small twig, using it like a tiny brush, he started the intricate pattern.

Time passed and the sun was just settling on the horizon when he finished the last strokes of the tattoo. He recognized the smell as the same ointment that his elders had used to make his chest patterns. He placed the now empty jar on the ground and looked at his handwork. Gwenelle turned to look over her right shoulder and it was as if the creature turned with her and looked back at Mandeler. A chill ran down his back as their eyes connected. Now she glowed with a green tint and those eyes were as deep as pools of crystal water.

She mind-spoke: *They are with me, the old ones. I can feel their memories.*

She seemed to look through him and she continued: *I can hear the crystals calling and I know why we need them.*

Without waiting for Mandeler, she reached out with her mind to the large green male. Almost at once he reached back to her and soon the air shook with the thundering wingbeats of the mated pair as they gently touched down in front of them, kicking up a shower of fine sand.

Mandeler was on his feet, following Gwenelle, as she quickly mounted Rachaner. He called to Labeena and she came to join him soon after. He caught up with her on the ledge where Gwenelle and Kateena were waiting for them.

Kateena limped towards Gwenelle feeling the excitement of the moment. The young woman reached out and took the little raptor's face in her hands mind-speaking: *I can hear them. I can hear the crystals calling, just like you described them. They sing to us and beckon to me.*

What can you hear? Mandeler interrupted.

I know in my heart what we need to make the exploding powder. Ever since you brought me Norwata's stone and then when you put the raptor on my back, I could hear the special crystals calling to me. Kateena could hear them all along but I could only imagine the tune. They are here, close, and they're the major component in that special exploding powder that Captain Larson showed us. I think the puzzle is starting to reveal itself to us. Oh Mandeler, I feel such hope for our quest.

In the fading light, he could see the tears in her eyes as she spoke passionately about the riddle. Gwenelle did not pause to explain but took him by the hand and led him over the boulders to the narrow slit that was the small lower cave. The entrance was narrow but this time she did not have to pause to let her eyes adjust. As she clutched her amulet the crystal wall began to shimmer with a bright blue light, all the while the air was filled with a tune that her fingers had found on the flute days before. Gwenelle stood letting the throbbing light and sound wash over her.

Gwenelle had not taken the time to dress before she rushed up the mountain. Now standing in this glittering chamber, she turned to look back at him. From Mandeler's place, wedged in the narrow entrance, all he could see was the raptor tattoo as it seemed to flex like a living creature. Gwenelle started to turn and bob to the unheard music. It was a timeless dance that only she could sense. Kateena's head squeezed in beside him and she mind-spoke: *She is dancing with the crystal song.*

The unreality of it all still washed over Mandeler and in this moment he could not imagine how he experienced all that he had to, only to find himself side by side with this dazzling woman.

Gwenelle became aware of Mandeler so she gracefully glided over to him taking his hand. Slowly she drew him near and placed his other hand upon the crystal that lay between her breasts. Just as he had shared images with her before, now he was drawn into her world. There was an explosion of light and sound as he became connected to this moment in time. They danced together in the shimmering light and the music of the crystal song.

Norwata sat quiet in a cross-legged position. It had taken some time but the dreams had come. First they were filled with the dark images of a cave, as a large creature stirring within, but eventually they changed and she could see a young woman stripped to the waist, a green raptor tattoo snaked up her back ending behind the right ear. She danced to unheard music before a wall of shimmering light. She had never seen Gwenelle but she recognized the amber crystal pulsing on her chest. She could almost feel the weight of it on her own breast as it had lain there for decades.

She took in a deep breath and opened her eyes. The injured denzel lay before her, his good eye directed at her. He mind-spoke to her: *Where have you been healer?*

At the end of life it is gratifying to know that you can still do a good turn for your fellow woman and perhaps our races as well.

Alheeza replied: *I would have counted the resetting of my leg as a good turn but if you can help to save our race, I have to admit that it does sound like a good turn.*

The old healer made a choking noise that turned out to be laughter. Through that wrinkled face she smiled broadly at her old friend. *It does me good to spend this time with you.*

Mandeler had removed his tunic and using it as a makeshift sack, they had collected an armful of the glimmering material. He was not sure how long they were in the cave together but when the three of them emerged it was dark. The vibrant little stones had been alive with light within the cave but standing in the moon light, they were as dull as a bag of salt. Without the light and song of the cave, Mandeler was filled with overwhelming doubt. It was like his strength was drained away, leaving an empty shell. How could they possibly do anything that could change the centuries of Raptor predation?

Gwenelle broke into his thoughts: *What is wrong?*

His euphoria within the cave had melted away and he staggered as his world spun in a blur around him. He did not even feel the ground come up as his body collapsed in a heap.

In the Mix

All was dark but he could hear the sounds of water lapping against the hull. There was the familiar smell of the mold that could only be the Sea Quester. Mandeler was snug in the coarse blankets of their bed. He was relieved to be on board Larson's vessel. He moved his arm and it came up against a warm body that turned towards him. Gwenelle wrapped herself around him in that way that only intimates can do.

"You're finally awake. You slept for two days and had all of us worried out of our minds!"

Slowly he traced his fingers around his head and made out the metal shape of the helmet that the elders had given him. Sensing what he was trying to do, Gwenelle continued, "You must have been exhausted from your quest to the Raptor cave. I was so taken up by my gift of Norwata's crystal that I missed how tired you were. I thought if I put you back in the helmet you might finally get the sleep you needed. How do you feel?"

Fine, I think.

He carefully slipped the precious helmet from his head only to meet those intense blue eyes looking back at him. He also felt a warm hand exploring his thigh.

How good do you feel?

When they emerged on the deck, sometime later, they were still grinning and holding hands.

Sea Quester was leaning into a fresh wind, and making good time. Captain Larson stood at the rail, his grey fringe swept back by the wind. At the sight of Mandeler, he strode towards them grinning. Much to Mandeler's surprise he gripped him in a crushing hug, then stepped back saying, "I thought we would never see you again. Imagine flying into the Great Raptors own territory and plucking that skinny denzel of yours out from under their noses. I'll bet they are still raging over that!"

"Ah, well, I can assure you raging is the right word. The folks at Earlsbee are a wee upset too," said Mandeler.

"Now Gwenelle tells me you are planning something bigger. She told me to head to the Smoking Mountain for more of the stinking rock."

"This time she knows more about what we are planning than I do. Apparently I have slept through a great many preparations."

Mandeler turned to look at the woman at his side. She had always been a striking woman, with a great mane of dark hair, and today it streamed out in the wind exposing the raptor tattoo as it snaked around her neck. The amber crystal gleamed at her breast, exposed by the deep V of her billowing blue blouse. She was magnificent.

As he gazed upon her she mind-spoke to the pair of them: *I have been working with the singing crystals and your supplies to see if I can make sense of the puzzle surrounding the exploding powder. Norwata's gift of memories is still very new to me, but it is often vague with moments of clarity and then nothing. I have been experimenting in the galley to see what I can make. It is a little like making a cake with half the recipe.*

Larson broke in, "It has stunk up most of the deck below, but what have you learned?"

Let me show you. She pulled a small pouch from her braided belt and poured the grey lumpy contents onto a shallow dish. *It still needs some time to dry in the sun and then we can put it to the test.* She stroked the grey mixture into a thin layer and patted it with the palm of her hand. *With this wind and the sun reaching its zenith soon, I should think that by the time we have had some lunch it will be time to put it to the test.*

To most, lunch would have been seen as a simple meal with

traveling supplies augmented with fresh roasted leaping gleamer, but to Mandeler it was a feast. He was still so hungry after the ordeal of the past days. Larson wanted to hear all the details of the flight and the encounters with the dark ones. Mandeler would wolf down a few morsels and return to his tale. It was almost like waking from his dreams, telling his strange tale of flight and terror. It sounded more bizarre than the legends the elders used to tell in the dark nights of winter. In the end Larson seemed content with his telling, but it was plain by his furrowed brow that the details had left him worried.

After the meal, they gathered at the rail, watching as Gwenelle scraped the now granular material into a pile. She produced a hand glass and focused the strong sun into a tight beam in the middle of the pile. It fizzed and sputtered, followed by an orange flame that gave off a thick white smoke, which burned their nostrils. Gwenelle's mouth turned down as she studied the scorched plate.

Give me a little more time in the galley and I will see what I can do.

The silence grew, but just as Mandeler was getting ready to say something supportive about Gwenelle's alchemy, there was a green blur, followed by an enormous splash just off the port side. The wind carried the salt spray over the deck, soaking the crew where they stood.

A familiar olive head appeared and a pair of large violet eyes locked onto Mandeler. Labeena mind-spoke to him: *Your floating transport travels so slowly, I thought you might have been farther away by now.*

How did you find me?

A few hands of time ago I felt your presence and I came at once. The sun came and went twice; all the while everything about you was quiet. It was as if you stopped being.

Gwenelle broke in*: I put the dream blocking helmet on him so he could sleep. Mandeler was so tired after the long trip with you that he slept for two sun cycles. I expect it was the helmet that blocked him from you. Were you not tired as well?*

Rachana brought me fresh offerings from the sea and in a sun cycle I felt renewed. Why is it that Mandeler takes two such days to recover?

It was Mandeler that responded: *I am just not as tough as you. I bow to a superior being.* At which point, Mandeler swept one hand into the air while bending at the hips into a deep bow.

If an olive raptor could smile, she did so now. Then she mindspoke: *If you are strong enough there is something you may want to see.*

A Glimpse Ahead

Mandeler was astride Labeena as she pumped with all her might to gain altitude. In their short time as flying partners, they had never climbed above the fluffy afternoon clouds into the blueness that was the sky above. The ship had long since been lost to sight as they flew onward and upward. A deep chill started to seep into every seam of Mandeler's heavy traveling tunic. Even the hood seemed to leak drafts that chilled his ears. If it had not been for the warmth of Labeena he would be frozen stiff.

It seemed like half the day had passed and then Labeena broke the silence: *Can you see it?*

Mandeler was shaken out of his reverie: *Where, what do you mean?*

Straight ahead, do you see the great mountain above the clouds? Today there is no smoke, but often there is.

It took a few moments, but through the haze he could just make out a faint white triangle rising above the scattered clouds. It was hard to see the details and even harder to believe a mountain could be that big. *I think I can make out a single coned shape, is that the smoking mountain?*

Yes.

It must be a great distance ahead. Can you fly that far?

Once a great storm carried my grandsire that way, and he waited for fifteen sun cycles until there was a strong enough wind to carry him all the way back. He was the strongest of our race and none of us has set foot on that rock again.

There was a long silence between them as they flew on. Finally

Mandeler mind-spoke: *What if you were to rest on the Sea Quester and finish the journey the next day? You would be safely out of the water and out of the reach of the long- necked sure-death.*

Again the silence between them grew, and finally Labeena telephathed: *We will need to see how we can fit on the floating thing you call Sea Quester.*

Gwenelle had busied herself with her experiments in the galley the moment Mandeler left. It was funny how there was some sort of connection between them that seemed intangible. Yes, they could mind-speak but if he was within a certain range she could feel his presence. It comforted her just to know where he was.

The work with the exploding powder was vexing. She had these dreams of how the stuff was made, but it was like looking through a steamed up window, for it lacked all detail. The charcoal and the singing crystals were a sure thing, but how to mix them with the sulfur and get it to do more than just burn and stink. On a whim, she decided to make the proportion without thinking. She just poured some of one, then a dash of another, then put the whole thing in a pot with some strong brew to boil.

It took several hands of time to distill the mixture down to a sticky goo, but it had changed the color and something more. She just could not put her finger on it, but it seemed right. She wrung the whole thing out in a cloth and spread it out on a clay baking pan. Even while it was still wet, it had a granular texture unlike anything she had made before. Now she placed the pan in the oven, and kept checking to see when it was dry.

It was late afternoon when Mandeler circled down towards their ship. Gwenelle was already on deck, so he telepathed his plan to her and the crew. He was going to attempt a landing on the stern of Sea Quester while they were under way.

The crew had lowered the large stern sail and put the row boat off the davits where it trailed astern. The ship had slowed under head sails alone and Captain Larson could be seen pacing anxiously next to the mizzen mast, his anxiety telegraphing up through his stiffened body and each rigid step.

Labeena approached just over the water from downwind of the starboard quarter. She had always been so calm and confident when approaching a touch down, but Mandeler could sense an element of tension in her being. All he could do was maintain his contact with her and try to calm himself as well. Just as they were about to hit the ship, she rose abruptly into the air taking several strong strokes of her magnificent wings and touched down delicately on the rail of the vessel. It settled in the water as it took her weight. She brought her wing knuckles down along the deck and if an olive raptor could look relieved, she did.

Mandeler stepped deftly down to the deck where Gwenelle rushed to embrace him. The tall woman looked him straight in the eye mind-speaking: *I think I have it!*

What are you talking about?

The puzzle is solved.

The exploding black powder?

Yes, what do think I am talking about?

She laughed and kissed him on the lips. He tightened his embrace and the kiss lingered.

It was Larson that interrupted, "I hate to break up a homecoming but what news do you have?"

They both started to speak at once, but Mandeler raised his voice saying, "Labeena has taken me far and high to see the mountain that we seek. We might have a plan that could cut our travel time in half."

Gwenelle added, "And I have just finished a fresh batch of powder, and this time I know it will work!"

Mandeler moved into mind-speak and open speech to include Labeena: *If Rachaner and Labeena join us on Sea Quester in two sun cycles we could be close enough to launch a flight to and from the mountain in one day. Using the ship as a base it would help to extend their flying range. It is too far from their island to the smoking mountain, but from the ship the round trip is possible. That is why I wanted to see if Labeena could land onboard.*

"If at the beginning of this voyage you had told me you planned to land and roost a pair of raptors on my very vessel, I would have had you tossed overboard, thinking you were a raving lunatic. But now young master, you have my ship to use as you need," laughed Larson.

Gwenelle telephathed: *My turn.* And from her shoulder satchel she pulled out a wooden plate and a tempered crucible. She went to the downwind rail and started to set up her demonstration. First she poured a small amount of powder into the middle of the plate, and then carefully trickled a small trail of granules along the rail. Then she placed the pot over the plate. Finally Gwenelle took out her glass, and while leaning to the side, she focused the afternoon sun on the far end of the granular trail. It burst into sparkling flame that rushed into the plate. Grey smoke engulfed her, along with an ear splitting concussion. The pot blurred upward and tumbled out of sight above.

It was hard to tell who was more surprised, the astonished men or the trembling raptor. As the small cloud of smoke was swept away with the wind, Gwenelle turned with a smirk: *Can I cook or can I cook?*

As the sun rose above the horizon, Mandeler and Gwenelle watched Labeena wing her way back towards her island. They stood comfortably leaning into each other with his arm around her waist and hers draped casually over his shoulder. He turned to look at her. She was dressed in a blue shimmering blouse that he had never seen before. She had always worn practical clothing, not too bright, coarse and strong. All well suited for the rough time they had getting this far, but he liked the look of this. The vibrant blue matched her eyes and the fine silver swirled about giving the fabric an inner light. Even the rising sun was adding a red highlight to her hair. The way it flowed in the wind made her look regal. Her strong cheekbones added to the strength, but it was the way the dark raptor tattoo came around her neck that was the final touch. She needed no jewelry, she was magnificent. She turned her piercing blue eyes to his, and he felt a chill run down his spine. *What?* she mind-spoke.

You have changed.

And you have not?
Ah, well you have me there.
Come, let's go back to bed.
Without our breakfast?
We can have it later!

Captain Larson had not forgotten what it felt like to have a raging Great black Raptor perched on his vessel bringing death and destruction. The olive raptors were by nature a much different creature, but when Mandeler landed with the strong female on the stern rail yesterday, it had brought back those fearful memories. Mandeler seemed to communicate with it in his silent mind speech, but still the way the ship had lurched and settled into the water did not feel right. Now in two days there was going to be two of them using his boat as a perch for the night. Never in his dreams had he expected to see this.

Or worse yet, he was sailing his precious ship towards that terrible mountain. He had only heard about it from a distant trader but even that had come with tales of foul smelling vapours and a huge mountain that trembled and shook. On the positive side, if Mandeler could fly his creature there it would save the risk of approaching it with his ship. Maybe this was all for the best.

The Queen of the Great Raptors could not settle. Her scaly shoulder abraded the cave wall while her sharp claws dug into the living rock, scattering her victims' bones as she turned and turned, trying to find comfort. There would never be comfort as long as 'the one' was alive. Ever since the small one had taunted her by flying a hideous green raptor so close to their sanctuary, she could not rest.

So far, her every attempt to snatch him had been thwarted. But that was about to change. She could feel his proximity, even at this great distance and he was starting to plot her death. Unimaginable, how could something so puny cause her harm, but she felt it. She must move quickly, if she was to harvest his juices before the others sensed his danger.

Mandeler awoke covered in sweat. It had been days since he had a dream of connection with the Queen but this was unsettling. She knew he was planning something and she had plans herself, but he did not know the details. A feeling of deep foreboding washed over him and he dreaded the next step. None of this was going to be easy. How was one young man supposed to take on all of the Great Raptors and change history? It couldn't be done!

He felt a hand caress his back and then she was in touch with his mind: *You have me. You are not alone against this wicked thing. We are together and we have an edge, I can feel it. That is why Norwata sent me this stone. I am here to help guide your quest. Yes, it will be difficult but we have hope.*

Two days had passed since the dream cycle and Mandeler had seemed to settle a little but Gwenelle worried constantly about their task. Her amber stone brought comfort and in some way their journey to the Smoking Mountain was pivotal.

She had spent much of her time sitting on the foredeck fingering her amulet. There were faint sensations, but nothing like the bursts of insight mixed with the ancestral memories, that led to her breakthrough with the exploding powder. Still she sat cross-legged feeling the warmth of the amber stone. How could she have lived without this remarkable thing? What a gift it had been, and she had never even met her benefactor.

She did not feel him coming, so Mandeler's light touch made her jump.

He telephathed: *I am sorry, I did not mean to scare you.*

You never scare me anymore. Your hands were cold is all.

I've been working the leather straps that I plan to use on the greens to hold our packs better. Sea water seems to help shape them, and my hands must still be cold.

She clasped his hands: *Tell me about Norwata again. I want to hear you speak of her.*

As I have said, she was old with wrinkles upon wrinkles and not too clean, I am afraid to say. She had a deep respect from her people that seemed unshakable, even though she was not much bigger than a child. It was like she saw right through me as I entered the hall. I don't think there were any other mind-speakers in her village, for she welcomed me in our way of speaking right away. As for the raptor tattoo, I did not see any hint of it when we met because of all the layers of shawls and her long grey hair. There seemed to be a tremor about her but when she touched me, her hand was steady. Alheeza had known her from long ago, and she proved to be an experienced healer, for she set his leg with great skill. For me, the most moving part was her gift of the stone to you and her insights into the dark ones and myself. She had such a depth of insight. I can't image acquiring that amount of knowledge in a lifetime.

Was she kind?

Oh my yes. Through those watery eyes there was such understanding.

Was she …dying?

I believe so.

A silence hung in the air.

Finally Gwenelle mind-spoke: *What now?*

I can feel Labeena and Rachaner approaching. They will be here very soon.

She beamed at him with delight and jumped up. As they made their way to the rail small dots on the horizon could be seen. Soon the dots had become raptors, and not long after that they had landed in the water next to the ship. Larson had stalled the vessel sideways to the wind to allow the pair to come closer.

Olive raptors could innovate, and this time they clasped hold of the stern rail on each side of the transom, pulling themselves smoothly onto the deck. It was not as dramatic as the stall landing Labeena had made days before, but it let the ship settle gently in the water. Even Larson looked relieved at the easy transition to a raptor's roost.

The Smoking Mountain

In the predawn, the leader of the olive raptors felt Mandeler's restlessness in the cabin below. Labeena and Rachaner had spent the night on the back deck of Sea Quester with their tails coiled on deck and their necks turned to let their heads rest on their dark green backs. They slept close to each other, digesting the feast of red fins from the previous afternoon. Now to the untrained eye they looked asleep but they were fully awake. As Mandeler stirred, he sensed their readiness.

He and Gwenelle were intertwined beneath the coarse blankets, skin to skin and amulet to amulet. They too had been awake for some time waiting for the first hint of dawn. Their gear had been prepared in the days before, and was stacked carefully next to the door. She kissed him tenderly on the lips: *It is time isn't it?*

Yes.

He reached up and shook a glow globe, sparking the inhabitants within to light. It was going to be a long flight and they each took a turn in the ship's head before pulling on their layers of warm travelling clothes.

As they pulled on the last of their packs and pouches, they shared a handful of the stringent acava berries that would sustain them for the first part of their trip. Wordlessly they headed for the companionway.

Larson had been on deck all night, nursing his precious ship along in the dwindling breeze. He had clever ropes strung below deck to handle the rudder so that the raptors would not be disturbed in their narrow roost. He sat in the companionway nudging the steering bar that operated the rudder. Larson rose stiffly from his vigil when he heard the young people mount the steps beneath him. The sky was showing the first purple glow of the coming day as the two silhouettes stepped over his steering rig and onto the deck.

Mandeler turned towards him, “Captain Larson, please turn the ship beam on the wind for our departure.”

The big female was the first to uncoil to face the wind. In silence, the young man swung upon her neck wrapping his arms and legs about her. She stepped to the rail, reached out with her neck and spread the wide leathery wings. The ship lurched as she pushed off reaching into the air with her powerful wings. Larson could hear the heavy wing strokes of the departing raptor. The sounds of her wing tips hitting the water soon were replaced with the rising silhouette of the green raptor and her young rider.

In a couple of breaths of time, Gwenelle astride the other raptor, pushed off in pursuit. In the predawn, they were soon lost from sight. Larson stood on the rolling deck of his ship. He had been witness to many departures in his sailing career. These young people had come aboard only weeks before, bringing with them the terrors and wonders of the raptor’s world. He had become entwined in their quest and now wondered if he would ever see them again.

It was barely dawn, the eastern sky was just aglow but the stars were still out in the west. A light haze seemed to obscure details near the horizon, but Gwenelle could see the pattern of waves below picking up the new dawn. It was exhilarating to feel the throb of her powerful companion climbing with each stroke to catch up with the others. Ahead Mandeler and Labeena were mere silhouettes on the brightening sky.

It had been some time since she had flown with Rachaner, and she felt the exhilaration as he pumped, climbing after his mate. Mandeler had made the long flight inland to the Great Raptor’s nest, but she had never done more than a turn or two around the green’s island. It was exciting, although she also felt trepidation about their task and destination. Perhaps if she ate a few more mouths full of food, her stomach might settle. She reached down for a filet of the dried gleamer they brought to supplement the acava berries. Its rich flavor filled her mouth and it was satisfying. A sip from her water skin washed it down and she felt more settled. As they climbed the morning chill intensified, making it necessary to tighten her hood and tuck in her cuffs. The warm raptor felt comforting as she pressed close to his neck. So she fell into the rhythm of the day's flight.

Not long after takeoff, Rachaner had exerted himself to fall in behind his mate. He flew just below and to the side of her flight path. They had known through the generations that this allowed two or more raptors to conserve their energy on a long flight. Soon it would be his turn to lead and give Labeena a much needed break. They flew on into the brightening day.

This is what Mandeler needed, action! Ever since his last dream of the tormented Queen, he could not settle but now he was mounted upon Labeena and they climbed into a new day. The dim haze of the morning gave way to a spectacular sunrise. Its first rays lit the distant side of the Smoking Mountain, turning it red. As he watched, the colors turned from emerald to gold and finally a brilliant white. In a few hands of time they would see it up close. Then it would be time to seek out the burning stones and collect enough to make their exploding powder. The morning fear that had lingered in his heart was giving way to hope.

As before, Labeena was climbing higher, she mind-spoke to him: *There are many unknowns about our trip today and if I fly higher we might be able to get a better view over the horizon. I sense some hidden danger but cannot make any sense of what it might be.*

You have never told me about sensing hidden danger before!

I did not feel them. Also on those flights I relied upon your memories and insights to guide us. Today, I only have what stories have been passed down from the women that have gone before me, but there is an uneasiness that I cannot explain.

I trust your feelings. I suppose all we can do is keep our eyes open, but surely there are no Great Raptors on the mountain ahead.

I did not say that. All I know is something feels wrong this morning.

As this conversation came to a close, Gwenelle urged her mount to pull up parallel to the lead raptor. She mind-spoke: *I got that. At first I thought it was just the excitement of the flight, but I can sense a stirring within.*

She had assumed the smooth flight posture where her body clung tight to the olive raptor's neck. Carefully she reached inside her tunic and clasped the amber crystal. All she could feel was the deep rumbling from somewhere far ahead. It was only a feeling with no clarity at all. Time passed, but the distant tremor did not resolve itself. Finally she telepathed: *I don't know, there is some deep stirring in the ground ahead but I cannot tell what is happening.*

Rachaner moved forward to take his turn in the lead. They flew on in silence. To know that both Gwenelle and Labeena were unsettled bothered Mandeler very much. It seemed to take even longer for the distant mountain to draw near. What could it be that was causing their discomfort?

The sun was approaching its zenith when the flight of raptors drew near the great smoking mountain. Today it was not smoking at all. The apex of the silent giant simply shimmered with its fresh crown of snow. A shudder ran down Mandeler's spine.

He mind-spoke to the group: *What now, we're nearly at our destination and how do we find the burning stones?*

All I know is that we're getting closer all the time, so I suggest we just fly around it to see how it feels. Gwenelle responded.

It took another span of time for the group to fly part way around the immense peak. What greeted their eyes was not an expanse of ocean behind the sleeping giant, but two more mountains, each progressively smaller. They were cone shaped too with peaks that were chopped off and the last one had a concave crater.

As they came into view Gwenelle shrieked, "It's on the little one!" *Oh Great Azimov, I can feel it! Somewhere near the top!*

The sun was quite high in the sky as Gwenelle led them down to land on the crater rim of the last mountain. Jets of steam rose from within and the air stunk like burning stone. The olive raptors fidgeted as the young couple pulled on their gear. Gwenelle picked her way through the rubble telepathing: *It think it is just over the edge. It should be a short climb down to gather our precious rock and quick as ever, climb back up.*

If you think so, let's do it.

Labeena mind-spoke: *We will circle above the stink until you are ready to return.*

The olive raptors faced the sea breeze. Each one pressed down with their wing knuckles to move their center of balance back onto their short back legs. The wings unfolded and they took to the air.

Mandeler and Gwenelle stood side by side, with their backs to the sea, looking down into the wide rocky depression with intermittent plumes of steam coming from hidden fissures below. It looked like a wasteland where nothing could ever live. As they stood there a tremor shook the ridge. It was not strong, but the pair felt a shaking come up through the rock and then it was gone.

Mandeler telephathed: *What was that?*

I don't know, but it's gone now. Let's get down this slope and find our burning stone.

Quickly Gwenelle led the way over the ledge, picking her way down through the bulging nodes of black stone. It was steep but the footing was good. The rock seemed warm to touch, even at this altitude. Gwenelle saw the yellow rock protruding ahead. It was thrilling to see the bright yellow stone oozing out of the rock wall like a small frozen waterfall.

She reached out a hand to the precious outcrop. It felt smooth to the touch. She pushed on a corner of it but nothing happened. As she stepped back to ponder the situation, Mandeler leaned forward with a black rock in hand. Using it like a hammer he pounded down on the same protrusion. "Clack!" A chunk the size of her hand clipped neatly off the edge of the outflow.

Very nicely done, now just keep it up and we'll have our packs filled in no time.

That is just what I had in mind. He responded.

She stepped back to give him more room to swing the hammer stone. In no time, Mandeler was making real progress chipping hunks of sulfur and tossing the pieces back to her. She loaded them into their bags and was almost done when a cloud of foul smelling gas crept up the slope. It burned her eyes and made her gag. Gwenelle coughed and gasped in the swirling stench. As she reached for Mandeler, the sky seemed to spin in a yellow mist and then everything went dark.

Mandeler was wheeling his hammer stone while standing in front of the crouching Gwenelle when he felt her fingers clutch at his waist. In that moment, he was enveloped in the stinking cloud himself. The gas bit at his eyes, nose and mouth. He turned crying out, “No! No! This can’t be!” *No! No! This can’t be”*

Holding the rest of his breath he crouched to shake Gwenelle. She did not respond!

Oh, Great Azimov, what am I going to do now!

All he managed was to draw Gwenelle’s limp body to him. His lungs screamed for fresh air, but with the acid fumes he dared not breathe. Just as his vision started to darken around the edges, the air boomed with the thundering stokes of a descending raptor. The downwash from Labeena’s wings swept the foul cloud aside, and Mandeler drew in a great lung full of clear air.

Moments later Rachaner came swooping over bringing another wash of clean air from above.

Gwenelle was a ghastly grey with very shallow breath. Pushing aside their packs, he slid an arm under her waist and hoisted her headfirst over his shoulder. Clasping her thighs firmly he started to mount the rugged wall. Soon his legs burned with the added weight, as he mounted the treacherous path to the summit. Time stood still as he labored up the steep incline but finally he broke over the edge to be greeted by a cool ocean breeze. Mandeler dropped to his knees, rolling Gwenelle gently onto an open part of the rough ground. He pulled off his heavy tunic, rolling it into a crude pillow, and placed it under her head. Kneeling beside his unconscious partner, he picked up her hand and studied her face. Her once rosy lips were now thin and grey and she was barely breathing.

Oh, Gwenelle!

Fear and sorrow were overwhelming him. Mandeler had faced

so many tests since leaving the estate, but how could this be happening? He was always able to keep a clear head through all the troubles, but now his throat tightened and he could feel tears welling up. All hope seemed to be draining away from him. He sat there, despair taking hold. He did not even hear the raptors land nearby.

Labeena's warm snout pressed on his shoulder. She telepathed: *You can help her. Just let your heart lead the way.*

Without being aware of why he was doing it, he let go of her hand and reached under her tunic to clasp the amulet between her breasts. The warm crystal seemed to come alive in his hand. With his other hand he reached into his shirt to clasp his own crystal. In that moment he was connected to Gwenelle. Suddenly, he felt their spirits soar some distance above the lip of the rock strewn crater. Below was a blond young man with sinewy arms crouching over a tall, slim, dark haired woman clad in men's pants.

She spoke wordlessly to him: *Mandeler my dear, you plucked me out of there just in time. My spirit was making ready to leave, but there is still time to bring me back.*

How? He seemed to ask.

Put aside your sorrow, and remember your healing hand with the crystal. As Labeena said, once you still your heart, you will remember how to heal me.

In that moment he was back on the ground looking down at her, still clasping their amulets. He took a deep breath and closed his eyes. Still holding his own amulet, he slid his hand down onto the bare skin of Gwenelle's abdomen just below the heart. Taking a deep lung full of air, he willed his breath into her. She responded with a deep intake of air. Every time he took a deep breath, she followed, with his hand gently rising and falling with the deepening breaths.

Nice work, he heard. Looking up he met her startling blue eyes looking back at him. They were still rimmed with red but she was definitely awake.

I thought I had lost you.

Not this time big boy, but it was a near thing just the same. No one else could have pulled me back from that distant place.

How do you feel?

Like I tried breathing fire and it still burns…

As she drew the next breath, it provoked a round of coughing so severe that she drew up her knees and rolled to her side. Finally the hacking subsided and Gwenelle drew in shallow lungs full of air. It provoked no further coughing, and she lay there catching her breath.

Mandeler searched his side pack and was rewarded with a small rind of copeander fruit. He mind-spoke: *Chew this, and you will feel stronger soon.*

As he watched her chew the tough piece of dried healing fruit, color seemed to return to her face. She was able to sit up and take in her surroundings again.

He mind-spoke: *I need to get you down to the beach because the air is thicker down there and you should breathe a little easier.*

It took a little longer, but he helped Gwenelle onto Rachaner's shoulders. As a precaution, Mandeler took a short length of cord from his side pouch and tied a safety line around the raptor's neck connecting it to Gwenelle's ankles. Then he handed her the end of the line saying, "Once you land on the beach, just pull the end of this to set yourself free. Otherwise there is no way you can fall from his back."

He reached up to kiss her, then turned back towards the lip of the crater.

"Aren't you coming too?"

"I'll just get our packs and then join you. After all it was the burning stones that we came for."

Rain of Terror

It was late afternoon when the young couple took inventory of their situation on the black sand beach. They had taken time to eat some traveling food and look over their collection of burning stones. Gwenelle picked through them, selecting the purest of color, while discarding the rest. It made for one firm travel pack of pure sulfur. She was still pale with red rimmed eyes, but her spirits were good although she still had a rasping cough.

Labeena telepathed: *It will be very late before we reach the floating craft. If Gwenelle can manage we must hurry now.*

They were standing by the raptors, loading their gear over their necks when the whole beach seemed to shake all over. They staggered as the black sand shifted under foot. Then everything was still.

Mandeler mind-spoke: *I don't like that.*

Labeena and Gwenelle seemed to answer as one: *This is part of the greater fear we sensed.*

The ground convulsed again, this time so violently that they lost their footing, throwing the travelers against the staggering raptors.

It was Labeena this time: *The mountain, look what is happening to the mountain!*

About a quarter of the way up the great cone, the side of the peak was starting to bulge. The once pristine white crown seemed to dissolve into a mottled grey. Unbelievably, the tip and side exploded outward, filling the sky with an expanding black cloud. From beneath it the mountain top dissolved, racing towards the ocean in a great avalanche of stone. In a matter of breaths the roar of the detonation hit them with deafening force.

As they staggered on the beach, Labeena insisted: *We leave now!*

Mandeler pushed Gwenelle onto Rachaner's shoulders. The big green arched his back, spreading his wings, and he beat down driving them out over the water.

Mandeler caught a quick look over his shoulder as he vaulted onto Labeena. As his green thrust forward, following her mate, he saw the ocean convulse as a huge part of the mountain hit the sea. It raised a wave that looked gigantic even at this distance. He leaned even farther forward, willing his flying companion on as fast as she could fly.

He kept looking over his shoulder in disbelief. At one moment it had all been quiet and then the Abyss of Azimov had gaped wide, spewing black billowing smoke into the sky. It was expanding and climbing higher as he watched. It was spreading so fast that day was turning into night.

Mandeler was tingling with the adrenal rush of their departure. Labeena was following Rachaner, at his wing tip, just clearing the waves. It was their fastest and most efficient way to fly. Tears streamed from his face as they raced on in the growing gloom.

He could not resist one more glance over his shoulder. *By the Sacred Fire! Climb, climb hard before we are crushed by the wave!*

He could feel his body pressed against Labeena as she pulled abruptly into a steep climb, pumping harder than he had ever felt. Just before she stalled in flight, the steep wall of water rushed under them so fast that it made it look as if the raptors were flying in reverse.

How could it get worse, Mandeler thought? Then small stones started to fall from the darkening sky. They landed in the sea around them. Some bounced off Labeena but when one hit him in the shoulder, he was surprised it did not hurt more. They must be very light, more like being hit by a herman nut. Even so, they could do real damage if they hit the eyes.

Labeena telepathed: *Put your head down and shut your eyes.* As she said this, she flinched from an impact on her eye ridge.

Moments later a volcanic stone hit him on the top of his head.

Raptor Dung that hurts!

Labeena responded: *Please do not take our names in vain.*

Sorry.

Mandeler put his hand under his hood and it came away sticky and red.

Gwenelle, are you alright? He asked.

If you mean is it alright that I am getting beaten up, yes I am alright!

He felt his mount quicken her pace once again, as she veered north east towards the light. As she strained onward, the rain of small stones began to dwindle. Soon they were flying over calm water, with the cloud behind them. Labeena altered the course one last time in the direction of the ship.

Gwenelle how are you now?

A few more glancing blows, but I'll be fine.

And everyone else?

Rachaner telepathed: *Nothing that will keep me from flying on.*

He started to relax and then it hit him that the Sea Quester would be facing that wave, and soon.

Gwenelle, I have to reach Captain Larson before that crushing wave hits him unaware.

But we are such a long way away.

He thought for a moment and then replied: *You know how sometimes you can sense me at a distance. I'll have to try reaching him that way.*

Focusing inward while clasping his amulet, Mandeler pictured Larson's rugged face with its fringe of grey hair. He could not tell where he was for sure but he repeated over and over in his mind the message:

WAVE! BIG WAVE!!

WAVE! BIG WAVE!!

WAVE! BIG WAVE!!

Then all was silent. He had not expected Larson to reply, he couldn't, but still he wished he knew if the message got through.

Finally he asked Labeena: *Do you need me to help you find the Sea Quester?*

Perhaps, I think I can get us close, but then it is up to you.

The flight of raptors had long since returned to fly just above the waves. They had outdistanced the black cloud filling the sky behind them, and now the real night was about to descend on them. Gwenelle was just barely hanging on, and it was only with Rachaner's great care that she rode easily on his shoulders, draped along his neck. Everyone had cuts and scrapes from the stone shower, but things were growing critical as the exhausted raptors pressed on towards the little ship. Their olive mounts had been flying most of the day with little rest, no food and there were limits to their endurance. Mandeler knew all this but what lay ahead was the final challenge of the day, trying to find the Sea Quester in the full dark. What if Larson had not made it through the giant wave. Could they survive a night in the open sea?

Mandeler marked their time flying in the dark by how far the moon, Izaic, had climbed into the heavens. It must have been well before midnight when he first sensed life on the Sea Quester.

A small dot of light appeared on the horizon. Except for the smaller moon and the star field, this was the only light to be seen. Before long the dark shape of Sea Quester could be seen on the rippling water.

Mandeler telepathed: *Captain Larson, we have returned. Prepare for our boarding.*

Of course Larson could not reply in kind, and it was left to the company to approach the ship as best they could. Labeena took the lead, coming in low and slow on the downwind side just to have a look. The little ship had turned broadside to the breeze and seemed to be dropping sail. As they passed the stern rail a man hoisted a glow globe, shouted and waved a greeting. Behind him the crew appeared to be hauling in the mizzen sail. It was far too dark to land on board so they both circled until the boat stopped moving and they splashed down nearby.

"Mandeler and Gwenelle are you alright?" came Larson's distinct voice.

"I think so!"

*Mandeler, I don't think I can swim…*Gwenelle added weakly.

"Gwenelle will need some help to get up on deck though." He shouted.

Several more glow globes appeared as the rest of the crew came to the rail. Birdard and Allenz stood on either side of Captain Larson, watching the foursome in the water.

In the dim light Rachaner swam to the edge of the ship with Gwenelle still clinging to his back. His wing knuckles slipped from the water to grasp the rail. As he held tight the ship healed towards him. Despite his fatigue, Rachaner levered himself up the side of the hull, as the crew quickly scrambled out of his way. He paused with his shoulder clear of the rail and mind-spoke: *Tell them to come fetch you off my back little one.*

"It's OK, he will stay still while you come and get me." She said weakly.

Birdard and Allenz advanced slowly, and then gently lifted Gwenelle from her riding perch on the olive raptor's back. She could not stand on her own, so they carried her to the far side of the deck.

"Get the pack draped over his neck too."

Birdard slowly circled Rachaner and finally got up the courage to pluck the double pack from the green's neck.

Rachaner withdrew, allowing Labeena to approach. She unloaded Mandeler and his gear in much the same way. He too was so tired that standing was almost impossible. When he was safely away, Labeena used the last of her strength to hoist herself onto the deck. The humans went forward to make room for Rachaner to mount the deck from the opposite side. Soon the large pair were coiled on deck with eyes closed.

Captain Larson directed the men to take Gwenelle down to his cabin. A wobbly Mandeler followed behind.

Recovery at Sea

"Don't you two look a sight? Great Azimov but I was worried when we saw that mountain explode. Then the funniest thing happened, it was like a little voice had told me to watch out, like there was a storm or something coming!" Captain Larson had been talking non-stop as his visitors settled into his cabin.

Gwenelle lay collapsed on Larson's bunk, Mandeler propped at her side. They both looked like victims of a brawl. The Captain rummaged in his trunk pulling out a nearly full bottle of orange liquid. He quickly splashed two little glasses full, handing them to the young couple. "Drink this, it'll perk yah right up!" he said, while taking a swig from the bottle.

Mandeler quickly took a gulp that blazed all the way down his throat. Before he could warn Gwenelle, she took a sip of the potent liquor. It exploded from her mouth, spraying Larson and provoked a round of coughing. Mandeler took the glass away and held her until the spasms subsided.

Then he said, "I am sure this was meant to help but I don't think Gwenelle is strong enough to handle it yet."

"I can see that now," said the dripping Captain.

"Can you boil some hot water so I can make a healing tea for Gwenelle?"

"By all means!" said Larson, as he dabbed at his face with a grey towel.

Mandeler went out to get his healing chest from their cabin while Larson set about getting his little stove chugging for tea.

When the young man came back, he had a handful of long dried leaves and a crucible of salve. He dropped the purple leaves into the pot then popped the lid off the salve saying, "Can I have that little towel and some water to clean her up?"

Sitting on the edge of the bunk, he started sponging off the crusted blood, then dabbed the salve on the multitude of little cuts that covered her face and arms. It must have been soothing because she visibly relaxed. She was probably bruised under the tunic but that could wait until later. Larson handed a cup of the steaming tea to Mandeler and he helped her to sip it slowly. She was soon asleep, so he covered her and took away the nearest glow globe to darken that side of the cabin.

As Mandeler settled into a chair opposite Larson, the older man handed him a warm wet towel saying, "You don't look any better than she did, use this."

He buried his face in the towel. It was heavenly to feel the warm moisture penetrate his punished skin. He worked it up to his scalp and that is when he found the wound in his hairline. It had hurt like blazes when it happened, but then he forgot all about it. When he took the towel away, it was stained with old and new blood.

Larson said, "With all that blood on your face, you looked like someone tried to kill you and failed. Let me put a little of that special salve on the cuts for you."

As he dabbed the ointment on gently he said, "If I had not heard that little voice warning me, the ship would have been lost. As it was we got the sails down and a loop of line out the stern. Then a wave, the likes I've never seen before, came rushin' upon us. If we hadn't been facing away, as if a storm was coming, we would have been pitch-poled head over heels. We ran down the face of it, dragging that great loop of line to break our speed. I'll tell you, it scared the tar out of us all. I didn't know the ship would run that fast down a cliff of water. When it finally broke over us, I was tied to the wheel and all the hatches were tied fast. It swept over the deck and I thought my lungs would burst and then we broke free to the surface. Anyway, we were putting things to right when dark fell but we still had no idea if we would ever see you again." He paused for breath, "And then you were there on those big flyers of yours."

The Captain stared at Mandeler for a while then said, "What caused all these cuts anyway?"

“Stones that fell out of the sky after the mountain exploded. It was like a summer storm, you know the ones with the big drops that start to land here and there, except these weren’t water but little rocks. Kind of light, like hard bread that has been left to dry, but they still hurt as we flew into them.”

They sat in silence for a while then Mandeler added, “There is more.” He went on to fill Larson in on the poisonous cloud, Gwenelle’s close call with death, their rescue and witnessing the eruption with its catastrophic consequences.

“Raptor dung that is one hell of a day!” the captain said.

Mandeler sat quietly on his chair while the captain took out some ground herman nuts and dried fruit. On the same little stove he brewed up a passable porridge, much like breakfast at the estate. With a warm bowl in his hand, Mandeler spooned the hearty gruel into his mouth, thinking he had never tasted better. When it was gone, he looked at Gwenelle knowing that she should not be moved until morning. He slipped into mind-speak: *Can I leave her here tonight?*

“I was going on deck to keep watch myself. You can take a blanket and curl up anywhere you like. I’ll wake you at dawn,” replied Larson as he strode from the cabin.

Sleep came quickly.

She was flying high in the dark sky. No other Great Raptors flew at her wing. The huntress knew this area for she had hunted the mountains, valleys and shores time and time again. There was plenty of prey and she could still taste the night’s kill on her pallet, a hump-backed swamp bellower. It was a good feed. She would not have to kill again for another week or more. These were her rich lands for as far as she could fly, and she could fly a great distance.

It had been fifteen season cycles since she was exiled from the colony, no more than a fledgling. Her guardian had raised her to hunt and care for herself but there never was contact with the colony again. The guardian had died a few sun cycles ago and she had been alone since. There was no one left to communicate with, no teacher, no friend, and no enemies. She had been instructed never to cross the narrow sea, stay in her territory and grow to maturity. A day would come when she would be called to a greater need, but she had no idea what the call would be or how it would sound.

Mandeler bolted awake. He had no idea what time of day it was, it was still dark and he had forgotten to put the dream-free helmet on.

He sat there breathing hard, damp with the familiar sweat of his dream cycles, but this was different. This was a creature he had never felt before. She was one of the Great Ones but she felt different. Then it dawned on him, he had felt the anguish and torment of the Queen, as well as sensing the presence of many of the individual male hunters, but this was the first female other than the Queen that he felt. She was different, much different and somewhere apart from the main cave and the terrible Raptor Queen. Not for the first time he wished Alheeza was there to talk with so he could try to figure his way through the puzzle.

He finally fell back into fitful sleep.

The Queen's Wrath

Gwenelle woke up entwined in Mandeler's arms. He was still asleep with the dream-free helmet snuggly over his brow. In the dim morning light of the cabin she could see the little cuts on his face scabbed over, the swelling all but gone. If she did not move, nothing hurt. Thanks to the purple tea her lungs were healing nicely. It had been four days since the olive raptors had returned to their island. After their departure, she had spent some time in the galley working with her collection of burning stones, charcoal and the singing crystals. She had carefully followed the recipe that she had made the last time and before long she had some grey mash ready for drying. In the days that followed she had grown stronger and the work in the galley yielded a couple of large crocks of dry granular black exploding powder. She still had a big problem to solve, how to set it off at a distance so that she and Mandeler could avoid danger.

Mandeler shifted as if finding a more comfortable angle to sleep but his hand started to caress her back. She kissed him knowing there would be no more sleep this morning.

Later that morning Gwenelle was sitting in the sun puzzling through her problems. During the head long dash to leave the erupting island, she had dropped their flingers on the beach. It was not until they took inventory that the precious weapons were missed. Now she needed to focus on what was at hand, but a school of little gleamers was leaping from the waves by the hundreds. As they moved on into the distance she found that she was playing with a loose thread on her heavy tunic. Looking down a thought came to her. She jumped up and went back to their cabin. Gwenelle found what she was looking for, her old baggy sweater. With a little persistence she loosened a length of the soft twine, and then she went back to the galley. She took a handful of the powder and softened it in some spirits. The twine was soaked with the thin paste and hung up to dry.

She found Mandeler sitting on the foredeck, looking into the distance. *Do you have any of your fire-sticks left?* She mind-spoke as she leaned over wrapping her arms around his neck.

I have exactly three left but they got wet and I don't know if they still work.

Can I have them?

Sure.

The Great Queen brooded in her cave. Something unseen had crept from the north, just a smudge at first but within a day the sky was blotted out with heavy black clouds. Fine dark dust had started to fall the day after that. Her best hunters skulked within the cave peering out at these strange happenings. All night she could think of nothing except ways to find and kill the one, that puny little creature that had taunted her and brought death to some of her best.

Sunrise only brought a dim glow through the darkness. Day had been turned into night. She thrashed about her cave, her bulk scraping the raw stone as bones crunched under foot. She had been entombed within these walls since before the arrival of these scrawny creatures. Her body ached with the need to bring her eggs forth, but she still needed one more infusion of rich telepathic blood to complete the cycle. The one could do it, but he was not the only choice. He must die just so she could be rid of his threat. She must act now in a bold strike across the sea. The new darkness would give her hunters the extra range they needed for a surprise attack. It must be now! Kill him or die trying.

Gwenelle placed the length of enriched twine into the little dish of powder. She carefully put a small bowl over it and started walking backwards, trailing out a length of the twine hand-over-hand. The sun was now brightening the sky, so she took out her glass and focused a beam on the twine. In just a few breaths it caught fire and flared into life. It snapped and sparked its way across the deck to the dish where it blasted the bowl into the air with a sharp bang and puff of smoke.

She turned with a grin to look upon the viewers. Birdard and Allenz were open mouthed with surprise, Larson smiled but Mandeler had slumped onto the deck just as pale as if he had seen the dead rise. Alarmed, she telepathed: *What is it?*

The Queen, she is sending a raid upon us.

How can she, we are days out to sea and they can't make the round trip this far out.

It's the volcano, it has brought night to the day and they can fly where they could not before.

She went to kneel next to Mandeler mind-speaking: *This changes everything. We were supposed to make a surprise attack on them but now what do we do?*

I haven't got a plan yet. Let me think.

"What is it?" Larson asked.

Gwenelle looked up and answered, "There is an attack coming and we have to prepare as best we can."

The new leader of the hunting pack squinted trying to keep the gritty dust out of his eyes but they still burned making it hard to see ahead. His Queen had sent all of them forth under the darkness of the black cloud, it should have been late morning with full sun but at best it was twilight. With this extended night time, his pack could range far out to sea, searching for the one. The orders had been clear. Try to retrieve the one but failing that make sure he was dead. As for him and his hunters, they were to succeed or die trying. There was no second chance, this must work.

Captain Larson was sweating, as he worked alongside his crew to rig extra support lines to the two masts. He had been toiling frantically since the warning about the Great Raptor attack had come through. From his experience with these two, he knew this was no false warning. The worst of his fears was going to arrive after dark. Not for the first time he thought he should never have left Portside with its selection of handy pubs.

He glanced over the rail, noting the changing color of the horizon. In his haste to strengthen Sea Quester's rigging, he had not noticed the purple haze climbing into the northern sky. That alone would have been a bad omen, but weather was the least of his worries now.

Gwenelle and Mandeler had discussed in detail what they could do together to hold off a determined assault by the night marauders. She knew from his stories of Earlsbee, that if they were to immerse themselves in the cold water they might avoid detection. There had been two reasons for not taking that as the first choice. One was that the crew were scared to get in the water and second, Gwenelle had felt another threat approaching. She could not sense clearly what it was, but going in the water would be suicidal. In the end she had taken on the task of making two flare pots that would burn brightly on the deck. Hopefully the light from these would hinder the approaching Raptors. Her hands shook as she poured a mixture of oil and singing crystals into the heavy crockery pots. They were lashed down by their handles and would not shift on deck, no matter how much the ship heeled. She paused to check her work. All looked in order so she stepped back and reached for her amulet. Just like with the Smoking Mountain she began to feel some deep foreboding about the pending encounter. She was sure the flare pots would make a good strong light but there was something else, some unseen threat coming. She placed the fiber lid in place and turned to go below.

Try as she might, she could not make sense of her foreboding. A sense of urgency came over her so she telepathed Mandeler: *I am going to repack all of our essential supplies in case we survive the night. I don't want to forget anything else.*

Good plan.

Mandeler had taken action soon after he sensed the pending attack. The obvious thing was to change course directly away from the threat, increasing the distance from the intruders. Once more the crew started to reinforce the ships standing rigging. He thought the best defense tonight would be to pull down sail, lash the tiller and send all below. Without his flinger there would be no heroic stance on the deck.

He drew his amulet, closed his eyes, searching with his senses for any trace of the hunters. A few breaths later he could feel the rhythm of their coordinated wingbeats far off. It would soon be sunset. They were still flying under the cover of the black cloud off to the south west. There was a solemn determination about this group. It did not bode well.

As any good captain would do, Larson made sure his crew had a stomach full of warm food before things turned bad. Mandeler and Gwenelle had eaten as much as their nervous stomachs would allow. The next meal was very much an uncertainty.

They sat cross-legged facing each other on their cabin bunk, amulets in hand. There were no words left, just that uneasiness that comes from knowing real danger approaches. Wordlessly they brought their foreheads together, feeling a better connection.

Finally Gwenelle mind-spoke: *There is something else sinister approaching. It's not like the mountain. This time I feel another presence coming our way and it is not a good one.*

I feel it too.

Oh raptor dung!

I'll second that…

They sat there for some time just touching foreheads. Then they felt the ship heel from the first gusts of wind. It was not long before the ship creaked and groaned as it strained with the rising waves.

Time for the foul weather gear: Mandeler telepathed.

As they got dressed Mandeler tried to estimate how far the hunting pack still had to fly to reach them and when they might arrive. He could not be sure, but the feelings were growing stronger.

On deck it was full dark with just a single glow globe illuminating the mizzen mast. Birdard was just lacing in the last storm reef on the sail. From the whistling in the rigging and the salt spray in the air, Mandeler knew this was already a gale. Captain Larson waved him over to the tiller.

"How much time do we have before they get here?" the captain shouted.

"My best guess, a few hands of time. What about this storm?"

"The storm we can handle, the Raptors I could do without."

"Me too!"

Larson turned to Gwenelle who had just joined them. "Can you get those flare pots lit if this get worse?"

"As long as it is not pouring rain they should light."

Larson gave her a doubtful look.

Time passed slowly as the little ship labored on. Mandeler had his hand under his rain gear continually checking for the hunting pack of Great Raptors. Then he felt them closer...

The leader was drawn by the strong pull of the one. His eyes still burned from the terrible beating they took from the volcanic dust, but he could see the floating vessel ahead with its glowing entities. His wing mates could sense the building excitement as their prey came into view. The wind was directly ahead of them and it had taken longer to reach these creatures. It had been the longest single flight he had ever made, but the one the Queen sought, above all others, was now within reach.

"They are here! Take cover everyone!" Mandeler shouted as he reached to help lash the tiller.

Gwenelle rushed forward, pulling two burning lamps from under a bucket. She threw off the lid and smashed the glass globe onto the flare pot. It burst to life before her. The air was filled with shrieking as she lit the second flare pot. Quickly she popped open the forward hatch and ducked below just as a dark shadow flashed over the deck.

Through the screaming attack she heard it, a few random thumps and then the full torrent of a rain storm pounded on the deck. Her flare pots would never stand up to this, she thought, and then the ship jerked as something hit the tall mast telegraphing the impact through the deck. Gwenelle made it to their cabin as the second impact shook the Sea Quester.

Mandeler crouched in the companionway, watching the dark hunters streak by overhead. Each pass they came closer until he felt the thumping impact of the mast being struck. He watched, hoping the crystal charged flare pots would be so bright that the monster could not gain the deck. With the sudden rain, his hopes drained away as the pots flickered, sputtered and then all went dark. He reached under his rain smock drawing out his amulet. His crystal flared with green brilliance but still it could not penetrate the heavy rain. He felt, rather than saw, wave after wave of the giant flyers swooping down to hit the ship and then retreating.

The ship reverberated as bits of wood and rope rained down on the deck. The sails shredded, leaving the vessel to wallow in the waves. There was a frenzied feeling about the way these creatures threw themselves at the ship, that made his stomach churn with fear.

The cabin above him shuddered as something large hit it. The sound of thumping and scraping claws came nearer. Splinters fell on his head as he retreated to their cabin.

The young pack leader circled above the others. Rain was not a problem for the Great Ones, they thrived in the dark. He would wait until the others had spent themselves beating the floating craft to bits. Within was his prize, that which his Queen sought above all things. She had not given him reasons, only orders, fetch the one, spare no hunter or if all was lost, kill the one. He would do his duty to the end.

By the soft glow of the glass globe, Gwenelle saw the grim look of Mandeler's face as he came into their cabin. She did not have to hear him say that all would soon be lost, the sounds of hammering on the deck had risen to a terrifying level. The deck seams opened up, letting water drip from the ceiling upon her as she had gathered their water proof gear together. How this would play out was an unknown.

Mandeler's face was grim as he started to pull their individual packs on. The small ones were slung over his shoulder, hanging under his arms. The large backpack held wax sealed packages of the precious exploding powder and lighting twine. When he looked up, Gwenelle was similarly decked out in their necessary gear, food, water, medicine, clothing and more of the powder.

When I was at Earlsbee, the cold water made me invisible to the hunting pack. Here the problem is they are between us and the water. Mandeler telepathed.

All we can do is be ready if a chance offers itself.

The ship lurched suddenly throwing the pair of them against the bunk. The sound of waves crashing on the deck above told them that the ship was forcibly heeling into the oncoming waves. They held onto each other straining to hear what would happen next.

Over the din, Gwenelle telepathed: *They will breach the hull won't they.*

It is only a matter of time and not that much time either!

Hold me...please.

He had been watching from above, and when his hunters had nearly rolled the craft on its side he became hopeful that the end was near. The Raptor that had been clinging to the top of the stick lost his grip, splashing into the heaving water. Unable to take to the air again, he thrashed wildly trying to stay afloat but soon sank beneath the waves. Even in the heavy rain he could see the struggle his pack mate had, before the sea swallowed him. The floating thing righted itself again dislodging two more hunters, flinging them into the frothy sea. As their struggling shapes vanished below the waves the leader made his decision. He would dive straight down and break the back of this shell that hid the one.

Without further thought he pulled in his wings, diving down to the wallowing vessel below. Through the driving rain he got a glimpse of the broken mast coming up to meet him. Unable to veer aside, the great hunter plunged chest first onto the splintered mast. His heart burst and he died impaled upon the main mast.

To Mandeler, the crash was deafening. Timbers groaned and shattered under the impact. He could hear water gushing from somewhere below. More scratching and thumping from above, and the vessel slowly heeled to port.

He saw Captain Larson scramble past throwing open floor boards as he went. Then he heard him, "Ah f'r Izaic's sake, we're holed. Now we're done for!"

Birdard and Allenz were there in the passageway when Mandeler looked out. Their faces were white with terror. The ship was at a thirty-degree angle and slowly getting worse. Sea water gushed from the floor boards around the main mast. It had been driven through the hull and now they were sinking.

"She'll go down by the bow, best make it back to my cabin!" shouted Larson.

Water was rising above Mandeler's ankles as he clung to the cabin doorway. When he looked back into their cabin, a glow globe was already afloat in the corner. Taking Gwenelle's hand, he pulled her up through the leaning doorway and toward the stern cabin.

Many times they had gathered in the warm little room to share meals, strong drink and shared plans. This time it seemed smaller, darker, slanted at an uncomfortable angle. The simple furnishings seemed odd, tipped up on edge, still standing where they had been screwed to the floor. The shivering crew crouched on the low side while Captain Larson perched on the edge of his table. The young couple worked their way through the door, sliding down beside the others.

Captain Larson spoke, "We're done for lads!"

There was the sound of something sliding along the side of the hull, and then the ship lurched to the side spilling them together on the floor. The pitch of the Raptor's screams suddenly changed, and there was a hasty scrambling on deck. Mandeler knew the Raptors were themselves under attack. Clinging to Gwenelle he mind-spoke: *Remember the feelings that something sinister was coming? Well, it wasn't just the Raptors. The Ixopods are here, Labeena called them the Sure Death.*

We need our amulets! Gwenelle replied.

Simultaneously, they clasped their precious crystals and held onto each other. There was that momentary wave as they connected to each other, then came the scene from around them. Swimming creatures, far larger than the Raptors encircled the boat. The Raptors fought back but they were outnumbered by long necked predators armed with powerful jaws and razor teeth. Those that had already slipped into the waves had vanished below and those left, clinging to the deck, were being dragged off one at a time. Suddenly the deck was quiet, just the sound of rain and waves beating on the hull.

Mandeler sensed one lone flyer heading away from the calamity.

Captain Larson asked the obvious question, "What in Azimov's abyss was all that about?"

So Mandeler told him.

The one threat had been averted, but it was replaced with another very deadly one.

Into the Drink

How long did they have? That was the question on Mandeler's mind, as he scrambled to the cabin door, clutching a glow globe. Its light seemed to be eaten up by the sodden passage way where the black water crept up the walls. Sea Quester was definitely sinking, bow first.

Behind him, Captain Larson said, "It sounds like we could get back up on deck, but will we just be killed like them black Raptors?"

From his perch, Mandeler replied, "I think I want to go on deck and have a look for myself, and then I can call back down when I know more."

"Flipp'n crazy is what I say," muttered Birdard.

"I'll come too," said Gwenelle.

Sea Quester was wallowing in the big waves making the slippery stairs, covered in splinters, even more dangerous for the young couple as they made their way back up. At the top, the dog house lay shattered exposing it to the wind and rain. The ship's bow was awash and the deck slanted forward and to port. Debris lay strewn everywhere about the vessel, but the most prominent feature was the dark body of a Great Raptor impaled upon the splintered mast. As he held the glow globe higher, Mandeler could see that something had bitten its head off, as well as most of the left wing and part of its tail. Yellow blood was being washed into the ocean.

Mandeler felt his stomach start to heave so he turned to Gwenelle. She pulled her crystal free and it glowed with renewed light as she placed a hand upon his brow. Instantly there was a calming effect so he clasped his own amulet. Sending out his senses, where he found the Sure Death feasting below the waves upon flesh of the dead Raptors. He shuddered as he remembered Labeena saying that she would never spend the night floating at sea because of these ravenous predators.

If they abandoned their ship, would they ever live to see tomorrow? Then he saw the row boat, half submerged and upside-down, laying some way astern. It rode up and down with the waves, but it looked intact. It must have been knocked free from its davits. On a sunny day it was an easy swim to the boat, but with the storm raging and ravenous killers in the water, it was a probably a suicidal swim.

Captain Larson said, "I've seen those Ixopods before, they feast on anything they catch. For some reason they do not recognize our boats as prey, and they have never touched any of our fleet unless someone was foolish enough to go swimming."

"It may be our only chance, we are sinking after all," stated Mandeler.

"Oh that sounds logical, but we three don't swim. Never learned," answered Larson.

Gwenelle could not believe this, "You can't swim and you live on a ship?"

"Don't fall off was always my thought," quipped Larson.

"How long till Sea Quester goes down Captain?" asked Mandeler.

"I expect we are halfway there now. So you can be the judge of that yourself."

Mandeler ventured, "I'll try to make it to the boat first and if I succeed I'll come back with it."

"If you can right it, if it still has oars and if you can bail it out before Sea Quester sinks?"

"Yah, all of that!"

"I'm coming too," Gwenelle blurted.

The rain had stopped and wind had started to die as he stood again on the deck. It was a brave statement that he would swim out to the partly submerged row boat, but now as he stood on the sloping deck he felt very much afraid. In the time they had been below, Sea Quester had sunk further into the sea. Time was short now. As he looked back he could see the crew at the head of the companionway staring towards them. Gwenelle had a firm grip on his arm as they edged down the deck toward the pulsing water.

The water felt colder than he remembered as he stepped cautiously into its depths. Slow easy movements were the only plan he had, so they made their way unhurriedly forward. Soon they were fully immersed, some of their travel packs providing floatation. Hand in hand, they took gentle strokes to carry them away from the hull. Mandeler's raptor vision had become intermittent at best since entering the water. Gwenelle was totally blind in the dark. If it was not for Mandeler's presence she could not have found anything afloat.

Lay still in the water for a moment while I get a reading on our neighbors: telepathed Mandeler.

Below and around them he could sense the great ocean predators still feasting. So far they did not seem to be aware of them. They continued on at a very slow pace towards the bobbing row boat, which had drifted farther away. It seemed to take forever to reach it, and when they did, it was slippery and hard to hang onto. Scared of making too much noise, Mandeler worked his way carefully around the skiff until he could get a good hold on the keel near the stern. Gwenelle had been following his lead.

Let's pull gently but firmly to see if we can roll this thing, Mandeler telepathed.

Together they strained and finally the boat started to roll. All the while Mandeler was afraid they would attract the hunters from below. As the boat started to roll, he reached as far as he could, just being able to grasp the opposite gunnel. With a swoosh, the little craft rolled upright... Mandeler could hear his heart beating over the sound the waves about them. He clutched his amulet in the cold water, searching for any approaching threat, but all was quiet.

Still holding his amulet he scanned the little vessel for damage. It was a miracle that it was in one piece with a bailing bucket held fast by a line. Gwenelle was soon at work bailing water. It was then that he looked back at Sea Quester. She was now almost two thirds submerged with the stern riding high. She could go down very soon. The three others were standing at the stern rail holding a glow globe aloft. They looked forlorn with the faint blue light being eaten up by the surrounding sea. Larson called, “Is there any hope?”

“She will float but we have no oars to get back to you in time.” Mandeler called back.

“We’ve collected a couple of barrels and bit of timber for a small raft. We’ll try to make it out to you. She is sinking below us and there is no other option left!” he shouted back.

There was a splash as the little makeshift raft was dumped from the settling stern. The men scrambled after it. It would not hold all their weight, so they dangled their legs in the water, kicking to propel it. Birdard lost his grip and would have drowned if Captain Larson had not reached over the edge and pulled him back up.

As Mandeler watched the men struggle towards them, through the waves, he suddenly became aware of something else. **“No, stop kicking, you’re making too much noise!”** They must not have been able to hear him or they felt so close to safety, because they thrashed on. That was when Mandeler first saw the massive head break the surface behind them. Silently it opened its broad mouth with its double row of irregular teeth. It made hardly a wave as it slipped upon the immersed men. Birdard and Allenz vanished in a single snap. The raft disintegrated, plunging the screaming Larson into the cold dark water. Silence followed, as a single barrel bobbed to the surface, but no one could be seen.

Mandeler and Gwenelle clung to their boat in disbelief. One moment they had been there and the next they were gone. A cold shudder ran down their spines as they realized they may be taken at any moment.

Hold my hand and breathe. Steady deep breaths, calm your mind. It is our only protection: he telepathed to Gwenelle.

Gwenelle, usually the tough and street experienced one, slid closer to him in the water. Clinging to the boat with one hand, he embraced her. Their chests came together and with that, the connection with the amulets. They could sense things vividly all around them. Larson was just below the surface. He had gulped a lung full of air before going down. The Ixopod had continued on, taking its prey deeper into the darkness.

Mandeler mind-spoke as he pushed off: *Captain, hold that breath. I am coming for you.*

Releasing his grip, he swam in measured strokes, only raising his head every now and then. At the last moment he dove down, coming up under the limp Larson. As their heads broke the surface Larson gulped air.

Mandeler added: *Quiet, do not struggle Captain. We don't want to invite the Sure Death back again.*

He felt Larson nod. Taking great care in his movements, Mandeler started to tow the captain towards the row boat. It was slow going but safety was at hand. That was when he heard the groaning sounds of Sea Quester sliding beneath the sea. In the silence that followed, the skiff ahead of them seemed smaller than ever.

Moments later they were gathered around the refloated row boat. Quietly they scooped the last of the water out and then, counter balancing each other, they took turns helping one another over the gunnels and into the safety of the little boat.

Three Up

Dawn found the three of them numb and exhausted after their nightmarish experience. The seas had calmed overnight but the early morning rays did little to dispel the deep chill they felt. Bits of debris floated in the water around them, a constant reminder of the tragic end of Sea Quester and her crew.

Mandeler felt a strong sense of loss for the two sea men that died in the dark, but he was puzzled by his feelings over the Raptors' death. They had come to ravage and kill but they in turn had died a painful and terrifying death themselves. Why should he feel any pity for them?

He and Gwenelle were laying together in the bow. No one had spoken since they had refloated the skiff. Captain Larson's grey face looked as if he had aged twenty years in one night. Mandeler finally broke the silence, "It is all my fault for hiring you to come all this way."

Silence hung in the air but finally Larson replied, "It would be easy to put all the blame on you, but I am a grown man and I accepted your payment for transportation. No one forced me to come on this quest."

Hesitantly Mandeler replied, "I did not ask you to forfeit your ship, your crew and possibly your life."

"Those are the risks every time I put to sea. This time I paid the full price for my folly."

Gwenelle sat up and rummaged in their travel gear. Soon she pulled out a water skin and a handful of acava berries. For something so spartan it felt like a feast. As the sun rose it started to warm the survivors.

The sun had climbed through its zenith and was working its way down the sky. Mandeler was sitting cross-legged against the gunnel, eyes closed, clasping his amulet when he first felt them. He turned to his companions mind-speaking: *Look to the east, soon you will see them.*

"Who?" Captain Larson asked.

That would be the return of the olive raptors, added Gwenelle as she started to braid her long hair in preparation for flight.

"That is all well and good for the pair of you but I have no hope of reaching safe harbour with this crippled boat."

"There is still a chance for all of us," answered Mandeler.

With that, silence returned to the boat while the occupants turned their gaze to the east.

As so many times before, the first sighting of the approaching raptors looked like a flock of smaller flyers on the horizon but as they watched they grew bigger and bigger. There were twelve of them in the flight. Mandeler had known Labeena and Rachaner would come as soon they sensed his need, but he had never dreamed a full dozen would show up. They circled and splashed down around the tiny vessel.

"Aren't they beautiful!" said Gwenelle.

"On this lonely sea even a flock of green dragons are a welcome sight," added Captain Larson.

Labeena seemed to smile as she approached Mandeler telepathing: *Could you not keep out of trouble while I was away?*

It is not as easy as it sounds. Trouble came looking for us this time: answered Mandeler and then he quickly related the night's events to her. He also added his concerns about the captain's safety in the crippled row boat.

Can he hear our thoughts? She asked looking directly at Captain Larson.

"What's this all about, thoughts and all?" Larson said.

"Labeena wants to know if you can understand any of her thoughts that she projects to us." Mandeler added.

What color am I Captain? telepathed Labeena.

The look on Larson's face was quizzical, and he said to the group, "For some reason the color green just jumped into my head. What's going on?"

"It appears that you can understand some communication with our olive raptor friends. As with us, you can't seem to speak, but you are a receiver of wordless speech."

Are you thinking what I am thinking? Gwenelle cut in.

What choice do we have?

"Oh come on, spell it out, I am in no mood for puzzles today!" grumped the captain.

Labeena, who amongst your flyers is best able to carry our captain?

That would be Rozzella, she is our strongest. Not our fastest but a good flyer.

"Bloody Azimov, you're going to put me on one of those green dragons, aren't you!"

Would you rather sit out here in your little boat and wait for another offer? added Gwenelle.

This changed Captain Larson's pallor for he was now a rosy pink and looked about fit to jump up and down. All the while Rozzella had been swimming towards the skiff.

Gwenelle built the captain's confidence by showing him how to mount a raptor. Rozzella stretched her neck over the boat so the captain could be helped into position. They used a short length of line to secure his feet, that way Larson could not be parted from his ride.

Gwenelle mind-spoke: *As I have said, Rozzella will do all the flying. Your job is just to hang on and not fall off. Simple?*

"Simple, I think not, but I'll give it a go!"

Now wait your turn and we will be off.

"Where to?"

Didn't I say? The closest land is the Smoking Mountain. We should be there near night fall: Mandeler added.

Return to the Smoking Mountain

Larson had stood on the deck of his ship in a raging storm, faced angry mobs with only a blade in his hand, and seen the worst that Great Raptors could bring. He would never forget the first time sitting astride an olive raptor feeling the release of her bunched muscles that launched them into the sky.

In raptor style they flew in a wide line behind the leader's wing tip. The evening sun shimmered on the swells as they skimmed over the waves. The three coned island was growing closer all the time. The Smoking Mountain looked disfigured from the eruption, but a new mantel of dark material was replacing the missing top. Smoke still chugged from the vent but the flow was greatly reduced. Clouds of steam could be seen along one shore. It seemed serene compared to the last time. They were headed for the same black sand beach they had been on before. Although the wind had changed, their end of the archipelago was untouched.

Throughout the flight Mandeler and Gwenelle had been in constant dialog with the lead pair. Although they had managed to bring their essential supplies, food and water were going to be in short supply, especially with Captain Larson along. Labeena decided to send three of the fastest young raptors ahead in preparation.

It was dusk when the flight of raptors touched down on the beach to be met by the three scouts.

Gwenelle quickly dismounted and ran to help Larson. He could hardly stand when he slid from Rozzella's back. On wobbly legs, she helped him up the same beach where just days before she had watched the catastrophic eruption.

Mandeler called her over after Larson stretched out to rest.

"Look what the scouts have left for us," he said pointing to a pile of red fins glistening on the dark sand.

"How did they do that?" she asked.

I think the word is regurgitation.

You're kidding! Should we tell Larson?

Nope.

I'd sure like to cook one.

So would I.

I dried out the three fire sticks that you gave me. Could we use one to get a cooking fire going?

Tonight I think a fire would be a cheery thing all around. I'll go up the beach and see if I can find drift wood while you make things ready here.

The setting was surreal but beautiful. They had selected a site well up the beach within easy reach of driftwood. A pile of smaller pieces served as fuel for a generous fire while they lounged on larger chunks. A large red fin sizzled on a stick, dripping fat into the fire. Gwenelle had found pools of fresh rain water to refill her skins. Behind them stood the three peaks of the Smoking Mountain Island, the two smaller ones were just silhouettes while the large one's shattered cone throbbed with a red glow that lit the column of rising smoke. From the mouth of the giant a tempest brewed, its giant cauldron was a boil with liquid rock which oozed down the mountainside where it was finally quenched by the sea.

By the light of the fire, the three tired people ate their meal in silence. The olive raptors had shared up the last of the swimmers for their evening repast and now they lay curled on the beach away from the fire. Three smooth forms just visible in the red glow.

Larson finally spoke, "What now?"

"The plan has always been to return to the Queen's nest and try to isolate or kill her. My guess is that the remaining hunters will back down if we succeed, at least that is my hope." Mandeler said.

“As we said to you in the beginning, when you showed us the exploding powder, we could use it as a weapon to equalize the fight.” Gwenelle added.

“Do you still intend to take the fight to her?” Larson said.

Yes, they replied.

The silence hung in the air and then Larson said, “I want to come too.”

“Are you sure? We leave at first light,” answered Mandeler.

“Then I better get some sleep.” he said.

Gwenelle and Mandeler left the captain curled up by the fire and went to look for their raptors. Labeena and Rachaner were curled up next to each other. The Leader telepathed: *We were expecting you. Settle next to us and share our warmth. Tomorrow will be a very long day.*

The old one had lived almost as many sun cycles as his Queen. He still remembered the old ways, the only one left that did. After the last hatching, his wing mate had fled the cave, never to return. He was the best hunter and often wondered what became of him.

Within the inner cave his Queen howled her rage at the failure of the last raid. It had gone on for longer than any rant in the past. He lumbered out of the stinking cave to stand on the edge of the cliff. The dark cloud that had hung over them had moved off leaving a star field in the sky. The ground was still covered in a fine dust but the air was sweet and fresh for the first time in ages.

The two other remaining hunters skulked about the outer cave trying to avoid her wrath. He knew she would send them out one last time trying to eliminate her nemesis. When the little being she referred to as the ‘one’ had come to their mountain on a green, he was surprised to see how small he was but he had the heart of a true hunter and something else. He had come to collect the denzel from the cliff. He cared about other beings, something his Queen did not even do with her own kind. Was this a weakness?

Mandeler awoke puzzled by the old one in his dream but he was so tired that he snuggled back around Gwenelle falling asleep again.

The Queen's Nest

They stirred as the eastern horizon turned purple. For Gwenelle and Mandeler there was little to prepare. They were dressed in the only clothes that they had and their gear had been carefully selected before Sea Quester went down. As with the day before they shared acava berries and water to break their fast. It had been arranged that the young ones would take the lead while those carrying their people would take the easier places at the wing tip vortexes.

They were still just silhouettes on the beach when they lined up for departure. One at a time wings unfolded followed by the thunderous sound of a raptor taking flight.

No matter how many times they had flown together, nothing matched the exhilaration of takeoff. Mandeler's stomach churned with anticipation of the day to come, but the wind on his face and the steady pulsing of Labeena's wings soon settled him.

For Gwenelle, her trepidation did not abate with their departure. She had sought the wisdom of her crystal, seeking how the day might unfold, but nothing had come. So much was riding on her precious exploding powder and yet so much was untried. All she could do was cling to Rachaner's neck feeling his strength in flight. Her own raptor tattoo seemed to tingle as she pressed her chest against his neck. They were going to fly as one today, no matter what.

Captain Larson was not as well dressed for the chilled morning but the little extra weight he carried would have to make up the difference. His flight on Rozzella's back the previous day took away some of his fear. Falling off was not a concern but riding with the ease of the others was beyond his skill. The young couple took to the air as if they were raised with the colony. For him he knew he would always be just out of sync with his obliging flyer. But he would get to the destination in one piece and it was only yesterday that he thought he would die of thirst in an open boat. Today he might die anyway but there would be no lingering.

She knew they were coming and sensed it would still be daylight when they arrived. The best of her hunters had died since the coming of the 'one'. Her three remaining killers were either too old or too young to be reliable. They would have to do, and their lives were of no consequence anyway. What she carried in her belly would rebuild the colony if she could just get one more infusion of the precious blood. If need be she would come from the cave and deal with this herself.

It was the longest day in Mandeler's life. Labeena flew on, her wingtips sometimes clipping the wave tops. Since the two of them had flown to the cave together there was no problem directing the flight of raptors to the dreaded cavern. The closer they came to the peninsula the stronger his sense of foreboding. He sensed the Queen making ready for them.

Gracanna did not know what drew her to that forbidden place but she had seen something in a waking dream. The guardian had told stories of old, when a smaller raptor had shared their land. They had been hunted until they were gone but in her vision she had seen a group of them flying. The dark green ones had round heads that sprouted winglets and this time some carried smaller creatures on their backs. One seemed to be staring back at her as if he could see her. At his breast glowed an emerald stone. This one was a hunter and carried something terrible to her race…

She had no choice, she felt compelled to make the journey even in the brightness of day. Today she had left before sunrise climbing into the sky. She flew east, climbing to a great height, so that as the horizon brightened she had closed her eyes on the day and felt her way forward, knowing that at this altitude there would be nothing in her way. She could feel the pull growing stronger.

Mandeler was startled by the image that passed before him. He had felt her once before, a lone great flyer and now he knew two things. She was aware of them and secondly she was pressing on through the brightness of day to the same place they were going. An involuntary chill ran down his spine knowing this was not a chance happening.

He telepathed from his flyer: *Gwenelle, there is another female raptor approaching from the west.*

In the day light?

Yes. She feels different from the Queen. She is the only other female that I have sensed. This must have to do with us but I have no way of knowing what this could mean.

Grim tidings but we must keep on, mustn't we?

I'm afraid so.

Mandeler flew on in silence. How had he dreamed that he could take on all of the Great Raptors at their own cave? He must have been dazed to think he could pull this off, but now he was astride one of a dozen greens headed straight for the Queen and her hunters. Would they get there before dark and even if they did could they vanquish her? Maybe they should have taken one more day to rest. He had never had these doubts before. Finally he shared this with Gwenelle.

She responded: *Me too. I was hoping to sense our path ahead but it is all a blank today.*

I fear the new raptor must have something to do with this but it just adds more to worry about.

I am here with you to see this to an end. I don't think it was just chance that put us on this path together.

I needed that: Mandeler telepathed back to her.

The smile he got back said more than words.

It was late afternoon when the peninsula came into view, reminding Mandeler that dusk would follow them to the cave, and then the advantage would shift. It had been a very long day for the olive raptors, who were nearly exhausted. They followed the coastline until the delta came into view.

Let's take the lead: telepathed Mandeler to Labeena.

They started to climb as they crossed the lowland leading to the mountains. It was all a different color now with its coating of grey dust on everything.

Darkness was approaching and with it their dominance of the sky. The Queen called her hunters and the three of them came to the passage way. They would make a stand at the entrance and with the coming darkness they would attack. This time she would join them. The Queen felt the dismay from the old one but his opinions had never mattered. They would move to the cave entrance and make ready.

Her wing knuckles scratched on stone as she heaved her great bulk awkwardly towards the outer cave. As she entered the passage way her folded wings became pinned by her enormous girth against the cave walls. Her rage boiled over as she thrashed to move forward. She stopped, breathing heavily, and then gathering her strength she thrust forward with more scraping and crunching under foot. Her progress was halted soon by her sheer bulk compressed in the narrow passageway. How long had it been since she left the sanctuary? Had it been in the last hatching cycle or the one before? The Queen heaved with all her might, but could not move. As she let out a long breath of despair, she felt movement. If she held her breath, she could edge forward. There still might be a chance!

Mandeler felt the Queen's movement. She was coming out to

challenge them. "Time is running out." He mumbled to himself.

Dread filled him as the cave on the mountain side came into view. Even from this distance he could see a single Great Raptor, with neck swaying, standing on the cliff face.

He looked over his shoulder to see how far the sun was from the horizon but the mountain range blocked his view. It was still full light but this side of the range was now in shadow. Time was limited and they must be decisive when they arrived. Still he had no clear plan.

It was Gwenelle that broke in: *I need to get close to the mountain, preferably above the cave.*

For Mandeler it was decisive, for now he could act. He telepathed: *Have the others circle above the cave while the three of us scan the area.*

With that, the flight of raptors broke formation, with the three humans being carried up and towards the rock wall. The others started to fly in a tight circle, one behind the other, well above the lone hunter on the cliff.

Gwenelle was clasping her amber crystal trying to draw from her ancestral memories. She longed for some sort of sign that they could act upon. They had drifted back and forth in a zigzag pattern searching the rugged terrain when suddenly she saw it. There was a fissure that cut the stone parallel to the rock face. She could feel that it ran deep within the mountain.

I have it. Land me on that ledge, she sent out.

The big fliers took turns approaching the rock face and with the skill honed over a lifetime of flight, they pulled up at the last moment stalling at the lip to touch down on the ledge.

Gwenelle launched herself from her mount landing on the coarse surface. The ledge was about two raptors deep and about ten wide. She walked purposefully to the back where she inspected a slit in the stone about as wide as she was tall. Clasping her precious amulet, she studied the crevasse. Mandeler came to stand beside her, followed by Larson.

"What do you think?" Mandeler asked.

This crack runs almost to the cave below. I am sure this is what we are looking for.

Larson was down on his knees peering into the dark slit, "How are you going to get your explosive down there and light it?"

"I don't know yet," she replied as she got down with Larson to look more closely.

"I've made a burning twine that will light, but my best guess is that it will go off within fifty to ninety breaths, and there is no way we can climb down and back out in that little time!" she answered.

"Can we drop it in and make a run for it?" asked Mandeler.

"Too risky, it might come apart as it bounces its way down, and we only have enough for one try," she answered.

"Raptor dung!" Larson said emphatically.

Mandeler looked around and saw the sun was setting. The mountains on the far shore were capped in pink, and as he watched long shadows crept up their slopes bringing dusk to the land. The Great Raptors could take to the air any moment.

"I'll do it!" said Larson.

"What?" replied Gwenelle.

"I'll shinny down there and light the sucker myself. If I get out, I get out, if I don't I don't. You said it, this is our only chance. Now give me the powder, fuse and something to light it." said Larson.

"No, absolutely not!" interjected Mandeler. "This has always been my quest! I'll do it."

Are you out of your flippin' mind? screamed Gwenelle into his head.

"Wait, I have an idea," Captain Larson added. "Mandeler always carries a length of strong light line in his pouch. Let me tie it to him and help get him get down and then back out of the crack. Once I have him back out, we make a break for it."

"Could work," added Mandeler.

Are you out of your minds, this will probably kill both of you!

What are the other options? It's getting dark, Raptor night is coming and we have nothing else to fight them with: mind-spoke Mandeler.

She stood, head down breathing hard. Finally she up looked at her friend and lover saying, "Alright, but I don't like it."

OK, let's do this. Give me all the powder and its lighting twine. You take to the air, and Labeena and Rozzella get ready for a quick takeoff.

Things happened all at once. Gwenelle hurriedly pulled their explosives out of the packs, lacing the two bags of powder together. She neatly tied the burning twine to the protruding fuses. Mandeler slung them over his shoulder as she handed him the two remaining fire sticks. Larson pulled out the fine line and looped it around Mandeler's waist. As he knotted the end, the air split with the shrieking sound of a Great Raptor taking to the air.

Below them, the big Raptor had taken flight. It was that transition time at sunset where there was enough light for the Greats and the greens to both see briefly.

At the same moment the circling greens dove down upon him. As the old one pumped to gain speed, he heard the whistling sound of something from above. The young olive raptors had dived, with speed on their side, knocking the old one about causing him to fumble in flight. Never in his life had he been attacked. He dove and pumped for all his worth, making for the valley below.

The two young hunters were about to leave the cave when they witnessed the attack on the old one. They may have been young but they were not stupid. Over the past moon cycles they had seen how the experienced hunters were being killed off, just a few in the beginning but after the last raid only one had come back and now he was under attack. They shuffled nervously around the entrance. Suddenly from behind them, their Queen bellowed her rage. She was almost free of her confinement, only her left wing remained jammed in the sharp rock.

Mandeler threw his leg over the edge searching for something to put a foot on. He let himself down almost as far as he could, finally his toe found a protrusion. *Let me down some more.* The rope slackened and he felt his way farther down. It was dark down here so he paused, clasping his amulet for a better look. There, below him, were a series of rough steps, a bit far apart but he should be able to manage. A thought came to him so he drew out his amulet and placed it sideways in his mouth. It started to glow a soft emerald color, now he could see his way to the bottom.

He reached the end of the rope just before the bottom. He undid the line and stepped down. There was some rubble at the base but a section of the crack was just visible. Unslinging the sacs he pressed them deeply into the slit. Then keeping the burning twine clear, he piled stones around the charge. When he felt that was the best he could do, he pulled out the fire sticks. Carefully he drew one across a pebble. It sputtered, flared and went out. *Raptor dung!* Taking the last one, he struck it across the same stone. This one flared and stayed alight long enough to ignite the end of the fuse. It came to life, illuminating the narrow crevasse. Like a scared muzel, he leapt for the dangling rope. "**Pull with all your might**!" he shouted as he clawed frantically up the wall.

On the surface, Captain Larson, threw all his weight into hauling on the line. Hand over hand he labored until kicking and scrambling, Mandeler appeared over the lip throwing the line aside.

"Go, Go!" Mandeler screamed launching himself towards Labeena.

In one smooth movement Mandeler leapt onto Labeena's neck and they were off. Larson stumbled as he was trying to mount Rozzella. She ducked her head as low as she could to nudge him onto her shoulder. As she turned, lifting her wings for flight, the whole shelf behind them shook with the explosion. The sound was deafening, as rock and grey smoke shot into the air behind them. With Rozzella's last push she felt the narrow cliff dissolve beneath her.

The Great Queen lurched free from her entrapment. The moment had come to reap revenge upon this insignificant one. Into the air, you spineless creatures, she roared her hatred.

Then the mountain shook and groaned. Rocks fell from the ceiling in front of her…

As the narrow cliff face spouted smoke and dust, Gwenelle felt the mountain quake in her heart. She watched it all while circling above with Rachaner. She had felt helpless after giving over the explosives to Mandeler and the Captain. Why she had agreed she would never know. She should have been the one to go down, not Mandeler, but it was all too late now. Time seemed to stand still after she saw him go over the lip with the charges. Forcing herself to breathe she waited for what seemed forever until he vaulted from the crack to jump upon Labeena. Larson was slow to get away and she thought he was lost, until they came flying out of the debris cloud.

Gwenelle had watched in wonder as the face of the mountain, above the cave, seemed to slide down the mountain, turning to rubble as it slid over the cave mouth. In the dim light the side of the mountain was covered in a rising cloud of dust. It only seemed to take a few breaths for the landslide to sweep down the slope, roaring as it went. As she continued to circle, details below slowly emerged. Where the Great Raptor's cave had once been there was only a smooth scar on the mountain's face.

The New Face of Darkness

As the last of the light faded, Mandeler led the way down onto the low lands where there was a large hill that stood out from the others. They landed on its rocky exposure, above the trees. His feet had hardly touched the ground when Gwenelle bowled him over, throwing her arms around him and covering his face with kisses.

Larson lumbered over and said, “Nobody ever gave me that kind of welcome!”

They did not seem to notice him as the shower of kisses turned into one long deep shared kiss.

The young olive raptors had come back to join the others. They were bobbing and ducking in excited conversation.

Finally the young couple parted and sat up. Larson plopped down beside them saying, “You did it!”

“I can’t believe it. I thought we might blast a few rocks loose and at best block the cave, but the whole cliff face cleaved off.” Mandeler replied.

“How did you know how to pick that spot?” asked the captain.

Gwenelle turned towards Larson and as she did so her raptor tattoo seemed to come to life on her neck. “Thank the wise women that came before me. They gave me this crystal to see and understand things better.” She pulled the glimmering stone free of her travel tunic. It was radiating a warm amber glow.

“The both of you are amazing!” Larson said holding his arms wide.

They hugged the old seaman, holding the embrace Gwenelle adding: *You’re pretty surprising yourself.*

As they drew comfort from each other Mandeler sensed her coming. He stepped back looking towards the dim glow of the western sky. Her silhouette was just visible. *Everyone draw together, danger is approaching.*

The olive raptors saw her too and they shuffled about nervously on their wing knuckles to form a tight group. The three people moved to join them. They stood there anxiously awaiting their fate.

She grew larger as she approached. There was no doubt this was a Great Raptor and she was a big one. Fear now spread through the group in the darkness. She did not circle or dive straight down on them but came in at an ever slower pace, touching down on the edge of the hill in a thundering rush of back strokes.

Mandeler could feel his heart pounding in his chest as he stared at the huge shape in front of him. He made his feet move forward as he lifted his amulet into the air. It flashed to life with an emerald brilliance, brighter than ever before. It illuminated the entire hill top. Its brilliance seemed to blind the large predator for she turned her head as if to avoid the light.

Mandeler stopped halfway between her and the group, still holding his crystal high in the air. As he stood there, he could feel the tremor that shook his body from within. Carefully he steadied his breath and studied his opponent.

The big female slowly turned her head towards him, squinting into the radiance of his gleaming stone. They faced each other down, a small man with only the gift of a crystal confronting the biggest Raptor he had ever seen. He was torn between the screaming need to run from her, and a fascination of her very presence.

They stood there studying each other, not moving so much as an eyelid. There was something about her that seemed different than the others. First of all she had not charged them with teeth bared. As he stood there it dawned on him, this one did not reek of death and decay.

Finally he telepathed: *I have known that we would meet today.* He trembled but stood his ground.

A grating voice appeared in his head: *My mind's eye has seen you as well.*

Where do you come from and why are you here?

I have lived in exile from this colony since I was a fledgling. My guardian secreted me away where he could teach me the old ways of our kind. He told me there would come a day when I would be called to return to the place of my hatching. That call came today.

You know that the Great Queen has been killing my kind as well as the denzels and the olive raptors.

My guardian could not live with the foul ways of his Queen. It was her way to kill all of the females after a hatching. My guardian hid me and carried me far away to live in the old style.

The Great Queen is dead.

I know. I felt her death and the passing of her corrupted ways.

As they were mind-speaking, Mandeler became aware of another dark shape approaching at an altitude from out at sea.

He continued: *There is a dark hunter approaching from the sea. Where does he stand with you?*

I do not know him.

Gesturing to the people and greens huddled behind him, he added: *We fear his approach as we feared yours.*

My approach? It is you that should be feared above all others!

That took Mandeler back for a moment. He went on: *Me! I am but a small human and you fear me?*

You came carrying death to the cave of my ancestors. Before my eyes you killed the most powerful of our kind, as well as the last of her hunters. Would that not make you the most dangerous creature on this hill?

Time stood still as Mandeler digested that last statement. He, the most dangerous creature on the hill, and that from the largest predator he had ever laid eyes upon. *I see your point.*

He thought for a moment and then continued: *Peace is what we want. The people, denzels and the olive raptors want to live their lives without being preyed upon by your kind.*

How would you think that is different from my needs?

I would not know!

I come from a land far to the west where I hunt for my own needs only. The forests and plains are rich with wild life. Why would I come here to harass your kind?

If that were to continue, I think we have something in common. Lowering his amulet he telepathed: I am *Mandeler Freedahson, from the southern Mulestead Estate.*

The Great Raptor lowered her head fractionally: *I am Gracanna, the last female of my race.*

He looked up seeing the old hunter circling far above them. On impulse he telepathed to him: *Join us on this hill to make peace.*

Cautiously the old hunter arced down, landing at the edge of the field behind the other raptor. She turned to him repeating: *I am Gracanna the last female of our kind.*

The old hunter replied: *My name is Grundler and I have lived longer than the Great Queen. I too remember the old ways but have not practiced them for almost four hundred season cycles. Are you the one that escaped the nest? If so, I knew the one that you called your guardian. He and I were wing mates and we trusted each other.*

Will you take me for your new queen and embrace the old ways?

He bowed his head very low, answering: *It would be an honor my queen.*

Then the first thing I would have you do is go to the sea shore and bathe until you no longer smell of the corrupted ways.

Yes my queen. He lifted his torso, spread his winds and with a mighty heave, lifted into the air.

How did he do your bidding so easily? Mandeler asked.

It is in our blood.

Mandeler felt his fear subsiding, leaving behind the fatigue of his long journey. Without thinking he found himself telepathing: *I would like to know you better.*

Then perhaps it will happen so.

May I introduce the others?

I have lived alone for so long that I find conversation, even outside my kind, to be pleasing.

What followed was the strangest meeting of all. Gracanna lumbered forward on her wing knuckles and was introduced to a beaming Gwenelle, a slack-jawed Larson and the whole nervous olive raptor clan.

Homecoming

Despite their fatigue, the events of the day were too exhilarating for them to sleep.

Above them the star field filled the night sky. On each horizon a moon rose to cast their dim light upon the hill. The ringed Argil was nearly full in the east while Izaic was a golden crescent in the west. Their lives had been so full that the beauty of the heavens had escaped them.

Gwenelle hugged Mandeler's back, her chin hooked over his shoulder. He reached down and stroked her thigh, telepathing: *Could you imagine such a sight?*

It's amazing, just amazing!

Below them the sea was alive with ripples caught in the moon light. The land masses were black silhouettes between the star field and the sea.

Gracanna added: *Night is our time to fly and sometimes I would fly high in the sky just to savor the beauty and quiet of the star field.*

It's beautiful: chimed in her flying companions.

Gwenelle mind-spoke: *Do you think Labeena and Rachaner will forgive us for flying with Gracanna?*

They were far too tired to care what we did. This is just a joy ride with a new friend.

She squeezed him tight. *Yep!*

The day was sunny and bright. On the edge of the hill shaded by the ragged forest, Gracanna and Grundler were curled up and appeared to be sleep. The air about them was sweet and clean. The old one must have spent the whole night cleaning off the stench of the cave.

The young couple quietly approached them.

We are leaving and I wanted to say goodbye: Mandeler telepathed.

Without opening her eyes, Gracanna mind-spoke: *We will wait until full darkness and leave for my lands in the west. I plan to rebuild our colony in the cycles to come but you need not fear us.*

Go in peace.

In the two days that followed, the young greens returned to their island while the rest traveled to Earlsbee and Portside to spread the news of the Great Queen's death. Both settlements had suffered damage from the tidal wave. The protective harbors had broken the force of the wave, but flooding had drowned several residents. Grieving and cleanup was well under way when the travelers arrived.

People gaped as the three olive raptors carrying their people landed at the end of town. Their amazement was replaced by awe, as they learned about the death of the Great Queen and the end of their reign of terror. Mandeler felt it was best not to mention the presence of Gracanna and Grundler. The time would come to reveal them but not now.

As they met the town's people, Captain Larson boasted of the feats of bravery that the blushing young couple had accomplished. When they finally came to Portside he was installed in a comfortable pub where he told his stories of danger and adventure over and over, with cheerfully refilled mugs of ale.

Outside, the sun was setting as Mirra washed a freshly pulled batch of orangkins. She had always kept the door closed and barred except during the full light of day. In the sun cycles since Almar's taking, and all the trouble that followed, she and the girls no longer tended the orchards and fields, keeping only to the large garden near the lodge. She was startled by a thrashing noise outside, followed by the sound of voices. No one ever visited in these dark days. It just was not safe to travel.

Tap-tap…tap-tap, came the rap on the door.

She recognized the tapping sequence, but knew in her heart that it must be some sort of mistake. She cautiously slid the viewing port open and peered outside. The sun was in her face, making the two standing on the steps hard to recognize. Their faces were in shadow, while their hair was lit from behind giving them an ethereal glow.

The blond bearded one spoke, “Aunt Mirra, we have come home.”

She burst into tears, as she unbolted the door and flung her arms around her nephew’s neck. Sobbing she said, “I thought I would never see you again.”

Holding her gently Mandeler said, “I have someone for you to meet.”

As she stepped back the tall slender woman put out her arms saying, “I am Gwenelle.”

“Oh, he told me all about you the last time he was here.” She answered as she threw her arms around Gwenelle.

Tearfully Mirra said, “Come in, come in. You must tell us all about your adventures.”

It was when the young couple were about to pass her on their way inside that she saw the two olive raptors sitting in the middle of her yard. “Am I to believe that you flew here, on those…”

“It beats walking all the way from Portside.” Mandeler said, as he led the way inside.

The End

The following is an excerpt from the next book in the Mind-Speaker series:

The Return of the Queen

Rebirth

In death the Great Raptor Queen spurned fate. The dust had long since settled from the rock slide that eradicated her lair. The people that had brought this fatal blow had gone feeling assured that her kind would never darken their lands again.

Now her mangled body lay pinned under a gigantic rock. Only a leg and part of her belly was exposed in the rubble. From her torn abdomen a dozen leathery eggs spilled out. With the evening shadows spreading, the largest of the eggs tilted and cracked. Pecking could be heard from within and moments later part of the shell broke open. A little black head with strings of mucus emerged, her tiny red eyes blinking at the dim light. By twisting and thrashing she pushed one and then the other of her leathery wings free of the embryonic encasement. The shattered egg fell backwards as she broke completely free. Crawling on her wing knuckles the fledgling made its way to the edge of her new domain. A crusted flutter bug landed awkwardly in front of her. Without hesitation her long thin neck shot out. The unsuspecting bug vanished in three bites. The miniature Raptor spread her wings and screamed a high note of triumph.

Behind her, several more eggs started to crack. On their isolated island, hope blossomed for her kind.

64 years later, across the ocean on the mainland:

Elvie Ericson knew it was his task to empty the compost bucket but he had been putting it off for most of the day. It was well past dark when he had finished a tankard of his wife's fine dark ale and conceded that it was time to finish his chores. With the wooden bucket in hand, he headed to the settling bin. It had been such a good harvest and things could not have looked better for the short winter months ahead.

The clear sky held a multitude of stars that shimmered in the chilly fall evening. Elvie did not notice the dark shadow that seemed to be sweeping towards him, making the stars blink out in its passing. The only warning he had was a whistling that seemed to come from above and behind him. The great talons that tore into his back, hurled him forward and up as huge wings carried him aloft. Through the searing pain, Elvie's last thoughts were, *"This can't be happening, the last of the Great Raptors were killed years ago!"* And then darkness engulfed him.

Far to the south Mandeler awoke from a nightmare. He sat up sweating in his twisted sheets.

To be continued.....